CHICAGO PUBLIC LIBRARY

TEEN

VOLUME

Teen Volume is made possible
through generous funding from the
Chicago Public Library Foundation

Chicago
Public
Library

something

A Horatio Wilkes Mystery

wicked

ALAN GRATZ

DIAL BOOKS

DIAL BOOKS
A member of Penguin Group (USA) Inc.
Published by The Penguin Group
Penguin Group (USA) Inc., 375 Hudson Street, New York, NY 10014, U.S.A.
Penguin Group (Canada), 90 Eglinton Avenue East, Suite 700,
Toronto, Ontario, Canada M4P 2Y3 (a division of Pearson Penguin Canada Inc.)
Penguin Books Ltd, 80 Strand, London WC2R 0RL, England
Penguin Ireland, 25 St. Stephen's Green, Dublin 2, Ireland
(a division of Penguin Books Ltd)
Penguin Group (Australia), 250 Camberwell Road, Camberwell, Victoria 3124, Australia
(a division of Pearson Australia Group Pty Ltd)
Penguin Books India Pvt Ltd, 11 Community Centre, Panchsheel Park, New Delhi - 110 017, India
Penguin Group (NZ), 67 Apollo Drive, Rosedale, North Shore 0632,
New Zealand (a division of Pearson New Zealand Ltd)
Penguin Books (South Africa) (Pty) Ltd, 24 Sturdee Avenue, Rosebank,
Johannesburg 2196, South Africa
Penguin Books Ltd, Registered Offices: 80 Strand, London WC2R 0RL, England

Book designed by Jasmin Rubero
Text set in Century Old Style
Printed in the U.S.A.

1 3 5 7 9 10 8 6 4 2

Library of Congress Cataloging-in-Publication Data
Gratz, Alan, date.
Something wicked : a Horatio Wilkes mystery / Alan Gratz.
p.   cm.
Summary: In a contemporary story based on Shakespeare's play *Macbeth*
Horatio Wilkes seeks to solve the murder of Duncan MacRae at the
Scottish Highland Games in Pigeon Forge, Tennessee.
ISBN 978-0-8037-3666-5
[1. Murder—Fiction. 2. Highland games—Fiction. 3. Scottish
Americans—Fiction. 4. Great Smoky Mountains (N.C. and Tenn.)—Fiction.
5. Pigeon Forge (Tenn.)—Fiction. 6. Mystery and detective stories.]
I. Shakespeare, William, 1564–1616. Macbeth. II. Title.
PZ7.G77224Sop 2008
[Fic]—dc22
2008001722

For Jon Manchip White, for whose class I first created Horatio Wilkes seventeen years ago

"By the pricking of my thumbs,
Something wicked this way comes."

-MACBETH, Act 4, Scene IV

CHAPTER ONE

—*/*—

History is full of guys who did stupid things for women. Paris started the Trojan War over Helen. Mark Antony abandoned Rome for Cleopatra. John Lennon gave up the Beatles for Yoko Ono. You can say I'm a dreamer, but they're not the only ones. Like my friend Joe Mackenzie: He was about to jump off a five-story building just to impress a girl.

"Come on, you wuss!" Mac's girlfriend Beth yelled. "If you don't jump off that tower, you're not getting any more of this!" She lifted her sweater up over her head, showing her bra and her extraordinary breasts to Mac, me, Banks, and the five or six other people milling around Kangaroo Kevin's Bungee Jump-O-Rama in Pigeon Forge, Tennessee. They actually inspired a small round of applause. I won't say what they did to me, but Beth's fun cushions certainly inspired Mac. With a Scottish war cry he charged the end of the platform and jumped headfirst, screaming all the way down. His kilt opened like a daisy as he fell, and everyone saw his stamen.

"Woooohooooo!" Beth called.

"Oh, for the love of Dirk Diggler," I muttered. "Only Mac would go bungee jumping in a kilt without any underwear on." I chose to look at Beth instead. She had covered herself back up, but the image of those perfect breasts was burned into my retinas, like when you look into a lightbulb too long and all you see for the next five minutes is the blinding after-glow of the filament.

"Get a good look, Horatio?" Beth asked.

"Of *Mac*, yes. If you could do that sweater thing again, though, I would very much appreciate it."

Bashful Banks looked away in case Beth took me up on it, which wasn't likely. Behind us, Mac's screams turned to laughter as he and all his dangling parts bounded into the air on the bungee cord. Beth proved she could multitask, watching Mac bounce and giving me the finger at the same time.

"Not even if every other boy in the world was covered from head to toe in zits and back hair," she told me.

Beth *was* out of my league. She was so far out of my league, in fact, that she was the New York Yankees and I was the Weehawken five- and six-year-old tee-ball B team. She was built like the top half of a lingerie model grafted onto the bottom half of a ballet dancer. She was also a freshman in college, and she suffered us high school juniors like a goddess among the muck-farmers. Beth's dad and Mac's dad were business partners, which was how they'd met, but beyond his male model good looks I'd never understood why she dated beneath herself.

Mac bungeed to a stop, and Beth ran to give him his earthly reward.

"Man, would you ever do that?" Banks asked.

"Not even for those marvelous Dolly Partons," I told him. "That boy is seriously whipped."

Banks sighed, and I wondered if he wasn't thinking right now that he'd be happy to be whipped if it meant having a girlfriend. Don't get me wrong—Wallace Banks was a great guy. He was also some distant relative of Mac's, which automatically let him run around with the king and queen of the Highland Games. But no amount of being nice or being Mac's second cousin once removed or whatever could ever really overcome wearing a white button-down short-sleeve shirt with a pen-filled pocket protector. He was also wearing a red tartan kilt and matching pom-pom beret, and just below his pasty knees he had on white woolen hose held up with ribbons. That we were in town to attend the Mount Birnam Scottish Highland Games made the getup somewhat excusable; that Banks wore this outfit on a daily basis made him a total geek—but a lovable one.

Mac came wobbling up with Beth wrapped around him. She was breathing harder than he was.

"I can't feel my legs!" he said.

"I think you've lost feeling in your brain too," I told him.

"There is a *cushion*," Mac said. We'd had this argument twenty minutes ago. "It was completely safe. They wouldn't let you do it if you could get hurt!"

"Mac, you signed a waiver that said you wouldn't sue them if you *died*. Does that sound completely safe to you? And a four-foot-tall inflatable bag wasn't going to do a whole lot of good if that cord snapped."

"You're just jealous, Horatio. You've got to try it! Woo! What a rush!"

Mac's knees went out from under him and Beth couldn't hold him up. I caught him, and Banks and I steered him toward a bench while Beth bounced away to buy him a bottle of water.

"The next time you go bungee jumping in a kilt, wear some underwear, will you?" I told him.

Mac grinned. "A real Scot wears naught beneath his kilt but a draught, Horatio."

"You're not a real Scot. You were born in Chattanooga."

"I'm Scott*ish*. Besides," Mac said, flicking the end of Banks's kilt, "Beth likes me freeballing. Better access, you know?"

I held up my hands. "Too much information."

Where Banks's kilt was a fashion disaster, Mac managed to look studly in his skirt. It was blue and red and he wore it with a T-shirt that had the blue and white Scottish flag with the words "X Marks the Scot" underneath. And Mac would have eaten haggis before wearing the dorky white socks and ribbons Banks wore; instead he showed off his tan, muscular legs in nothing more than a worn pair of hiking boots. But for a short mop of brown hair instead of long flowing locks he could have doubled for one of those beefcakes on the covers of romance novels.

"Your dagger's showing," I told him.

Mac frowned and adjusted himself under his kilt.

"Not your metaphorical dagger, Spartacus. Your literal one." I pointed at his shoe. The little dagger he wore in his sock had come loose during the bungee jump. It was a Scottish thing; Banks had one tucked into his sock too.

"Your *sgian dubh*," Banks told him.

"Yeah. What he said."

Mac stuck the thing back in his sock. "Oh man, was Beth all *over* me when they unstrapped me. Just wait 'til tonight at the campground."

"Mac, you're always letting her make you do stupid things," I said.

"She's not making me do anything I don't already want to do."

"He's hooked on Beth Amphetamine," Banks said.

"Yeah. You need to kick the habit."

Beth came prancing up with a bottle of water. "What I need is a little more Beth," Mac said for her benefit. And his. She sat on his lap with a twirl of her skirt.

Of the four of us, I was the only one wearing pants.

"Gee," I said, "maybe someday I'll have a girlfriend who makes me jump off buildings too."

Beth played with Mac's hair. "One of those people who follows you around is talking again, Mac. Make him go away, will you?"

Mac lifted Beth off his lap and he stood, ignoring our sniping like always. "We've only got an hour before we need to be up the mountain. What else do we want to do?"

"There's a Tartan Museum we could go see," said Banks.

Beth looked at him like he had just grown a third eyeball.

"We could maybe set fire to the Gooder than Grits restaurant and hope it spreads to the rest of this tourist trap hell," I offered.

Beth started hopping up and down. "I want to go back to that fortune-teller's! The one we passed. What was it called?"

"Madame Hecate's?" I said.

"I want Mac to have his palm read!" Beth sang.

"Here, hold it out and I'll slap it," I told him. He held out his hands and I tried to smack them and make them red, but he pulled away in time.

"I don't want to go to some stupid psychic," Mac said. "Let's go get funnel cakes."

Beth pressed her boobs into Mac. "But I *want* you to have your fortune read, Mac."

"Okay, okay. We can come down the mountain and hit the Tartan Museum later," he told Banks. "And maybe we'll have time for a funnel cake before we go back. Right now we'll do Madame Hoodoo or whatever."

Beth took Mac by the arm and pulled him away.

"Meow," Banks said.

I made a sound like a whip cracking and we followed along down the strip.

Pigeon Forge sits like a scar in the earth, a gaping, brightly colored wound festering in the Smoky Mountain sun. It's not a town; it's an eight-lane abomination of go-cart tracks, mini-golf courses, and comedy barns, peopled with Elvis impersonators and neon orange fiberglass gorillas. The dappled green mountains in the background occasionally threaten to reclaim Pigeon Forge and engulf it like kudzu, but at the last minute some new developer will add another outlet mall or country music theater or pancake house and beat back the horrible darkness.

We found Madame Hecate's Psychic Readings wedged in between a funnel cake stall and an airbrush T-shirt hut. A sign in the window said: "Palms Read While You Wait."

Mac pushed his way inside and a bell tinkled, I suppose so Madame Hecate wouldn't have to waste any of her considerable psychic talents on predicting our arrival. The little room was decorated in a combination of Late Victorian and Pier 1. The walls were covered with old black-and-white portraits in gilded frames, and funky beaded lampshades draped with red handkerchiefs did what little they could to give the place some atmosphere. A plug-in fountain spewing clouds of dry ice bubbled in the corner, and in the center of the room stood a small table where it looked like someone had been playing solitaire with tarot cards.

"Excellent!" said Beth.

Something brushed my leg and I nearly jumped.

"That is Graymalkin, my, how you say? Familiar," said a voice.

The gray cat certainly was getting familiar with my black Converse. Meanwhile Madame Hecate, the source of the creepy accent, ran a hand up the wooden door frame on the other side of the room. I think she was trying to be mysterious. The fortune-teller was round like a crystal ball, and had her black hair tied back in a yellow bandana. She wore a long flowing gown that *shushed* as she shifted, and in the strange light I could see she had whiskers on her chin. It wasn't so much disgusting as embarrassing: Madame Hecate could grow a better beard than I could.

She slid her hand back down the door frame, then suddenly jerked it away.

"Ach!"

"What's wrong?" Beth asked.

The woman sucked a finger. "It is nothing. A splinter. I prick my thumb."

"Too bad she didn't see that coming," I muttered.

"Who comes to see Madame Hecate?"

At her invitation we sat in folding chairs around the table, and Mac gave her our names.

"*Horatio* your name is?" she said after I'd been introduced.

"Seriously," I told her, "you of all people do not want to go there."

"I want you to read Mac's palm," Beth told her.

"Is twenty dollars for full reading," said Madame Hecate. I snorted, but Beth already had a twenty out on the table. I shook my head. P. T. Barnum was still right.

In the only real magic she was going to perform that day, Madame Hecate palmed the twenty and made it disappear. Then she took Mac's hand in her own and began tracing the lines on his palm.

"Ah, yes, your fate line is strong," she said. "Very strong. But here—the heart and head line are fused. You think and act at same time, yes?"

"That's true!" said Beth. "He's very impulsive."

"Ah," she said. "And I see you are here for . . . some kind of festival. A competition."

"Well, kind of, yeah," Mac said.

"The . . . Highland Games?" she asked.

"What gave it away," I asked, "the kilts or the funny hat?"

"Hey," Banks said.

"A festival, yes, but you are not competing?"

"I didn't make the clan team," Mac confessed.

I had to admit, the woman's act was good. She certainly had Mac, Beth, and Banks snowed. They watched her work Mac's palm like she was revealing the hidden secrets of the universe.

"But make the team you will," she told him. "And not only will you compete, you will win!"

"You mean the Highland decathlon? I win it?"

"You're not even in it," I reminded him. To Hecate I said, "He missed the cut."

"For you, fate is sealed. You will compete, and you will win," Hecate said, ignoring me again. "And you will be king of the mountain!"

Beth gasped in delight and hugged Mac around his shoulders.

Mac nodded, happy with his fate. "King of the mountain. I could get used to that."

"What about me?" asked Banks. He reached into his sporran—a traditional Scottish waist pouch that was the ancestor of the fanny pack—and pulled out another twenty.

"Oh, not you too," I said.

Banks blushed and shrugged, but he still handed over an Andy Jackson.

Madame Hecate took his palm and gave it the same treatment.

"You, your life line is strong, but you are not athlete," she said. I huffed at her mastery of the obvious, but apparently no one was listening to me now. "For you, there is other competition? Music, perhaps?"

Oh, she was good all right. That had been a complete guess, but it was spot on.

"The bagpipes," Banks offered. "I play the bagpipes. There's this really important tournament, and the winner gets—"

"You are lesser than your friend, but greater," Madame Hecate told him. "I see you not so happy, yet much happier."

Banks frowned. "I don't—"

"While that one will be king of mountain, it is you who will *own* mountain."

"Me?" Banks asked. "Own Mount Birnam you mean?"

For all the laughing they'd done about coming here, Mac and Banks were deadly serious now. Beth crossed her arms and frowned.

"Is all I see." She turned to me. "I read your fortune, Horatio?"

I loaded up a short laugh with derision and disbelief and let her have it.

"Right," I said. "Let me guess. You see a crease bisecting my life line, which means I'll soon have some kind of big test or trial. And when I get to this great, vague, unnamed challenge, I should just listen to my heart, right?"

She took my palm in her hand and I rolled my eyes. I got a cold shiver, though, like the temperature in the room had just dropped ten degrees. I tried not to let anybody see me shake.

"Heart line is strong, yes, but head line is stronger. You think, think, think, which is good," she told me. "But this time you will listen *too much* to heart. It is head you must learn to hear again."

She was right about me thinking too much. I almost started to believe she had some kind of power, then shook it off. *Of course* she knew I used my head more than my heart— I'd been the only one playing the skeptic. As for the cold shiver, she'd probably turned up the air-conditioning when she heard us come in.

"I hope you're not expecting to get paid for that one," I told her.

"No. That one is free," she told me. "But you will be back. Then you will pay me."

"Right," I said. "Don't bet on it."

We sat through Beth's fortune—something vague about having gall for milk and a snake under a flower—and the mystic rose from the table. "Madame Hecate is tired now. Must, how you say? Recharge batteries."

"Wait, how do you know I'll—" Mac started to ask, but Madame Hecate disappeared into the next room.

"Happy now?" I asked them. "Sixty bucks for five minutes of flimflam. The next time you jokers want somebody to blow hot air up your kilts, let me know. I'll be happy to take your money."

Nobody was listening. Mac and Banks had fortune and glory in their eyes, and Beth was no doubt lost in some fantasy where she was wearing a tiara. We filed back outside and made for Mac's SUV. For a time, everyone was lost in their own daydreams.

Mac gave Banks a punch in the arm. "Hey cousin, you're going to own the mountain!"

It woke Banks up and he smiled. "And you're going to be king of the games!"

"And I'm going to be queen," Beth said.

"Right," I said. "Which is all just about as likely as me wearing a kilt."

They chuckled, but I could tell they didn't think it was funny. As we climbed into the car for the trip up the mountain, I saw Beth squeeze Mac's hand and pull him down to whisper in his ear.

If I'd been paying attention then, really listening with my head and not my heart, I might have heard it. It was the whisper of something coming.

Something wicked.

CHAPTER TWO

—/—

Mount Birnam stood 5,964 feet high, which isn't much for a Rocky Mountain, but for a peak east of the Mississippi, that put it right up there with the best of them. I tuned out the conversation from the front seat of the SUV and watched the lesser mountains roll by through the breaks in the trees as we climbed.

On a clear day where I lived in Knoxville you could see the mountains in the distance, but every now and then the Smokies would call to me and like some pilgrim I'd take a Saturday and make the hour-long *hajj* to the high country. The thing that impressed me most about the mountains wasn't their sheer size. What really awed me was the thought of the incredible forces of nature it took to push a million tons of earth and rock six thousand feet into the sky, and then the millions of years it took to smooth them out again. The high country made me feel small and powerless, and I think sometimes it's good to be reminded just how small and powerless we really are.

"I am so totally going to kick ass at the Highland decathlon," Mac said.

"You're not *in* the decathlon," I reminded him.

"Madame Hecate said he will be," Beth reminded me.

I let it go. Arguing with Beth was like debating philosophy with a See 'n Say.

Mac parked his car with a bunch of others in a large grassy field near the fairgrounds, about four-fifths of the way up Mount Birnam. A huge round rock rose from the ground in the center of the lot, defiantly reminding the 4x4s and trucks that grazed around it that this was a parking lot for stones long before it was a parking lot for cars. Another thousand feet or so above us, the top of Mount Birnam was hidden in the clouds. It was unseasonably cool and humidity-free up here for late July in the South and I took a deep, appreciative breath.

Mac honked the car locked and I jumped. Mac laughed. "I think Horatio's fallen in love with your mountain, Banks."

Beth pranced on ahead, her skirt flouncing in a way that made her impossible to ignore—and she knew it. I did my best not to think about how hot she was and focused instead on how *cold* it was.

"It's like ten degrees cooler up here than down in Pigeon Forge," I said.

"The mountain makes its own weather," Mac told me.

Banks did a 360, taking in the scenery. "It is pretty amazing, isn't it?"

"It's got a lot of potential," Mac said. He put an arm around my shoulder and gave me a manly side-hug. "So, who'd have thought we'd get Horatio to a Scottish festival?"

"Now all we need to do is get him into a kilt," said Banks.

"I'll eat haggis first," I told them.

Mac clapped me on the chest. "That can be arranged,

chum." Mac let me go, and we walked into the campground with Banks behind us.

"Chum?" I asked.

"I think *chum* is an underused word, so I'm bringing it back," Mac told us.

"You mean *chum* as in the bloody pieces of meat and bones they use to attract sharks?"

"No, no, no—like buddy. Pal. Amigo. What do you think, chum?"

"I think I wish Hamilton had come instead of me."

"Where is the artist formerly known as Prince, anyway?" Mac asked.

"At home in Denmark spending some QT with his GF," I told him.

Mac waved him off. "Screw the Dane. He doesn't know what he's missing, chums. This is going to be the best weekend ever."

I had known Mac and Banks forever, it seemed. Mac and I had grown up on the same street, once upon a time, and Banks would come and stay with him almost every summer when we were kids. That was before my parents had gotten divorced and my dad moved to St. Louis and my mom sold our house and moved us into smaller digs closer to the university where she worked. After that I hadn't seen Mac until the day we re-met in Freshman English at Wittenberg Academy and realized we had played Harry Potter in the backyard together when we were nine. Little Banks I hadn't seen since we made him be our house elf and carry all our spell books around. As we walked together toward the campground I had a strange sense of nostalgia for Batman action figures, Super Soaker water guns, and Nintendo video games.

The campground soon overrode my reverie with the smell

of grilling meat and the sound of vaguely Celtic music. Huge RVs were tucked back into the forest, and the leaves above formed a sparkling green ceiling in the late afternoon light. We dodged three different golf carts zooming around the little gravel paths, each driven by a festival official too lazy to walk. Deeper in, boys in kilts chased each other with wooden swords, families laid out hot dog and potato salad feasts, and friends gathered around campfires to laugh and sing. It was just like a football tailgating party, only the men were wearing skirts.

Mac's border collie, Spot, came bounding up to us with his tongue lolling out when we reached the Mackenzie family compound. There was an RV where Mac and his father slept, a covered picnic area, and a big guest tent where I was staying. Mac went into the RV to hit the head while Banks and I stayed outside. Spot ran circles around us until I bent down to give him some dog-love by scratching behind his ears and patting his belly.

"I think that dog likes you better than Mac," Banks said.

"Maybe he smells my dog on me."

Beth came out of an RV the next plot over. She was still wearing her Highland kilt, but she'd put on a pair of sweatpants underneath it and traded her sweater top for a sports bra. Spot immediately started to growl.

"What is it, Spot?" I asked, loud enough for Beth to hear us. "Do you smell something evil?"

Beth flopped a thick, smooth piece of plywood on the ground and swapped out her Crocs for a pair of dance shoes.

"Keep that mutt away from me while I'm practicing," Queen Beth commanded. Spot strained against my hands. I was sorely tempted to let him go after her, but I was afraid she might eat him. Beth pressed PLAY on a little boom box and started hopping around on the plywood to the prerecorded sounds of a bagpipe.

"There, Spot. Good boy. Good dog," I told him. "Don't let the horrible ogre bother you. Celtic music has soothed the savage beast."

"What is it with Spot and Beth, anyway?" Banks asked. "He's like a Tribble around a Klingon."

"Horatio?" asked a familiar voice. It was my older sister Desdemona—one of my *six* older sisters—waving to me from the path. Mona was tall and thin and pretty like the rest of my sisters, with a kind, open face that was sometimes too trusting for its own good. Mona was a beat reporter for the *Knoxville News Sentinel* and she looked the part: a photographer's vest over a white button-down blouse with rolled up sleeves, blue jeans, and sensible shoes. In one hand she carried a large-lensed camera and over the other shoulder she carried a stuffed duffel bag.

"Wallace Banks," I said, "this is my sister Desdemona Wilkes."

Mona's bag slipped off her shoulder when she shifted to shake hands with Banks and she stumbled, dragging him sideways with her.

"Oops, sorry."

I caught my sister before she could fall. "Mona, what are you doing here?"

"Fluff piece for the *Sentinel*. You know, the usual men in kilts throwing telephone poles kind of stuff. God, how I wish I got a real story for once and didn't have to cover bake sales and barbeques anymore."

Banks frowned like Mona had insulted his mother. "The Mount Birnam Highland Games is the longest continually-running celebration of Scottish heritage anywhere in the country," he told her. "The Scots have a centuries-old culture that can be drunk, eaten, and sung. What other culture can you say that about? Without Highland festivals like this, all that might have been lost."

"Right. Of course. Sorry," Mona said.

"You'll have to forgive Banks," I told her. "He's like Captain Kilt or something. He lives and breathes this stuff. He and his dad do like a dozen of these every year."

"Actually I prefer Haggis the Horrible," Banks said.

Mac came down out of the RV and made his way over to us. I squinted at Mona, trying to figure something out.

"What?" she asked.

"Is the air conditioner in your car broken?"

Mona opened her mouth and then frowned. "How did you know that?"

"Your left arm is pinker than your right arm. You must have had your window rolled down the whole way here."

"Oh crap," Mona said. She compared her arms.

"Your hair looks like you dried it with a jet engine too."

"Nothing gets by you, does it, Horatio?" Banks said.

I reintroduced Mona to Mac, but she was too busy trying to fix her hair.

"You're a photographer now?" Mac asked. "Here—you want me to show you a Scottish warrior pose?"

"Sure," Mona said. "Okay." She gave up on her hair and fumbled with her camera.

"Lens cap," I told her.

"Right, right. I always forget that."

"I'll do like William Wallace did to the English at the Battle of Falkirk," Mac told her.

"Great!" said Mona. She got ready to take the picture.

Mac turned around and flipped his kilt up, mooning her with his bare butt.

Mona took the picture, then lowered her camera to her hip.

"Nice. Thanks. I'm sure that one will make the front page."

Mac's father and three other men—an old white-haired guy and a young twentysomething both wearing the same tartan patterns on their kilts and a small, thin, middle-aged man in a green kilt—came walking down the path just in time to see Mac being an ass. His father's face turned as red as the two matching men's kilts.

"Oh Joseph, for God's sake. Grow up."

Mac stood and straightened out his kilt. His father leaned in close to scold his son, even though we could all hear him.

"What would your mother say if she were alive?"

"She'd say, 'Help! What am I doing in this coffin! Somebody let me out!'" Mac patted the air like he was a mime trying to escape an invisible box.

His father raised up and took a deep breath, clearly making an effort to control himself. He smiled at the old man.

"I'm sorry, Duncan—"

"Boys will be boys," the old man said. "I daresay I mooned a few lassies in my day."

"That's no moon," the younger red-kilt said. "It's a space station!"

He and Mac laughed and did some kind of secret handshake. Banks smiled like he knew who they were too. I was feeling left out.

"I'm Beth's father, Chad Weigel," the man in the green kilt told me. "Joe's dad and I work together."

I shook hands with Mr. Weigel warily, on the off chance Beth got her personality from him. His handshake was quick and distracted, like he had somewhere else he wanted to be, but he seemed all right. That meant his wife was probably the monster who had spawned Beth, and I made a mental note to watch out for Grendel's mother if I should ever meet her.

"Oh, sorry," Mac said, realizing he was falling down on the introductions. "And this is my uncle Malcolm and his dad—and my grandfather—Duncan MacRae."

"Everybody calls me Mal," the younger red-kilt said. "You a Cards fan, Horatio?"

He meant my St. Louis baseball cap. "No," I told him. "I just wear this to confuse people."

Mal laughed, which earned him points. He seemed a little young to be an uncle, but coming from a big family I knew how looks could be deceiving when it came to relations. I shook hands with uncle and grandfather both, assuming the "any friend of Mac's" attitude and laying off the fact that both Duncan and his son Mal looked like kilted waiters. Their clothes were impeccable, down to the last ironed crease on their shirts. Above their skirts they had on white button-downs like Banks, but Mal and Duncan also sported plain green ties and blue maître d' jackets. And, like everybody else, they both wore daggers in their socks.

Desdemona stage-coughed behind me, and I introduced her to the newcomers.

"Mona," she said, ignoring Duncan completely and reaching out a hand to Mal. Her bag slid down off her shoulder again, but this time she wasn't able to catch it before it hit the ground and spilled its contents all over the grass. Mal bent down to help her pick things up. The way they were smiling at each other, I began to wonder if she hadn't done it on purpose.

Mac's father had the impatient look of a man ready to push women and children out of the way for the last lifeboat off the *Titanic*. He gave the old man a patronizing smile. "Duncan," he said, "why don't you and Chad and I step inside my trailer so we can talk business."

The old man held up a hand. "All in good time, William. First, I have some good news for your son."

"Great," Mac said. "What is it, Gramps?"

"I'm not sure if you're aware of it, but Donald McKinney got married this past April," Duncan told him.

"That's . . . great," said Mac.

"Donald married Cynthia McHay of the Clan McHay."

"Hey, hey, hey," Mac said, doing his best Fat Albert imitation. His father crossed his arms and frowned at him.

"Donald has decided to compete in the Highland Games for his wife's clan from now on, not for our clan team," Duncan explained.

"The traitor!" Mal joked.

Duncan smiled. "Indeed. You think you know a fellow. Regardless, I'm afraid the loss of Donald McKinney to our clan team leaves us a man short for the Highland decathlon—unless *you* can take his place."

Mac stood straighter. "You want—you want me to be on the clan team for the Highland Games?"

"Absolutely not," Mac's father said. "Joseph will just find some way to embarrass us. What about Alastair Cross? He's somewhat athletic."

Duncan shook his head. "I've had my eye on you for some time, Joe. I've seen you in the amateur competitions, and I think you're ready for the professional ranks. You're the one I want for the Mackenzie-MacRae team. What do you say?"

"I can do it," Mac told him. "I'll win that claymore for us."

"Translation?" I whispered to Banks.

"A claymore is a huge Scottish sword," Banks told me. "They give one out at the closing ceremonies with the winning clan's name engraved on it. It's the highest honor any clan can achieve."

I thought there were maybe a few better things a clan could win than some sword, but I didn't say it.

"I won't let you down," Mac told his grandfather.

Duncan put a hand on Mac's shoulder. "I know you won't, Joe. I know you'll do our clans proud. Congratulations—you've earned it."

Banks and Mal converged on Mac to congratulate him and I looked away while they exchanged more secret family handshakes and in-jokes. Just across the main road by a large message board I noticed a good-looking girl about my age who really did justice to the sweater and kilt look. The skirt was short and the sweater was long, with a high turtleneck that framed her pixie face between it and her short boyish black hair. The tall black go-go boots were a nice touch too.

The skirt and the sweater and the boots were the reason I'd taken a second look, but what stopped me in the first place were her eyes. I was too far away to see if they were deep eyes or playful eyes or clever eyes—but I could tell where they were pointed: at me.

Or not me, I realized. Her eyes shifted from just over my shoulder to my face, and she turned away and pretended to read the message board when I'd caught her staring. I glanced over my shoulder. At that distance, she could have been ogling any of the other people I was standing with—but knowing the effect my friend Mac had on women, I guessed it was him.

"How about we go and discuss that business of ours then," Mac's father suggested.

Duncan shook his head. "Later, William. Mal and I want to make the rounds first, get caught up with everyone."

"That's all right," Mr. Weigel said. "I uh, I have something else I want to do first anyway."

Mac's father shot him a nasty look. "Six o'clock then?" he said to Duncan. "So we'll be done well before the bonfire tonight?"

Mac's grandfather relented and agreed to the time. He congratulated Mac again for making the team and went on his way—but I noticed his son Mal didn't go with him. He was too busy chatting up Mona.

Mr. Mackenzie pulled Mr. Weigel aside. "Don't get weak on me. We've come too far to have you blow it now."

Mr. Weigel pulled away. "I can handle it," he told his business partner. Mr. Weigel left and Mac's father turned and saw I had been listening in. Out of nowhere he gave me attitude.

"What are you looking at?" he said.

I had about a dozen good answers for that question, none of which Mac's father would have liked. Out of respect for Mac, I didn't use any of them. I raised my hands instead like I surrendered. Mr. Mackenzie stomped off to his trailer and slammed the door behind him. Nice guy.

I tuned back in to Mac and Banks. "Hey, you're one-third of the way there," Banks told Mac.

"What?"

"The psychic's prophecy," Banks said. "She said you'd get to compete on the clan team. That was her first prediction, and it's come true. Now all you have to do is win and be king of the mountain!"

"Right. Of course! I'm gonna go tell Beth," Mac said, and he jogged over to where she was working out.

"And . . . he's gone," I said.

Banks shook his head. "Women," he said.

"Yeah," I said.

I looked back over my shoulder for my pixie, but she was gone.

CHAPTER THREE

Banks and I rocked back and forth on our heels while Beth snogged Mac, and Mal and Mona made small talk.

"How is it we're the only two guys here not hitting it off with girls?" Banks asked.

"Well, in my case, one of them is my archnemesis Beth, and the other one is my sister."

"Yeah, okay," Banks said. "Then why am *I* not hitting it off with any girls?"

"Because one of them is Beth, and the other one is my older sister," I told him.

I led us over to Mal and Mona.

"That is so interesting!" my sister was saying. She clicked off a little gadget in her hand. "Digital recorder," she told me. "So I don't have to keep fumbling with a notebook."

Instead she fumbled the digital recorder, and I caught it and handed it back to her. She hardly noticed.

"You know, I would love to get your number," she said to Mal. "So I can, you know, follow up with any questions I have about the Highland Games."

"Sure, yes, of course," Mal said too quickly. I shook my

head, but it was lost on the two Scot-crossed lovers. Mona dove into her bag and dug around until she found her cell phone.

"I'll just . . . program it in. So I don't lose it," she said.

I groaned. My sister was about as subtle as a personal ad. Luckily for Mona, her blatant overture gave Mal permission to be positively obvious too. He pulled his phone out of his sporran and they exchanged numbers.

"Wow, desperate much?" I asked when Mal had left to find his dad.

"Oh shut up, Horatio. I knew you'd have something smart to say." Mona hefted her bag to her shoulder and walked with us over to Mac and Beth.

"He certainly looks like he'd be able to get you a good seat at a restaurant," I said. "And bring you the wine list too."

"Stop it. He's a really nice guy, all right?"

"And the skirt makes him look sexy," I guessed.

"Kilt," she corrected me.

"A man in a kilt is a man and a half," said Banks.

Mona grinned. "I'll say."

Mac and Beth had stopped sucking face, and the three of us walked over to the Weigel campsite to join them.

"I'm telling you, you should so totally do it. Think of the rush!" Beth was saying. She grabbed Mac by the shirt and heaved against him like she could barely contain herself.

"Beth's not talking you into jumping off a cliff or something, is she?" I asked.

Beth backed away from Mac like we had startled her. She rearranged her boobs in her sports bra and Mac popped his neck, and neither of them answered my question.

"You missed it," I told Mac. "Malcolm just beat your all-time record for getting a girl's phone number. He got her digits in fourteen seconds flat. They've even got each other on speed dial."

Mona punched me in the shoulder, but not hard. "Laugh it up, Horatio. You see how easy it is meeting people when you're not seventeen anymore."

I gave her my super-sad face. "Poor Mona. Is Tom your only MySpace friend?"

"Keep talking and I'll tell your friends about The Underwear Incident when you were six."

I figured Mac would jump on that one, but Beth pulled him away toward her family's RV. "Ooh, ooh!" she said. "I know how we can do it."

"What can I say?" Mac called, letting himself be dragged. "When the lady wants it, the lady wants it."

Banks and I were suddenly alone with Mona.

"Well, *I'd* like to hear about The Underwear Incident," Banks told her.

"It all started when Horatio got into Juliet's underwear drawer when he was six—"

"Annnnnd, we're out of here," I said, pulling Banks by the shirtsleeve. "See you around the games, Mona!"

Mona gave me a little wave and a smile of triumph, and Banks and I made our way down the main campground road toward the fair. The games didn't officially start until the opening ceremonies that evening, but some of the vendors had already begun to set up shop, and Banks and I headed in their direction. We walked for a while in silence. Pine trees whispered in the wind and the hills echoed with the strains of four different bagpipes playing "Amazing Grace"—and not together.

"Can you imagine having a dad like that?" Banks asked.

"A dad like what?"

"Like Mac's dad. Cutting him down all the time. Saying he's an embarrassment."

I shrugged. "I don't know. Mac's never seemed to care much what his dad thinks anyway."

"Are you kidding? It's *all* he cares about," Banks said. "He may not show it, but it completely eats him up that no matter what he does, no matter how hard he works, his father will *always* treat him like a failure."

What Banks said suddenly made a lot of sense. Despite his outward devil-may-care attitude, Mac had always been quietly driven. He wasn't the smartest kid in the class, but he always did his homework, always studied hard for tests, always took the extra credit. He wasn't the best athlete on the Wittenberg football team either, but he was by far the Bears' best *player*—and he did it by poring over playbooks and putting in extra hours in the weight room and on the practice field. Why hadn't I seen it myself? I thought I knew Mac better than anybody, but I guess being family gave Banks an insight I could never have.

"Banks, how is it we haven't found a girlfriend for you yet?"

"That's what *I* keep asking!"

"All right, if ever there was a place for you to find a soul mate, it has to be the Highland Games. Or at least a one-night stand."

Banks blushed. "I was hoping that maybe—"

"Maybe what?"

Banks looked away as he said it. "Maybe this would be the games where I—you know."

I didn't know. "Where you . . . what?"

"You know. Did . . . it."

"Oh. You mean, you haven't done . . . *it*?"

"Horatio, I haven't even done anything remotely *like* it."

"Aha," I said. We walked along to the strains of "Amazing Grace."

"I mean, I *would* have done it by now," Banks said. "I've just been waiting for the right girl."

"And what girl is that?"

"The one who says yes."

I laughed and put a hand on his shoulder.

"There may be hope for you yet, Banks. But you really are going to have to lose that pocket protector."

Banks put a hand to the black plastic case in his breast pocket. "But where will I keep my bagpipe reeds?"

When we were close to the vendor booths I caught sight of my pixie again. She was setting up a shop of her own. I wanted to cruise by, find out who she was and maybe what she was doing for the rest of her life, but not with Banks along for the ride. He'd already made it clear he was tired of playing wingman to somebody else's gunner. The pixie would have to wait.

"Oh no," Banks whispered.

"What?"

"Just be cool, all right? Be cool," Banks said.

"Okay. I'm being cool."

"Eleven o'clock," Banks said, his head bent toward the ground.

There had been real panic in Banks's eyes. I looked ahead of us. A bunch of teenagers wearing English soccer jerseys, torn punk T-shirts, red and black striped kilts, and black Doc Martens sauntered down the path like the Jets from *West Side Story*. Every last one of them carried a bottle of some kind of orange soda, and one or two actually had homemade pink-dyed Mohawks. I wished I'd brought my camera.

"What is this," I asked Banks, "a Sex Pistols reunion?"

"They're a pipe and drum corps," he whispered. "They call themselves *Hell's Pipers*."

I laughed. Banks shushed me.

"I'm sorry, Banks. I just find it a little hard to be intimidated by a pipe and drum corps. That's a little like being afraid of the Wittenberg marching band."

"Just don't antagonize them, please, Horatio? They mess with me every year."

"Look, I don't mess with anybody that doesn't mess with me. Or my friends."

Banks closed his eyes and shook his head.

We drew closer. Banks kept his eyes on his shoes while I searched the faces of the pied pipers, waiting for one of them to make a move. When we were a step away from butting heads they suddenly swerved, spilling around us like we were Moses parting a red-kilted sea. We moved forward against the current, but we never got wet. None of them even looked at us, as though to register our existences would be to give us too much credit.

Then one little fish swam right down the middle. The gang leader or drum major or something, I guessed. He wore the requisite red and black tartan kilt, unlaced army boots, a black leather jacket with the arms ripped off, and, in what I thought was a bold punk fashion statement, a plain white T-shirt without any band name or emblem on it. But the one thing that really set him apart from his piper posse was his hair—died dark red and pulled into a dozen pointy spikes that made it look like a sea urchin was devouring his head. Or maybe excreting it.

The sea urchin tried to look menacing by cleaning his fingernails with the tip of his little ceremonial knife. It was so threatening I almost laughed. He looked at me and I looked at him as he passed between me and Banks. One "accidental" bump from me and he'd lose a fingertip, but I refrained. I didn't want to get blood on my T-shirt.

The urchin's leather jacket brushed me as he passed— just a hint of a *schhhhk* where his ripped shoulder seam met my sleeve—but I kept on walking. He was baiting me, feeling me out, but I wasn't going to be the one to flinch.

When we were finally clear of the Ramones rejects, Banks let out his breath and turned around to make sure they weren't following us.

"Thanks, Horatio. You don't know those guys. They're bad news. It's best to just stay clear of them."

I nodded, but didn't tell Banks what I already knew: The sea urchin and I would be seeing each other again, and soon.

Banks ran a sweaty hand through his hair. "I should—I should be practicing."

"Banks, don't let those guys rattle you. You're golden. You've been rehearsing for this moment since you were ten."

"Seven."

"See? You live for the bagpipes. Don't freak out the day before the competition."

Banks glanced back at the disappearing pipe corps, and then at his feet.

"No—I think I better practice. This scholarship is only offered once every four years. This is my only chance at going to college, and I can't screw it up."

"All right," I told him. "But seriously, don't let those guys get in your head. That's their game."

Banks nodded, but I knew it was already too late.

"I'm gonna go practice," he said. "I'll see you tonight at the bonfire."

Banks took off for the campground, taking the long way around, out of sight of the pipers. I sighed and shook my head, then doubled back to see if my pixie was still setting up shop.

CHAPTER FOUR

The vendor booths were set up as a series of covered tents, with three or four stalls per tent. If it had anything to do with Scotland, it was being sold here: kilts, scarves, and hats in every tartan color imaginable, T-shirts and bumper stickers with corny slogans like "Real Men Wear Kilts," clan pins, Celtic CDs, broad swords, wooden swords, genealogy charts, and maps of Scotland. And just about every shop sold those little Scottish daggers that everyone wore in their shoes. It was quite a racket.

The pixie was still at work on her booth, but she had a junior partner now, a girl who looked to be a couple years younger than her. Same pixie face and dark black hair, but grown down to the shoulders. She wore the family kilt too, but paired it with a loose sweater and sensible shoes. They were sisters, I figured, but I couldn't take my eyes off the original model.

It felt strange, chasing a skirt. I knew a good-looking girl when I saw one, but I didn't go trailing after every one of them like a puppy. What was wrong with me? Just to prove I was still the boss of me I wandered up the hill toward a separate row of shops. See? I have willpower, I told myself, even though I was keeping one eye on where I was and one eye on where I wanted to be. The best view of the girls was from a booth selling more of that orange stuff the pipers had been drinking, and I stopped there and pretended to be interested in some of their swag. A Scottish tune full of violins and bagpipes blared from speakers and televisions all around the orange drink booth, but I was barely listening.

"*Feasgar math!*" someone behind me said. One of the orange drink flaks had caught me lingering at the booth. She was college-aged and perky, wearing an orange and black kilt and a T-shirt that had the letters "IRN-BRU" stretched across her Victoria's Secret chest. Her eyes sparkled and her mouth curled up at the end like I'd said something clever and witty, only I hadn't yet. I already wanted to buy every last bottle of orange soda from her.

"*Feasgar math* yourself," I told her.

"Och! You speak Gaelic too?" she said with a thick Scottish brogue.

"Only what I get from your lips."

The curl broke into a full-on smile and she held her hands behind her back and did that little bounce on her toes girls do to show you how much their boobs like you.

"It means 'Good afternoon'!" she said.

"And in one less syllable," I told her. I pointed at a speaker. "I like the music. Catchy."

"It's magic, innit? A traditional ballad from the old country with a wee bit of a modern edge to it." She nodded to one of the televisions, where a looped commercial played the song over and over again. "Iron-Brew's got a mad on for it. They've spent ten million pounds on this new campaign, trying to take the States by storm."

"Iron-Brew?" I asked.

She puffed out her chest and drew a finger slowly across the "IRN-BRU" stretched across her high beams. "'Iron-Brew,'" she read for me.

"Very effective," I told her. "You should rent out space."

She grinned. "Would ya like a taste, love?"

Oh, she was dangerous, this one. Like Flamin' Hot Cheetos. You wanted more even though you knew it was just going to burn your ass later.

The girl handed me a bottle of the orange stuff.

"The first one's free, huh?"

"You ken to that, come back and see me." She grinned and bounced on her toes again. "There's plenty more where that came from, love."

There was so much in that I almost forgot we were talking about soda. Was this girl really flirting with me, or was this like the crush you get on a cute waitress when she chirps you for a better tip? Whatever it was, I didn't need an orange soda right now. I needed a hot coffee and a cold shower.

I touched the bottle to my forehead in salute. "Thanks for the ego trip," I told her, then blew that pop stand before I did something stupid like ask her what her name was. I was feeling bolder, though. I was ready to talk to the pixie, whose name I *did* want to know. I cracked the cap on the IRN-BRU and took a swig on the way to her booth— then made a quick detour to power spit the mouthful into a trash barrel.

I hung over the can, hawking and spitting to try and get the taste out. When that didn't work I rubbed my tongue on my shirtsleeve. I glanced at the bottle. "Made with real iron!" it declared. It was just trace amounts, but whatever else was in it, I didn't like it. I dropped the bottle in the empty trash barrel with a *thunk* and tried not to think about how disappointed the IRN-BRU girl was going to be in me.

When I regained four of my five senses—taste was still down for the count—I found the pixie's shop. Only she wasn't there. It was just the younger girl. I frowned and looked around. She'd been there just a second ago, I was sure.

"Hi," I said to the younger girl. It wasn't the best cover ever, but I played it.

"Hi," she said back. She was good.

I smiled and studied their wares, like that was all I had come by for in the first place. There was a small selection of handmade jewelry with Celtic knotwork designs and various pieces of leather—bags, belts, bracelets—with designs punched and carved in them.

"I do the jewelry and my sister does the leatherwork," the girl told me.

"Oh, your sister?"

She nodded. "She'll be back soon, if you want to wait."

I eyed her. "Why would I want to do that?"

"That's who you came to see, isn't it? I saw you hovering at the IRN-BRU stand."

I closed my eyes. I must be losing my touch. I had been made by a—

"What grade are you?" I asked her.

"Ninth."

I had been made by a freshman. I told her my name and asked her for hers.

"Lucy. And my sister's name is Megan." She said it like "May-gan."

I cleared my throat. "Right. Thanks. She didn't, ah—"

"See you? No. I didn't tell her. I wanted to see how you were going to play it."

I nodded. "Ah. Thanks. I ah—I appreciate that. So, what, you guys run this with your parents?"

"No, it's just us. Mom and Dad spend the whole festival giving genealogy talks and helping people figure out what clan they belong to."

"Right. Well. I guess I'll . . . see you around then."

"Don't worry. She'll like you. My sister, I mean. You're cute. And you don't take all this too seriously."

"And how do you know that?"

"No kilt," she told me. "As for the cute part—"

I held up a hand and she smiled.

"Lucy," I told her, "there is someone I'd very much like you to meet. Do you by any chance like the bagpipes?"

After I laid the groundwork for Banks I bid Lucy adieu and told her I'd make my play for May-gan another time. I was even more resolved now than before. If her sister was half as smart as Lucy was, Megan and I were going to get along very well indeed.

I made my way down to the ring of clan tents that circled the playing field where the actual Highland Games would be held. It looked like a Renaissance fair, with multicolored tents and pennants flapping in the cool mountain breeze. There were maybe seventy or eighty tents in all, and each one had a Scottish-sounding name hanging from a banner at the top: Bruce, Campbell, Donald, Douglas, Gordon, Kennedy, Ross—and a slew of Macs: MacArthur, MacDougall, MacKay, MacMillan, MacPherson, MacBeth, and more. Some of the clans were already setting out suits of armor, family albums, maps of Scotland, and flyers and brochures about their clans. The women wore long skirts and the men wore short kilts, and each clan looked like its own private school with matching plaid uniforms. It felt like the cosplay parade when the anime convention hit town, only here it was parents and grandparents who played dress-up, not the kids.

A few tents down I spied an old man in a wheelchair trying to get a banner hung by himself. He wore the usual Scottish getup, with the addition of a red and blue plaid blanket wrapped around his legs, and two dogs like Mac's standing by his side. They weren't helping much with the banner. He'd managed to loop one end of the rope over the bar at the top, but the slack wasn't long enough for him to reach.

"Need a hand?" I asked.

"I've got two hands," he told me. "What I need is two working legs."

I pulled the rope down to him and he tugged the banner tight. It said "Macduff."

"There. Now tie that off," he told me. I was able to reach it without a chair, and I secured it to the tent crossbar.

"Here—there's a display back here too."

The old man pointed to a pile of PVC pipe that was supposed to go together like a big frame to hold a huge canvas map of Scotland with the Macduff ancestral lands highlighted on it. I raised my eyebrows to show the old man this was a bit more than I had offered to do, but he was already torquing his wheelchair through the wet grass to throw a tartan-patterned cloth over the folding table at the front.

What the hell, I thought. It'll be my good deed for the year.

The damn PVC frame took fifteen minutes to put together because it kept collapsing under the weight of the canvas map. The dogs kept sniffing at it and knocking the flimsy thing down too. Once or twice the old man looked back to watch me juggling the pieces, but he kept his mouth shut and didn't tell me how to do it. **Maybe** he sensed that would be the end of my assistance.

I finally got the thing to stand up on its own but I gave it a half a day before one of the dogs knocked it down again, burying the old man in his wheelchair. It would probably be another day or two before anybody even noticed. He'd have to send the dogs for help like Lassie.

I clapped my hands together. "Okay. There you go." I was already walking out of the tent. "Be seeing you."

"Wait," the old man said. I stopped and turned, ready to lie and tell him I had somewhere I had to be.

"Sit down," he said. "I'll get you something to drink."

He had already thrown the carriage into reverse and opened a cooler. It felt like as close to a thank you as I was bound to get from him, so I stepped back inside.

"As long as it's not that orange stuff they're selling at the vendor stalls," I told him.

The old man laughed. "IRN-BRU?" he said. "The only way they get anybody to drink that swill is to have big-breasted girls hand it out for free."

I laughed and sat in one of the metal folding chairs at the table.

"Root beer all right?" the old guy asked.

"My favorite," I told him.

He popped the top on a cold one and put it on the table.

"You not having one?"

"Doctor tells me I can't drink the stuff anymore," he groused. "It angries up my blood. Damn doctors. What's the point of living longer if you can't *live* while you're alive?" He nodded at my bottle. "Drink. At least I can enjoy it vicariously."

I took a long drink, and the old man licked his lips while he watched.

"Maybe I should videotape myself eating steak and drinking sodas and smoking cigarettes," I told him. "Sell them to old people as fetish videos."

The old man grunted a laugh. "What's your name, son?"

"Horatio. Horatio Wilkes."

"Jesus, Joseph, and Mary," he said. "You should sue for damages. My parents saddled me with 'Guy.' Guy Sternwood. Most people call me the General."

"Are you? A general, I mean?"

"Judge Advocate General, United States Army, retired. Glorified lawyer," Sternwood explained. "Technically a major general. Two stars."

I saluted with my bottle and took another drink for his benefit. One of his dogs came up and put his head in my lap, and I scratched it.

"My dogs are a good judge of character," General Sternwood said.

"What are their names?"

"Ross and Lennox." The dogs' ears twitched at the sound of their names.

"My friend Mac has a dog like this," I told him.

"Border collie," Sternwood said. He squinted at me. "Bill Mackenzie's boy, you mean? I trained that dog. Trained all these dogs."

The General whistled—a piercing sound that made me jump in my chair—and Ross and Lennox stood at attention.

"Come by," he said. The dogs ran out of the tent and ran for a couple of tourists walking the clan tent path. You could tell they were tourists because they were loaded down with cameras and didn't have a hint of tartan anywhere on them.

The woman gasped as the dogs ran toward her and clutched her husband's arm.

"Walk up!" Sternwood called. "Walk up!"

The dogs suddenly slowed to a walk, crouching low like they were hunting the tourists. The couple froze where they stood.

"Way to me," General Sternwood called, and the dogs circled the couple to the right. When they were behind them he barked, "Lie down!" and the dogs did. One of the tourists flinched like he might do it too.

"Walk up, walk up, walk up," he told the dogs. They inched toward the couple, herding them toward our tent.

"Take your time," Sternwood told the dogs. "Take your time. Now way back!"

The dogs jumped and nipped playfully at the couple, making them scurry into the tent.

"Ooh!" the woman squeaked, realizing now she wasn't in any danger.

"That'll do, lads. That'll do."

The dogs ran back to the General's side and he pulled a treat for each of them out from under the tartan blanket on his lap. The tourist couple applauded, and the man took a snapshot of Sternwood and the dogs.

"Border collie demonstration tomorrow morning at eleven o'clock on the main field," Sternwood told them as they went on their way.

"Mac never does anything like that with Spot," I told him.

General Sternwood *tsked*. "That's criminal is what that is. Hangable offense. Border collies are born to work. It's in their blood." Sternwood eyed me. "You a Mackenzie then?"

"What?" I'd already told him my name was Wilkes.

"Your clan, boy. What clan are you?"

"I'm not any clan," I told him. "I'm not Scottish. I'm just a friend of the family."

Sternwood harrumphed. "Everybody's Scottish, lad. They just don't know it yet." He twisted his chair so he could pull a large three-ring binder over to him on the table.

"Let's see. Your name was Wilkes, right? Wilkes. Wilkes." He ran his finger down a long list of names. "You Irish?"

"Some part, I guess. We're kind of nothing. And everything."

He smacked the book. "Heh. Whatdya know? No Wilkes—but 'Wilkie' is a sept of Macduff."

"A what?"

"A sept. It's like a smaller family that's been rolled into a bigger one. My name's Sternwood, but I've got a Randolph three generations back. The Randolphs are a sept of the Macduff clan, so I'm a Macduff. Understand? You're a Wilkie—or close enough—which makes you a Macduff too."

I shrugged. "Thanks, but I'm not really into all this stuff."

Sternwood flipped the book closed. "Neither am I. I put up the booth because nobody else wants to, but I'm mostly here for the dogs." Ross and Lennox perked up again, and the General scratched their backs. "I've been training border collies since I was your age, and these games, these festivals, they're the only place for it anymore. We need the games so we won't lose that part of us," he said, nodding at the book of family names, "no matter how tenuously we're connected to it." He looked around. "These mountains, that wind, those rocks—without all this we lose our sense of place. We need these games, these mountains, to remember who we were once and where we come from. To remind us how human we

41

are in spite of all our computers and gadgets and contraptions."

Sternwood smacked the armrest of his wheelchair and clutched both sides with his bony white hands. I gave him a minute for his words to be carved in the big stone of profound thoughts, then he looked up at me and grimaced.

"I must sound like a crazy old man."

"No," I told him. "I get it."

He could see that I did and he nodded.

"I better go," I told him. "I've got a summer reading book to finish. *The Sound and the Fury*." I stood. "Thanks for the root beer."

"Wait," Sternwood said. He worked the wheels of his chair around the table so he could be closer to me. Ross and Lennox followed him. "Do me a favor, will you?"

I looked around the tent, but I didn't see anything left to do.

"No, not that," he said, waving it away. "It's my niece. She needs looking after this weekend."

I adjusted my hat. "Look General, I'm with you on the mountains-are-bigger-than-we-are thing, and it's kooky that you like watching people drink root beer and all, but I'm no babysitter."

"No, no, no. It's not like that. My niece, she doesn't need a babysitter so much as a . . . a guardian angel. Someone with enough common sense to get her out of trouble when she gets in over her head. You seem like the right man for the job."

I waffled. "Yeah, thanks, but no. Look, if you want a rent-a-cop, there are plenty of guys with cowboy hats and walkie-talkies around here running people down with golf carts. Ask one of them."

Just then I caught sight of my pixie, Megan, coming down the path. I watched her get closer and closer, and then to my surprise she ducked into our tent and went straight for the General, leaning close to whisper something in his ear. Ross and Lennox wagged their tails at her and I was tempted to do the same. When she'd told Sternwood whatever it was she came to tell him she stood up, gave me the once-over with her eyes, then left the tent and went on her way.

I realized I had my mouth open and I closed it.

Sternwood knitted his fingers in his lap.

"My niece," he told me. "Megan Sternwood."

I opened my mouth again, and this time words came out.

"You know, I think I'll be able to help you out after all."

Sternwood smiled.

CHAPTER FIVE

—✒—

Dusk was falling and the clan tents and the vendor booths were emptying out. Everybody staying on the mountain was headed back to their campers to have dinner and get ready for the opening ceremonies. I left General Sternwood at the Macduff tent and followed his niece. I didn't have to be asked to keep an eye on her, but now that it was official I thought I'd make a point of introducing myself when she stopped at her booth.

But she didn't stop at her booth. She went instead to the campground, where I figured she was going back to her family's RV. I was wrong.

When the territory got familiar I closed the gap between us, and I pretended to be studying the huge Scottish flag hanging over the path when she took a quick look around and ducked off the path into the woods. A few seconds later I followed her into the rhododendron.

There wasn't much of a path, but I could tell from the break of the leaves where she'd been. I tried to move slowly and quietly, but made about as little noise as the Scottish Highland Regiment marching through the woods.

The thick undergrowth opened up behind a big RV on a campground site, and from where I was hiding I could see Megan crouching low against the trailer. She turned at the sound of my trailblazing and I froze. She must not have seen me, because five seconds later she stood on the toes of her tall black boots and lifted an ear to an open window on the back of the RV.

Mac's RV.

I squatted there and she stood there for only five minutes or so, but it felt like an eternity. Then something made her start and she pulled away from the camper and dashed off toward the woods again. She was coming right for where I was hiding, and there was nowhere for me to go in the twisted rhododendron branches, and no way to retreat without raising a ruckus.

Just when I'd thought of something clever to say when she tripped over me, Megan found a different path into the woods a couple of yards away. I could see the red of her skirt passing by through the leaves, but if she saw my khakis and white T-shirt through the green she didn't squawk.

Our introduction would have to wait.

At the risk of missing out on more sneaky fun, I let her go without following. I wiggled my way out of my nest and reintroduced my legs to the idea of standing up by moving to the spot where she'd been snooping. I didn't quite have to stand on my toes to hear Mac's father and Mac's grandfather Duncan.

"I understand your concerns," Mr. Mackenzie was saying. "But if you could just appreciate the time and work that we've put into this proposal—"

Duncan didn't say anything, but from the way Mac's dad left off I could tell the conversation was over. The RV rocked with movement, and I hurried around to the corner of the trailer to hear them come out. Spot came with them and immediately bounded around the corner to where I was hiding. "That'll do, Spot," I whispered, hoping what he remembered of the General's training might calm him down enough to not give me away. It worked—Spot sat down on the ground beside me, peaceful for the first time since I'd known him.

"I hope you'll at least accept the invitation to stay with us tonight," Mr. Mackenzie said. "It would be our honor."

Duncan sighed. "All right, William. All right. For old times' sake."

I wondered how much of this exchange Megan was seeing. She was out of the woods now and walking along the main road by the campsite and taking all of this in with a surreptitious glance. Her gaze shifted from the two older men to me where I was hiding with Spot. Our eyes locked for a moment, then she picked up her pace and disappeared down the road.

Mr. Mackenzie and his father-in-law said their good-byes. What was that meeting all about? And why was Megan Sternwood so interested? I waited a long beat while Mac's dad dialed someone on his cell phone. He cursed when the call didn't go through.

"Damn it, you idiot," Mr. Mackenzie said, presumably to whoever it was he couldn't get on the phone. "If you get caught we're both going down."

I chose that moment to come around to the front of the trailer with Spot. For some reason, Mr. Mackenzie wasn't happy to see me.

"What were you doing back there?" he demanded.

"Looking for Bigfoot," I said. He was just about to grill me again when Spot started to growl at Beth, who came out of the trailer next door. Mac followed wearing the same kilt and T-shirt he'd had on before, but Beth had changed into more formal cosplay: a white long-sleeve peasant blouse, white-trimmed blue vest, and a skirt in her family tartan with tall argyle socks to match.

"Waiting tables tonight at the Salty Wench?" I asked Beth.

"Spending the night with your right hand again?" she threw back.

"Mac, Horatio," Mac's father said, dropping my interrogation, "I have some good news. Duncan's honoring us by staying with Clan Mackenzie tonight. You won't mind sharing the guest tent, will you, Horatio?"

"No, of course not."

"Gramps picks a different clan to stay with every night of the festival," Mac told me. "He's got a house here on the mountain, but he likes to make the rounds with the other families. He's been doing it forever."

"I've got to go make some calls," Mr. Mackenzie said, giving me the eye again before he left.

"Tonight," Beth said to Mac. "It has to be tonight." She was giddy, practically bouncing. I hadn't seen her so spastic since she'd gotten Mac to go skinny-dipping in the fountain at the World's Fair Park back home.

"What has to be tonight?" I asked.

"I don't know," Mac said, but to Beth, not to me.

"You *have* to do it, Mac. For me. For us! Can you imagine the rush?" She was almost breathless.

Mac grimaced. "Can we talk about this later?" he asked. I could tell he didn't want to have this conversation with me around, but Beth wasn't letting him off the hook.

"No! Later will be too late, and you know it!" Beth reached

a hand under Mac's kilt and grabbed him. "Are you going to be a man for me? Huh? Are you gonna earn these?"

Mac's eyes went so wide I thought they would roll out of their sockets. Beth leaned in close and whispered, but loud enough so that I heard it.

"You think we've had fun up until now? You do this and you will have The. Best. Sex. *Ever.*"

Beth was breathing hard like they just had. I had wanted to run screaming from this strange conversation long ago, but Beth had as much of a grip on me as she did on Mac. Metaphorically speaking. She did something else under Mac's kilt and he stood up straighter and sucked in his breath.

"I know you want this just as much as I do," she told him.

"All—all right," he said. "I'll do it."

Beth pulled her hand away and Mac sagged like an empty puppet. She gave him a smack on the butt that fluffed his pleated kilt and she bounced off toward the main field.

I stared at Mac.

"What?" he said.

"I'm just waiting to hear you explain . . . *whatever* that was."

"Sometimes . . . sometimes Beth can just be a little . . intense. That's all."

"*Intense?* That's not the word I would use for it. How about *insane?* Mental. *Wacko.* Oh, here's one you'll appreciate: *nut-*job."

"Come on, Horatio. This is my girlfriend you're talking about here."

"Ods bodkins, Mac! I know she's hot and all, but sometimes Beth scares the ever-living crap out of me."

"Me too," he confessed. "A little. But she only wants what's best for me."

Mac walked over to a picnic table where food had been set out in plastic containers. We served up plates for ourselves and sat down by the campfire.

"So," I said. "Are you going to tell me what that was all about? Besides Beth making you her bitch?"

Mac cracked open a bottle of IRN-BRU and took a long drink from it. The flickering light from the fire mottled his face with flames, and Mac stared into it for a minute like it was consuming him. He shook his head.

"Nothing, it's—it's stupid. Beth just wants me to . . . to make up my mind about competing in the games. That's all."

"That's *it*?" I said. "No. No, I don't believe that. She wants you to do some crazy new stunt so she can get off on it."

"No, it's not—no. She just wants me to win the Highland Games and be king of the mountain and everything. I mean, I want it too, but—"

"You mean you're *not* going to do it?"

"I don't know," Mac said. "What's the point?" He ate a potato chip.

"What's the point? I thought you lived for stuff like this. You never wait for anything to happen to you—you always reach out and take it."

"Yeah," Mac said. "Yeah." He looked into the fire again. "It's like that this time too, like it's right there in front of me. I can see it, but when I reach out to grab it, it's gone."

Mac was getting deep on me. Mac never got deep.

"Is this about your dad?" I asked him.

"What?"

I'd broken whatever spell he was under. "You know. How nothing you ever do is good enough for him," I said, taking my lead from Banks.

"Jesus, when did this turn into a therapy session?" he said, his mouth full of hot dog.

"You're right, I'm sorry. It's none of my business."

Mac let his plate and his shoulders sag. "No. No—you're right. I mean like today, you know? You were there. When Duncan told me I'd made the team, all Dad could say was 'He'll just embarrass us.' I mean, what the hell? It's like he *never* takes me seriously."

"So *make* him take you seriously. *Make him* acknowledge you."

Mac looked into the fire and nodded.

"Look, I can't believe I'm agreeing with something Beth told you to do," I told him, "and I *certainly* won't go as far as she did to convince you, but I say go for it."

Mac's face hardened and he nodded. It had gotten colder, and I could see his breath as he spoke—not to me, but to himself.

"Yeah. Yeah," he said. "I mean, I do this—I do it right—and he'll have to acknowledge me. I mean, I will be *king* of this mountain. That's what the psychic said. And when I'm the king, he'll have to take me seriously."

"It's good to be the king," I told him.

The fire was out of Mac's eyes when he turned to me, but the mettle was still there. He was going to do it.

"Thanks, Horatio. I needed that."

I smiled. "Don't mention it, chum."

CHAPTER SIX

—🔪—

By nightfall it felt like someone had left the Birnam Mountain refrigerator door open. I had never seen so nice a day become so nasty so quickly. The wind picked up and I shivered in my short-sleeve shirt and kicked myself for not bringing a sweater to the opening ceremonies. I could have walked back to the campground to get one, but they were already ringing the bell to call the clans to Mac-Rae Meadow. Still, I guess I had it better than all the men in kilts gathering on the field. At least I was wearing pants. And underwear.

Mac and Banks were both down on the field somewhere with their clan. The audience for the night's festivities— myself included—was scattered about on a hillside facing MacRae Meadow. Most of them sat on blankets or brought those canvas chairs that fold up into a tote bag. I kept myself entertained by counting the number of people who fell down trying to wobble up the slope under their loads. For Highlanders, these people had an awfully tough time walking on hills.

I had taken shelter at the very top, under the lee of what

served as a review stand. More men in kilts—this time smarter than me and wearing heavy jackets—tested microphones and shuffled papers inside.

My sister Mona staggered down past me and I called to her. She trudged back up.

"Horatio, why aren't you wearing a sweater?" she asked.

"I don't like to sweat," I told her.

"You're going to freeze to death," she told me. She started to give me her photographer's vest, but I shook her off.

"I have a flashlight—see?" I clicked it on and rubbed my hands over it, as though it might warm them.

"How did it get so bad all of a sudden?" she asked over the howl of the wind. "I think it might even rain."

I shivered so hard my head shook. I pretended I'd done it on purpose.

"It's not going to rain," I told her. "It's going to snow."

"Go back to the tent and get a jacket."

"Go do whatever it is you're here to do," I told her. "If I'm cryogenically frozen by morning, don't thaw me out until everybody's driving flying cars."

"I'm supposed to be down on the field taking pictures of the ceremony," she said. She looked around. "I don't suppose you've seen Mal anywhere, have you?"

She threw it out casually, the way you throw a harpoon.

"You mean he hasn't been giving you a guided tour of his kilt?"

Mona rolled her eyes but didn't take the bait. "No. He isn't on the field with the others, and he's not up here in the press box either. No one's seen him."

"Maybe he's avoiding you."

"Drop dead," she told me. She turned and made her way back down toward the field.

I gave her a shaky salute. "Snow problem."

An arctic wind tore through just then, no doubt conjured up by our mother, who hated to hear her children bicker. Instead of snow, I was showered with papers from the review stand above me. I caught as many as I could and risked a case of frostbite to return them.

"Thanks, son," said a bearded man in a kilt and heavy jacket. "Aren't you freezing?"

"Me?" I asked. "I hardly notice. See? I can't even feel my hands."

A man beyond us with a walkie-talkie cursed. "I don't know where he is, Donald. And I can't hear a thing over this damn walkie-talkie. It must be the weather."

"Who are you looking for?" I asked.

"Duncan MacRae," the bearded one told me, "but we'd settle for his son Mal if we could find either of them. We need a MacRae to light the ceremonial bonfire."

"Duncan's lit the bonfire at the end of every opening ceremony for fifty years," the other one said. "I don't know why he didn't hear the call."

I stamped my feet to stay warm. "He's staying with the Mackenzie clan tonight. Have you checked their tent?"

The guy with the walkie-talkie tried to relay that information to his army of golf-cart jockeys, but all he got was static in return.

"I'll go see if he's still there," I told them.

"You'll miss the start of the ceremonies," the bearded man told me.

"If I don't get some warmer clothes on I'll be dead by then anyway."

The path back to the campground was cold and lonely. True to the bearded one's words, I could hear the drone of a bagpipe corps warming up behind me on MacRae Meadow. The ceremony was starting.

Farther into the forest, the hum of the bagpipes fell away and the wind screamed like a woman wailing. I had to lean into it or be blown away. Above me, the moon appeared and disappeared behind clouds that raced across the blackened sky. I took back all those poetic things I'd said about the mountain. This was a nightmare. A frozen nightmare. I kept my head down and my eyes on the weak circle of light from my flashlight. If I lost the path, I'd be slicing open my tauntaun by midnight.

The wind was so strong it had blown out a few of the campfires in the campground. I jogged the last little way, eager for at least the shelter of the Mackenzie tent.

"Who?" someone called, making me jump. I swung my flashlight in the direction of the voice. Two bright shining eyes gazed back at me—an owl, perched above the entrance to the tent. "Who?" it asked again, then spread its wings like a dark angel and flapped away into the night sky.

That's when I saw the tent flap was untied and whipping around in the wind.

"Mr. MacRae?" I called. "Mal?" It was as black as a telemarketer's soul inside, and I brought my flashlight up to look around. There was something dark splashed all over the wall, the floor, my cot. My shoe squelched as I pulled it up out of the sticky stuff to shine my light on it.

Blood. I was standing in blood. An ocean of it. More blood than a B-grade slasher pic. It was everywhere, on everything. I tried to make myself laugh, tried to believe it was some kind of elaborate practical joke, but the laugh came out like a wheeze. It was warm in there too, and I suddenly wanted it to be cold again. The hair on my arms stood on end.

Without moving my feet again I swept the room with my flashlight. I saw a toppled cot, a blood-soaked blanket, and, in the corner, a crumpled heap.

I had to know.

My sneakers slid as I crossed the room and I threw out a hand to catch myself on a tent pole. It was slippery with blood. My dinner came up in my throat and I swallowed it back down. There was nowhere to wipe my hand, though. I held it away from me like it was cursed.

I squatted next to the heap in the corner. His kilt was the color of Clan MacRae and his shirt was the color of blood. I turned the body over with my flashlight, and Duncan MacRae's blood-drained white face stared up at me in mute, dead horror, his throat slit from ear to ear in a grotesque imitation of a smile.

I staggered backward and crashed into an overturned chair. As I scrambled to my feet, my flashlight caught a word written in blood on the wall by Duncan's dying hand: "MAL-COLM."

Outside I fell to my knees and emptied my stomach into the dirt. I'd seen death and I'd seen blood—hell, I'd even seen a man shot before—but never like this, never so much of it, never so—

I threw up again, coughing and spitting when there was nothing left inside me. When I was finished I wiped my bloodied hand on the grass.

The door on Beth's RV one lot over opened, startling me. Beth's dad stuck his head out and looked around. He stepped out of the trailer, still glancing this way and that, and that's when I stood. He jumped when he saw me, slamming the RV door shut.

"Jesus, what are you doing here?" he asked. "You're Mac's friend, aren't you?"

"Horatio," I told him. "What are *you* doing here? Is there somebody in there with you?"

"What? No. I just—I just came back to use the bathroom. The Porta-Johns are already disgusting. Are you headed back? I'll walk with you," he said, his voice raised strangely.

This was all a little too suspicious. Had he really come all this way back just to use the bathroom?

"We can't go," I told him. "Duncan MacRae's been stabbed."

I watched his face. If he was ready for that, it didn't show.

"What?" he said, looking around. "Where?"

"In Mac's tent. There's blood everywhere." I brought the back of my hand to my mouth, trying to ward off another esophageal episode. "I need you to go for help."

"Go for help?" he asked. "Good God, is he still alive?"

"No. But someone needs to stand watch over the tent."

Mr. Weigel glanced back at his RV.

"I'll do that. I'll stay. You run and tell someone."

I wasn't so sure that was the best idea, but I didn't know how I could say no without making it a big deal. Besides, I'd been inside. I knew what I had seen. If he went in and changed anything, I'd know it.

"All right," I said. "But don't go in there, and don't let anybody else in, got it? It's a crime scene."

"Good. Yes. Go," he told me.

He was right: I had wasted enough time already. For better or worse, I left Mr. Weigel behind. There was one more thing I should have done right away, and as I ran I pulled out my cell phone and dialed 911.

My phone chirped back at me in protest.

I was out of range.

CHAPTER SEVEN

I ran like I was mad at the ground. The trees shrieked, but I didn't hear them. The wind cut through me like a knife, but I didn't feel it. The world had descended into chaos all around me, but I don't think I would have noticed an earth-quake. Every sense I had was filled with Duncan, bloody Duncan.

The emcee was busy introducing clans when I burst into the press box. The man with the walkie-talkie caught me. I told him what I'd seen, leaving out the name scrawled on the wall of the tent. He blinked like he didn't understand. I told him again, and he went as white as a suburb. He plucked his two-way radio from his belt and pressed down the button and opened his mouth, but nothing came out.

"Police," I told him. "We need real police, not rent-a-cops. A sheriff, a forest ranger—*somebody*."

He shook himself.

"Sonny—Sonny, do you read me?" he said.

His radio squawked, and miraculously Sonny answered.

"I need you to find me Sheriff Wood and send him to Bill Mackenzie's tent in the campground. He'll be in the audience, watching with his wife. And don't ask me why—just do it."

He clicked off, and Sonny 10-4ed that he'd understood.

"We need to find Malcolm MacRae," I told him.

"Mal should be on the field, with his clan."

"So should Duncan," I told him.

Together we ran headlong down the steep slope to the meadow named in honor of Duncan MacRae. Now it was a memorial. It was pitch-black on the field, except for the flickering torches held by the clans. One of the clan leaders was out near the unlit bonfire in the middle of the meadow, raising a thickly burning torch and telling the crowd about his family. We circled the gathered clans from behind looking for the MacRaes. The security guy pulled to a stop near a group with tartans like Duncan's.

"Mal MacRae?" he asked the group. "Mal?"

Mal came out of the darkness on the other side of the track and jogged over to us. He hadn't been with his clan.

"I'm here, I'm here," he told us. "It can't be time to light the bonfire yet, can it?"

The security guy pulled him aside and broke the news. Mal backed away, shaking his head. The security guy nodded, told him again, and Mal was off and running in the direction of his father.

"Follow him," I told the security guy. "Make sure he goes to the campground."

"Why?"

I told him about Mal's name written in blood. He turned white again.

I caught his eyes, making sure he was listening. "Don't let him go inside until the sheriff is there, do you understand?"

The security guy nodded and took off at a sprint, already barking into his walkie-talkie.

"What's going on?" one of the MacRaes asked me. "Is everything all right?"

I looked around at the hundreds of people gathered around the field, waiting to declaim for their clans. If word got out now it'd be chaos, and knowing now or an hour from now wouldn't make any difference. That still didn't make it any easier to lie.

"Nothing to worry about now. Nothing to worry about," I told them. I felt like the captain of the Hindenburg. I backed away and went looking for Mac. Instead I found Banks.

"Where's Mac?" I asked him.

"He just got here," Banks told me. "He and Beth were off fooling around in the woods or something." He saw my face in the darkness and he frowned. "Why? What's wrong?"

"Something's happened," I told him. "To Duncan."

Banks had just begun to ask what when the emcee called for Duncan MacRae to step forward and light the bonfire. I cursed. No one had told him Duncan wouldn't be lighting the bonfire again this year or any other year. A murmur grew on the meadow as the clans wondered aloud where their venerable leader was.

Banks began to understand. "Horatio, what's happened?"

"Maybe Duncan's gotten in out of this cold," the emcee joked. The crowd laughed politely. "How about the next generation, Mal MacRae? Is he here to raise the clans for us?"

I cursed again. Mal wasn't coming either.

"Where's Mr. Mackenzie? He needs to take charge."

"Mac's dad? But where's—?" Banks started.

Someone stepped out from the crowd, marching a torch

toward the bonfire in the center. The assembled clans grew quiet.

"That's not Mr. Mackenzie," Banks said. "It's Mac."

Lightning flashed—no, it was a camera, Mona's camera. She was out in the middle of the meadow, snapping pictures of Mac. The wind swirled his kilt, and he raised the torch high in the air.

"I am Joe Mackenzie of the Clan Mackenzie," he declared, "Duncan MacRae's grandson and heir." A mike picked up his voice and carried it across the glen. "When my grandfather bought this mountain all those years ago, everybody laughed. What was he going to do with a *mountain?* But now, sixty years later, that mountain is worth a thousand times what he paid for it—and more!"

The audience cheered, and I felt a swell of pride on Mac's behalf. He didn't know it, but he was giving Duncan MacRae a eulogy.

"Our two great clans—Mackenzie and MacRae—have been entwined for hundreds of years since first joining forces in the Scottish Highlands. Tonight I stand in for Duncan MacRae the way the Mackenzies have always stood for the MacRaes, and the MacRaes for the Mackenzies. The MacRae motto: 'With fortitude!' The Mackenzie motto: 'Save the King!'"

Mac bowed his head. Mona's camera flashed, capturing the moment forever.

Mac looked up. "For Duncan!" he cried, and the audience cheered again. "Now, lock up your women and hide your sheep—I hereby raise the clans for the fifty-second annual Birnam Mountain Highland Games!"

The wannabe Scotsmen surrounding us roared as Mac thrust his torch into the bonfire, setting it ablaze. Bagpipes launched into something other than "Amazing Grace," and kilted kinsmen rushed the field to celebrate. I lost Mac in the confusion, but I could still make out the flash of Mona's camera and forged my way over to her.

"Your friend Mac is quite the showman," she told me.

"Have you seen him? Do you know where he is?"

"No. What's wrong?"

"You know how you were saying you wanted a big story to cover?"

"Yeah?" she said, perking up.

"Be careful what you wish for," I told her. "Duncan Mac-Rae is dead. Murdered."

"What? Here? That nice old man? Oh, Horatio—no."

I nodded, searching the crowd for Mac. "In the Mackenzie family tent. The sheriff's on his way there right now."

"But how?" she asked. "Who did it?"

I almost said Mal, but then I remembered her kilt-crush on him and swallowed it. "Just go," I told her. "You're missing your story."

Mona didn't have to be told twice. She squeezed my arm to leave me with a little courage, and dashed off toward the campground. I wished she hadn't done that. She was going to need that courage when she went inside that tent.

I saw Mac making his way toward me with his arms in the air and a smile on his face like he was already king of the mountain.

"Were you there, chum? Did you see it?" he asked. He put his hands on my shoulders like he wanted to hug me, but I took hold of his wrists and stopped him.

"Mac!" I said, my voice almost drowned out in the celebration. "Mac, Duncan MacRae is dead."

CHAPTER EIGHT

Mac was faster than me, but he hung back so he could see the path with my flashlight. We were taking a shortcut Mac knew through the woods. It was unfamiliar territory for me. As the forest swallowed us up, we heard the emcee back at the meadow calling everyone to order and asking them not to leave the grounds until they'd spoken to the police. There'd been an incident, he told them. I wanted to laugh. It was one hell of an incident.

"What's he talking about?" Mac asked as we ran.

I frowned. Mac knew what he was talking about. "Duncan's murder," I told him.

"No, I mean, why can't anybody leave?"

The trail opened up into a large field of some kind, and Mac charged ahead in the darkness.

"Duncan was killed with a knife," I told him. "And since a few thousand people are wearing Scooby-Doo daggers, or whatever they're called, in their socks, they're going to need to check them all."

"Sgian dubh," Mac corrected me, but from the sound of his voice I could tell his mind was elsewhere. Probably on Duncan.

There was a *thunking* sound, a curse in the night, and suddenly my Converse were the only pair of shoes I could hear running. I skidded to a stop.

"Mac?"

I turned around and my flashlight caught him in a halo of light. He was kneeling on the ground, his hand stuck in his right boot massaging his ankle.

"Must have gotten it caught in a root or something," he told me. I swung the light around in the field but didn't see anything he could have tripped on. The only thing behind him was a sign that said: "Dunsinane Picnic Area." I brought the light back to him. He was already standing.

"I'll be all right," he said. "Come on."

We jogged more carefully now, the wind nipping at our shirttails as we left the picnic area and were swallowed up again by the small path through the woods.

"I saw you, you know," I told Mac.

"What?"

"I saw you go out there and say those things about Duncan and light the bonfire."

"Oh. Yeah?"

"Yeah. You did good."

"It doesn't feel so good now," Mac said. I almost couldn't hear him over the storm.

"I know. With all this—" We got close to the campsite. "But you really took charge out there tonight. That's exactly the kind of thing I was talking about. Making your father respect you."

I shined the light on Mac. His eyes were haunted, but he nodded his thanks.

We came out of the woods again right near Mac's campsite. Beth's dad sat by the smoldering campfire and a Highland Games security guard now stood watch by the door. Mac stopped.

"They're not going to let us in."

"You're his grandson and I'm the one who found the body," I told him.

"You—you found him? I thought it would have been one of the security guys."

"I went back to look for Duncan when he didn't show at the ceremony. Come on."

Mac shook his head. "I can't. I—I can't go in there."

I hadn't told Mac about the blood, but he must have had a vivid imagination. His eyes were wide as though he could see through the walls of the tent and there was sweat on his forehead even though it was zero degrees Kelvin outside. His breath came quick and he backed away.

"I get it," I told him. "It's okay. Just stay here then. You can sit with Mr. Weigel."

"What's he doing here?"

"He was in his trailer when I came back out. He might have been there during the whole thing."

"He what? He was in Beth's trailer the whole time?"

"Sit," I told him. "I'll see what the sheriff thinks."

I deposited Mac with Beth's dad and headed for the tent, hoping I wouldn't pull a repeat of my gastronomical explosion like before. The guard had a deputy's badge pinned to his jacket. I told him the sheriff wanted to see me.

"You seriously do not want to go in there," said the deputy.

"Yeah," I told him. "I wish you'd been here to say that half an hour ago."

I stepped inside. In the light of a kerosene lamp the tent was less bloody than it had seemed in the dark, but it still looked like a Jackson Pollack autopsy. I braced myself for another round of peristaltic pyrotechnics, but it didn't come. Either I'd emptied my stomach or I was getting used to blood-splatter. For the sake of my soul I hoped it was the former.

There were three other people in the little canvas room. One was my sister Mona, who was snapping pictures of the crime scene, probably at the sheriff's request. She'd been crying, and she was still fighting back tears as she worked. "Jesus, Horatio," she whispered, passing close by me to get a new angle on a shot.

The guy I took to be the sheriff was wearing jeans, not a kilt. He stood across the room with his hands in the pockets of a heavy sheepskin jacket that looked as warm and fuzzy as the big mustache crawling up his nose. He registered me with the quick eyes of a hunter, then flicked them back to Mal, who was quivering in the corner.

"But I loved my father!" Mal blubbered. "I would never—I could never do this!"

Mal's name still hung in bloody accusation on the back wall.

"Can you tell me where you been all night?" the sheriff asked him. His Appalachian drawl was slow and deliberate.

"You mean, like an alibi!?" Mal cried. He ran a hand through his hair. "I was—I was at the bonfire. The opening ceremonies."

"But you came late," I said.

Mal registered my existence in the tent for the first time.

"Horatio? What are you—"

"You got there after I discovered the body," I told him. "I ran all the way back to the meadow, and you were just getting there when security and I went looking for you."

"Care to tell us what you were up to?" the sheriff asked.

Mal paled. "I was—I was on the other side of the fairgrounds. Near the parking lot. I got a text message on my phone asking me to come there."

"A text message? From who?" I asked.

Mal pointed at my sister. "From her."

Mona stood, startled. "What?"

"You texted me," said Mal. "You asked me to meet you over by the parking lot."

"No I didn't!" Mona told us. "I was down on the field, taking pictures."

"Do you still have the text message on your phone?" I asked Mal.

"No," he said. He ran a hand through his hair again and cursed. "No—I deleted it. But look, I *swear* she texted me! We hit it off earlier, and I thought she wanted to meet and talk about hooking up later. I went to where she told me to meet her, but she didn't show. I waited as late as I could, then ran back to the meadow so I wouldn't miss the bonfire. I swear!" Malcolm turned to Mona. "Tell them!"

Mona flushed with embarrassment and shook her head. "I didn't send you any message."

"Well, it takes two to tango," the sheriff said. He turned to Mona. "Got your cell phone on you, darlin'? Let's have a look at it."

Mona went to her bag and dug for her cell phone. She frowned. "It's not here."

"What do you mean it's not there?" Mal asked. He took a step toward Mona, and I moved in between them. The sheriff put a hand on Mal's chest to stop him.

"Hold your horses there, son. It'll turn up. In the meantime, I don't suppose you saw anybody on the way who can prove your story."

"Prove my story!?" Mal cried. He could see where this was

going, and there was panic in his eyes. "No—no, of course not! Everyone else was down on the field, ready for the opening ceremonies! I *swear,* I didn't do this! You have to believe me!" He turned on the faucets and his tears ran like tap water.

"Just take it easy, son," the sheriff told him. "Sonny?" he called out. "Sonny, why don't you escort Mr. MacRae down the hill to the sheriff's station for me."

The guard from outside came into the tent to take Mal away. I could just imagine the mug shot Mal would take, all prim and proper in his immaculate Scottish costume, holding up a black slate with his criminal serial number on it.

"No, please," Malcolm begged. "I didn't do this. Why would I? I loved my father—"

The sheriff produced a pair of handcuffs from the back of his belt and slipped them on Mal before he knew what was happening. Mal stared down in horror at the chains on his wrists like his hands were covered in blood. Maybe they were.

The old sheriff sighed. "Better read him his rights while you're at it."

"You have the right to remain silent," Sonny told him on the way out. "Anything you say can and will be used against you in a court of law—"

I watched Mona. She was clearly shaken by everything that had happened, and she cast about trying to remember what she was doing here. The sheriff must have seen the same thing. He took a blanket off one of the cots and covered the body with it. "I think that's enough pictures of the crime scene, sweetheart. Thank you kindly. Would you do me another favor now and take some pictures outside, all around the campsite? Just anything will do."

Mona nodded blankly, then collected her things and left.

The sheriff shifted his keen eyes to me when she was gone. "Your sister?" he asked.

I nodded. He was observant. I liked that. "My name's Horatio Wilkes," I told him.

"Name's Wood," he said, introducing himself. "Inverness County sheriff."

He brought a hand out of his warm pocket and I shook it.

"Horatio, huh? Almost as bad as my first name. You catch much hell for it?"

"Only slightly less than if my parents had named me Angus."

Sheriff Wood's mustache fluttered as he blew out an approving snort. He eyed me again.

"It was you who found the body?"

I told him it was.

"That your puddle of puke right outside?"

I told him it was.

"Glad to know you're human then," he told me. "And glad to know I don't have to take a sample for the state lab. You touch anything in here?"

"That tent pole. The tent was dark and the floor was slippery. And I turned the body with my flashlight. Had to be sure I was running for the police, not an ambulance."

Sheriff Wood nodded, then turned his eyes to the grisly scene at our feet.

"Who's the fella you left watching the door?"

"Chad Weigel. He came out of his RV next door right after I spewed chunks. I told him I'd stay, but he insisted."

Sheriff Wood harrumphed. "We'll look into that. You tell Mal his name was scrawled on the wall when you found him down on the meadow?"

I shook my head. "Thought you or somebody would want

to see how he reacted when he came in. I didn't want to ruin it—and didn't want him running."

Sheriff Wood nodded at that too. "That was some smart thinking," he told me. He considered me for a minute before asking his next question.

"You think Mal did it then?"

I blinked. "You really want to know what I think? Why?"

"Well, one: You got a first name as bad as mine, and that counts for something. Two: I figure you and me are about the two smartest fellas on this mountain."

"Why's that?" I asked.

"We're the only two ain't wearing skirts."

I grinned. "Okay. Well, there's Mal's name written in blood by his father's dying hand."

"Always tough to beat," the sheriff agreed.

"And he certainly had opportunity," I went on. "That business about the text message is pretty weak." Maybe too weak, I thought—but I left it at that. "As for means, I didn't see Mal's dagger in his sock when I got here, but he was wearing one earlier."

Sheriff Wood nodded. "You got a good eye. I already scooped it up and put it in a little baggy for the TBI—although I don't know anybody who'd be stupid enough to use his own dagger, what with all them high-tech detective shows on TV."

"Then he could choose from one of the other thousand floating around this mountain," I told him. "Still, too circumstantial. As for motive—? I don't know."

"You're standing on it," Wood told me. I looked down at the bloody tent floor. "The mountain," he clarified. "Piece of land like this must be worth millions. It's the only one left around these parts that isn't covered with ski slopes and chalet rentals."

It made sense. Duncan owned the mountain, and with him out of the way Mal would inherit.

"It works," I told him. And yet—

"And yet," Wood said like he could read my mind, "and yet there's something not right about all this."

I nodded. I looked around at the bloodstained tent. "Like why isn't Mal covered in blood?" I asked.

"He changed his clothes?" the sheriff tried, like he'd already been kicking that question around. "But that takes time, and where do you hide them? The dagger too?"

"He had to hide them close by, if he wanted to get back in time for the bonfire."

"I've already got boys searching his tent, but there's not much hope of finding something out in the woods tonight if that's what he's done," said the sheriff. "Lot of ground to cover."

"But they're not going anywhere," I told him. "He probably figured he'd have all night to find them again and really get rid of them. He'd have to be a suspect, he had to know that, but he never figured on being arrested so soon. How was he supposed to know his father would point the finger at him from the grave?"

Sheriff Wood stared at the word *Malcolm* written on the wall of the tent.

"Something not quite right about that either," he said, "though I can't quite put my finger on it."

I shrugged. "Motive, means, opportunity: So he doesn't have all three. It's not tidy, but when the dead man writes your name in blood, two out of three doesn't seem all that bad. You find that dagger with Mal's prints on it out in the woods tomorrow and it's a done deal."

"Right," Sheriff Wood said. He turned and shook my hand

again. "Okay. Thanks for your help. You've got a good head for this, Horatio."

He walked me to the front of the tent and sent me outside.

"So, are you going tell me what *your* first name is?" I asked.

"Nope," he said, dropping the flap in my face.

Mac's father was trying to push past another of the security guards when I turned around.

"I'm sorry, Mr. Mackenzie. I can't let you in there," the guard told him. "It's a crime scene."

"But that's *my* tent," he told the man. "Horatio, what's going on in there?"

"Duncan MacRae's been murdered," I told him. I saw Mac behind him, staring at the smoldering campfire. Mr. Weigel had gone.

"I've gathered that much," Mr. Mackenzie told me. "I want to know who did it and why!"

"Go check out an Agatha Christie novel," I told him, brushing past.

"I see your friends are as useless as you are," Mac's father told him. "And I heard about your sheep comment tonight at the bonfire. We could have done without that."

"You're welcome," Mac said, but it was lost on his father. Mr. Mackenzie had already begun to badger the security guard again.

Mac poked a stick at some singed logs and I stuck my hands in my pockets. All the excitement had made me forget about my frostbite, and I wished the wind hadn't blown out the campfire.

"It's bad, isn't it?" Mac asked.

"It's bad," I told him.

We stood there for a while, Mac poking at the charred wood, me shivering. It wouldn't be long before the campground was crawling with angry men in kilts, but for now it was eerily silent, as though the earth had stopped spinning and time had been frozen along with my toes. There was no screaming wind, no hooting owls, no chirping crickets. Even Mr. Mackenzie was quiet. I stood waiting for something to break the spell, and then watched as a leaf broke free from a branch above us and fluttered to the ground. Break time was over. The world had started spinning again.

"The mountain's yours now, isn't it?" I asked Mac.

He looked up at me. "What?"

"Duncan was your grandfather on your mother's side, right? She's dead and Mal's been arrested, which means you're next in line."

Mac sat on a log. "I guess I never thought about it, but yeah. Yeah, I guess that's right." He looked up at me. "Did they really arrest him? Mal I mean? I saw them take him away in handcuffs—"

I sat down next to him. "That's usually a pretty good sign," I told him. "That and reading him his rights."

"I suppose he wanted the mountain," Mac said. "If he hadn't been arrested, it would have been his."

"That's what the sheriff thinks anyway," I told him.

Mac looked at me. "But you don't?"

I shrugged. "I didn't say I didn't. It's a good motive, but there are still a couple of things that bother me about it, like—"

I spotted something white among the black logs in the fire pit and stopped.

"Like what?" Mac asked.

"Give me your stick," I told him.

"What?"

"I see something in the fire. Give me your stick."

Mac finally handed it over and I pushed one of the smoking logs out of the way. Underneath it was one half of a charred white dress shirt like the kind Mal wore. The breast pocket carried the MacRae family crest. The bottom half was covered in blood.

"Never mind all that," I told Mac. "You'd better get the sheriff."

CHAPTER NINE

— ⚔ —

It was well after midnight when the deputy got done asking me everything the sheriff had—twice—and writing it down in his little notebook. The place was crawling with walk-by rubberneckers when the medical examiner from the next county over packed Duncan MacRae's body bag into his van, but now there wasn't much to see.

A hasty meeting was held to determine where the games should go from here, and I got dragged along. I had already met most of the people in the room. Mac and his father, Bill Mackenzie, were there as the next of kin for Duncan—at least the next of kin who weren't arrested—and Banks was there with *his* father, who represented the musicians. Beth was there too, with her parents. The resemblance to her mother—long legs, stacked chest, condescending attitude—was frightening. Rounding out the powwow were Sternwood, representing the clans, and Megan and Lucy, who'd been roped in as representatives of the merchants since most of the others who did twenty or thirty of these a year had left for their motels before the opening ceremonies. The only person I didn't know was Douglas McGowan, the president of this year's games. He was the first one to say it out loud.

"I think we should cancel the festival."

"I agree," Mac's father said. "And maybe this should be the *last* festival."

"Now hold on," Sternwood said. "I agree it's right to discuss whether or not we should continue with the weekend, but just because Duncan MacRae is dead doesn't mean—"

"We can't cancel the games," Beth's mother said.

"Of course we can," Mac's father said. "And we should."

"No. Beth put in too much rehearsal work," her mother said. "She needs this win to advance to the regionals." She turned to Mr. Weigel. "Tell them."

"*You* tell them. Bill's right," he said, siding with his business partner. "I think it's time we canceled the games. And it's time for you to stop living vicariously through your daughter's beauty pageants and dance competitions. It's getting old, Veronica. Just like you."

It was a cruel thing to say in front of an audience. Letting Beth's mother stand in vicariously for her daughter, I enjoyed it immensely.

Mrs. Weigel started to lay into her husband, but he simply walked out of the tent.

"Chad—" Mac's father called, using the same voice he used to show Mac how unhappy he was with him. I didn't get that, since Mr. Weigel had been toeing the company line with Mr. Mackenzie. But Mr. Weigel didn't care what Mac's father thought either. He was gone, leaving us staring uncomfortably at his humiliated wife. She closed her gaping mouth and set it in a hard, tight frown.

"The games must continue," she told us, bringing us back around to the discussion.

"There'll be a pall over the entire weekend," Sternwood

said. "The Highland Games are a *celebration*. How will anyone be able to celebrate anything after this terrible night?"

Beth pulled Mac's ear down to her mouth to whisper something at him. "But there's no danger, right? Duncan's killer has already been arrested," Mac said when she released him, no doubt repeating something she had told him. I was surprised she didn't just say it herself. Certainly nothing had stopped her before. She looked a bit shaken, though, and she clung to Mac's arm like it was a life preserver.

"Safety is obviously an issue," McGowan said, "but the *real* issue here is that Duncan MacRae was the heart and soul of these games. How can we continue without him?"

"But that's exactly why the games *should* continue," Mac said. He stepped into the middle of the group, rounding on all of them. "Duncan may be gone, but we can't let his legacy die with him. The Highland Games *have* to continue. What about all the merchants who spent money to get here, the dancers who practiced all year for the regional competition, the athletes who trained for the decathlon. Who will be king of the mountain?"

"I hardly think any of that matters now," his father told him.

"And what about the bagpipe music scholarship?" Banks asked.

McGowan put up his hands. "Everything can be postponed until next year. Nobody's talking about canceling the games permanently."

Sternwood glowered at Bill Mackenzie. "*He* is."

"I'm just saying that maybe these games have run their course, and we should let them die with Duncan."

"No!" Mac yelled, and the ferociousness of his voice startled everyone. "The games *have* to go on this weekend."

Nobody was quite sure what to say to that, since it was really more of a command than an argument. I didn't know where this sudden intensity was coming from in Mac. It could have been shock over the loss of his grandfather, but it felt like he was channeling Beth, even though she wasn't coaching him anymore.

"Well, there is the small matter of finances," McGowan said. "All the tents and staff and advertising have already been paid in advance. There's a good chance that if we can't recoup at least some of our losses, this might very well *be* the last Highland Games on Birnam Mountain."

"And it'll break the musicians who paid their own ways to get here if they can't have a chance to sell their CDs," Mr. Banks chimed in.

"The same with the vendors," Megan said. Our eyes locked for a moment as she scanned the small group, and then she moved on.

"There you go," Mac said. "And this way you won't have to refund anybody's tickets."

"Good heavens, I hadn't thought of that," McGowan said. "As much as I hate to say it, I don't think we have any choice. We have to push on with the weekend."

Mr. Mackenzie harrumphed, but there didn't seem to be anything left to say. He pulled Mac aside as the meeting broke up to give him the *Godfather* "Never take sides against the family" speech, and I used the chance to snuggle up to Beth without her boyfriend around.

"What?" she said, trying to destroy me with her laser vision.

"I don't get you."

"That's because you're a high school toad and I'm a sorority girl. You won't get sorority girls when you're in college either."

"That's just it," I said. "Why Mac? You could have any guy at college, but you still date a high school junior."

Beth walked away. I caught up, trying to goad her.

"What is it about him? There have to be good-looking frat boys you could date." I snapped my fingers. "*Of course.* Mac worships you and he'll do anything to keep you. No college guy is going to do that—no guy worth having, at least. That's what you really want, isn't it? Control."

Beth rounded on me with something resembling a growl.

"What I *want* is for Mac to reach his full potential. Besides Madame Hecate, I seem to be the only one around here who sees what kind of man he can be."

"So you're saying it's your mission to make him into a *man?* Is that it? That's very noble. Or is this part of a service? Do you have a card I can have? Because I've been thinking lately about becoming a man—"

"My mother made my father into a man," Beth said, "and I'm going to do the same thing for Mac."

"Yeah, and your dad really seems to appreciate that," I said. "I could *feel* the love between them."

Beth turned her back on me and joined up with Mac, who was finally free of his father. I let her go. I felt a little bad about cracking on her henpecked dad and her domineering mom, but not too much. Mac was in for a lifetime of the same thing if he didn't snap to his senses soon.

"Hey, Horatio—" Mona called. She had just finished interviewing some of the campers for their reactions when she flagged me down.

"Hey, Mona. Do you have a hotel room in town?"

"No—the paper just sent me up here for the day. I was supposed to be long gone, except for . . . you know. Why?"

"Well, my tent is a crime scene, and it's a little too close for comfort in Mac's RV with him and his dad in there."

"You mean you're staying on? They're not canceling the games?"

"They can't afford to."

Mona made a note of that into her digital recorder.

"Banks and his dad offered to put me up too, but they don't even have an RV. They sleep in the back of a pickup truck."

"Sorry," said Mona. "I need to get back to Knoxville tonight to give them my notes."

"Stop the presses, huh?"

"My big break," she said, though I could tell she had mixed emotions. I wondered then what it took to be a *real* news journalist, the kind who writes about drug addicts and child laborers and soldiers dead in the sand. To have your entire life be focused on documenting the suffering of others, day in and day out. To write a story, print it, line the kitty litter box with it, and then start all over again, constantly trolling for injury and malfeasance like a vulture circling for roadkill. Looking into my sister's haunted eyes, I wondered if she was hardened enough to do it—and if I even wanted her to be.

I said good night to Mona and woke up my 1986 Volvo 240 for the trip back down the mountain. Pigeon Forge was touristy enough that I figured I'd be able to find *someplace* close by to stay, but I hadn't figured on the Highland Games making it *too* touristy. There wasn't a decent motel within a ten-mile radius with a "Vacancy" light on, which just left the *in*decent ones.

The flickering neon light at the "Hillbilly Haven Motel and Wedding Chapel" let me know there were "Rooms to Let." A sign beneath that told me the rooms to let were "Air-conditioned by Nature," and that the wonder of "Color TVs" awaited me. I pulled into the parking lot. What can I say? It was one o'clock in the morning and I was desperate.

A gigantic freestanding hillbilly statue wearing red long johns under patched-up blue overalls greeted me with a wink and a bottle of moonshine. The woman I took to be his hillbilly bride—the sign did say "Wedding Chapel," after all—wore cutoff daisy dukes and a sleeveless flannel shirt with the tails tied together over her belly button. She cradled a shotgun in her arms and grinned at her bumpkin beau through a corn-cob pipe held in place by her three good teeth.

And Southerners wonder why the rest of the country thinks we're all rednecks.

The sign said open, but the door was locked. I peered in through the glass. A light at the front desk was on, but nobody was home. I knocked on the window. Nothing. I knocked louder. I thought I heard something thump inside and knocked again. A small middle-aged man with a scraggly beard remarkably like the one on the two-story-tall hillbilly outside staggered into the lobby wearing blue jeans and a black T-shirt with hot-rod flames licking up from the bottom. He stopped in the middle of the lobby, mumbling. He was half-asleep and talking to himself. I couldn't hear what he was saying, but he was having quite the conversation. I banged on the glass.

"Hey Jethro! Over here."

That seemed to focus him, and he located me with lidded eyes. He unlocked the deadbolt with a *chunk* and cracked the door.

"Knock, knock, knock," he groused. "You're gonna wake the dead."

"I wish I could," I told him.

"Whaddya want?"

"Sign outside says you've got a vacancy."

"Sign outside says 'Rooms to Let.'"

I took a deep breath. "The sign outside says you have . . . rooms to let."

The little man eyed me as though the Hillbilly Haven had standards, then must have remembered they didn't and opened the door. I stood at the counter while he tried to remember where he left the guest book. There wasn't a computer.

"'Air-conditioned by Nature,'" I said. "Does that mean the rooms don't have air-conditioning?"

He slapped the guest book onto the counter. "We got air-conditioning," he told me.

Despite the radical drop in temperature up on *top* of the mountain, mid-July in East Tennessee was hot, especially down here in the asphalt-covered valley. Even at one o'clock in the morning I was sweating. I glanced at the strange sign outside again.

"So, there *is* air-conditioning," I said.

He eyed me from beneath his brow. "It's air-conditioned," he told me, "*by nature.*"

"Which means . . . they're *not* air-conditioned," I translated.

He slid the book around for me to sign in.

I smiled, though I wasn't amused. "And I suppose everything else in town is booked up because of the Highland Games."

"Ayup."

"Swell." I took the pen from him to sign in. "So, is the plumbing also 'by nature'?"

He handed me a key and glared at me. "We ain't completely backwoods."

"Right. Thanks," I said. "I'll just see myself to my room. I can't wait to see what color television is like."

All the motel rooms opened onto the parking lot, and I found mine a few doors down from the office. The key was an actual key, of course—not a key card—hanging from a four-inch-long diamond-shaped piece of plastic that would make it a lot of fun to carry around in my pocket all weekend. I wrangled the door open and flipped on the light switch inside.

It was a simple room with a bed, a side table with a telephone, a chair, and a low bureau with a television on top. Both the telephone and the television had dials on them. A moist-looking, matted brown dog-hair carpet covered the floor, and a worn path in it led from the doorway to the bed to what I hoped was the indoor plumbing I'd been promised. There was a hole the size of a fist in the wood paneling on the far wall and a little plastic "No Smoking" sign in the ashtray next to the bed. Like I'd guessed, "Air-conditioning by Nature" meant "No Air-conditioning," and I opened the window to let nature air out the lingering smell of armpit and ass.

I threw the duffel bag with the clothes I'd been able to salvage from the Mackenzies' guest tent onto the bed. That's when I saw the stain.

I picked up the phone and spun the dial for the front desk.

"No refunds," the desk clerk answered.

"Yeah, this is Horatio Wilkes in Room 107. There's a stain. On my blanket. It's big and dark and—" I poked at it with my plastic keychain. "Crunchy."

"Yeah," the clerk said. "We don't know how that got there."

I closed my eyes. I was tired. Oh so tired.

"Yeah, see, I wasn't really calling to find out what it *is*," I told him.

"You want a new blanket?" he asked.

"Just—just forget it. It's hot enough I don't even need it."

I hung up and tossed the blanket into the corner, being careful not to touch the unidentified disgusting object on top. The white sheets beneath it were yellowed but clean enough, and I stripped down to my boxers and collapsed into bed. The mattress hugged me like a three-hundred-pound aunt.

One minute I'd been shivering on top of beautiful Mount Birnam, the next minute I was sweating it out in a seedy motel down in Pigeon Forge. One minute Duncan had been alive and kilting, the next minute he'd been carved up and left for dead, his devoted son now his desperate killer. Fair was foul and foul was fair.

And none of it made any sense.

CHAPTER TEN

I was sweating in my T-shirt and khakis when I left the motel, and shivering again two thousand feet up Mount Birnam. Mac and I had agreed to meet by the vendor area, and he was waiting for me in a blue Mackenzie kilt, black T-shirt, and a brown leather jacket. There were tree branches and leaves strewn all around the merchant booths, and some of the tents had actually taken damage.

"It was a rough night," Mac said.

"Yeah. No kidding." That was the understatement of the year. "So why the hell is it still so cold up here? The TV said it was supposed to be mid-seventies."

"Like I told you, chum: The mountain makes its own weather."

"Thanks. That's very helpful."

Mac wrapped an arm around my shoulders and shook me. "Ach, ye shoulda stayed with us, laddie! Then ye could run back to the camper fer yer woolens!"

"If you talk like that all weekend I *will* kill you," I promised him. I'd said it as a joke, without thinking, but in the moment that followed we both realized that maybe this wasn't the right time or place to joke about killing people. I cleared my throat and stepped back from Mac to see what new T-shirt he was wearing today.

"'MacGalla'?" I read. "What does that mean?"

Mac pulled his jacket open so I could see it better. "'Mac' means 'Son of.' Like 'Son of Kenzie'—'*Mac*kenzie.' And 'Galla' is Gaelic for 'bitch,' so 'MacGalla' means—"

"I get it, I get it," I told him. Mac grinned.

As we walked along, I could see the vendor booths weren't the only casualties from the night before. The Highland festival was officially open for business, but there was no one here. What had been busy paths the night before were almost deserted.

"It's like church night at the Roman coliseum around here," I said.

"Yeah. Late last night a bunch of the campers left, even though we told them the games were still on. Cowards."

It looked as though the regular tourists were staying away too. From the way Mac had described the games to me before coming, they had expected twenty thousand people to attend. Now they'd be lucky to get *two* thousand.

"I say good riddance," Mac said. "Less competition for me in the decathlon."

Again with the misplaced intensity. It bothered me that Mac could look around at the wounded Highland Games and see only good fortune for himself, and I wondered how much of that was Mac and how much of it was Beth, pushing him.

"Mac, you know that Beth is using you, don't you?"

"What? Where is this coming from?"

"I'm just looking out for you, like when you told me Helen was cheating on me. Beth is only dating you because she can control you, keep pushing you to do dangerous things."

"Okay. So she gets off on the chills and thrills. But man, when I do something crazy for her, she's like a *hellcat* in bed."

I put up a hand. "Seriously, enough. I'm sorry I said anything." At least I had tried.

We walked along in silence for a while until Mac found something else for us to talk about.

"So, um, last night, by the fire," he said, "when you found Mal's shirt—"

"Yeah?"

"You started to say there was something was wrong."

"I did?"

Mac put his hands in his jacket pockets. "You know, something that was bothering you about the murder."

"Oh. Yeah." There were a *few* things bothering me, things that had kept me tossing and turning all night. Or maybe that was just because I'd been sticking to the three-dollar sheets.

I stopped at a booth selling accessories for bagpipes even though I didn't know what I was looking at. The shopkeeper gave me a solemn nod, like we were passing through a visitation line at a funeral.

"Well, like what?" Mac persisted.

"Well, like Mal's alibi, for instance."

I told Mac what Mal had said about getting a text message from Mona. "Why would he use my sister as an excuse for where he was when he knew he couldn't prove it?" I asked.

"Well, we all saw Mona fawning over him in the campground. Maybe he thought she'd cover for him."

"But why not just say he was changing clothes in his tent? Or off going to the Porta-Johns or something? Why rely on somebody he just met? Why pick an alibi he couldn't prove?"

"Maybe he *did* get a message from her," Mac said. "Maybe he stole her phone and texted himself so he *would* have an alibi."

I looked askance at Mac. "You've got a devious mind. But if he did that, why did he delete the message off his own phone before anybody could read it?"

Mac stopped. "He did what?"

"He says he deleted it. There's no text message on his phone."

Mac searched the ground with his eyes. "He deleted it?"

"I know. Weird, right? Anyway, it's just stuff like that," I said. "It doesn't matter."

I picked up a flute-like thing from the booth and looked at it. It had little holes up and down it like a recorder.

"In the market for a new chanter?" a man at the booth asked me.

"A what?"

"A chanter. That's what you've got there. It's the part of the bagpipe the air goes out through." He showed me by attaching it to one of those big air bags pipers carry under their arms like footballs. "The piper plays it with his fingers, down here."

"All that sound comes from that little thing?" I asked.

"That and the drones." He pointed to the tall wooden pipes that stuck up out of the back of the thing like chimneys.

Mac laughed. "You thinking about taking up the pipes, Horatio?"

"I'm in the market for a new hobby and Mom says watching *Magnum P.I.* reruns all summer doesn't qualify."

"I can put you in a fantastic set of learner's bagpipes for a thousand dollars," the salesman said, his natural instincts overriding the grave atmosphere.

I made a sound like a bagpipe tuning up.

"My *car* doesn't cost that much," I told him. "Thanks, but I think I'll take up knitting."

"Oh, sweet!" Mac said. I had already lost him to the booth behind us. He was looking at a table full of those little daggers everyone carried in their socks. Meanwhile I was looking at Megan Sternwood. I spied her shilling leather goods in her booth two stops down.

"I've had my eye on this pretty little thing for a while now," Mac told me.

"Same here," I said.

Mac glanced up at where I was looking, and I quickly turned my attention to the dagger he held in his hands. The blade was small for a knife—about three inches long—with a pointed end and a serrated edge. The hilt was black leather with studs set along its length and a silver crown on top that held a blue gem stone. The price tag dangling from it said it was $129.00.

"What do you think?" Mac asked. "Damascus steel, pewter inlay, and I can get my family crest embossed on the scabbard."

I glanced at his empty socks. "What happened to your old dagger?" I asked him.

"It got taken up by the police last night, along with everybody else's. Seems like as good an excuse as any to get a new one, eh?"

The woman in the weapon booth smiled. "We've sold three dozen sgian dubhs this morning. I wish I'd known. I would have brought more."

"Yeah," I told her, "too bad somebody doesn't get cut up with a dagger at every games. Then you'd really make a killing."

The woman scowled at me and left us alone.

"There you go, Horatio. Maybe a weapons dealer killed Duncan, so he could sell more daggers."

I frowned. Some vendor from out of town being callous was bad enough—but Duncan's grandson?

"Oh, come on, Horatio. Lighten up. You know I'm kidding. You're just so convinced it wasn't Mal."

"I never said that," I told him. "I just have questions, is all. Go buy your toy."

Mac raised his hands and backed off like I might bite him. I certainly felt that way. I turned to see if my pixie had disappeared into the ether again, but this time she was staying put.

Mac came back and caught me staring. I tried to pretend I hadn't been looking at her, but he was onto me.

"Leave her be, chum."

"Who?"

"Megan Sternwood. I know she's totally hot in that elfish kind of way—"

"Pixie," I told him.

"Whatever. You don't want any piece of that."

It felt silly to be defensive about a girl I hadn't even met, but I was, and the look on my face let Mac know just how much.

"I'm serious, Horatio. She's trouble."

"Oh, really? What, kills men in their sleep, does she?"

Mac blinked and gaped like I'd slapped him. I'd just meant to match his hyperbole, but I'd really staggered him instead.

"Mac, look, I'm sorry. When you said that earlier about the weapons dealers, I thought—"

"Forget it, Horatio. And forget that girl. She's paranoid. She thinks everybody's out to get her."

I looked back toward Megan. She was having some kind of standoff in her booth with a bunch of punks in kilts—Banks's old friends from Satan's marching band.

"It's not paranoia if people really are out to get you," I told him.

Beth found us just then and stepped in between me and Mac like I wasn't there. She was wearing her dance sweats and glistened like she'd just come from a swimsuit shoot.

"We need to talk," she told Mac. *"Now."*

Mac started to protest, but all Beth had to do was raise her eyebrows and he relented. I thought again about the power she had over him, but if Mac didn't care, I didn't see why I should. Beth pulled Mac away to make him into a man, and I decided it was time for me to be a man too.

It was time to say hello to Megan Sternwood.

CHAPTER ELEVEN

Megan-called-May-gan's booth was three tables of jewelry and leather spread out under part of a tent with a cash register on a small stand at the back. The "Hell's Pipers" were scattered throughout the booth sucking down IRN-BRU and picking up anything in sight like preschoolers in a toy store. Megan stood in the middle of them all, taking things out of their hands and putting them back. Her little sister Lucy sat at the cash register, looking worried. She spied me coming around the side of the tent and cut her eyes at the pipers, just in case I'd missed that there was trouble. I hadn't.

"All right you douchebags, you've had your fun," Megan was saying as I got close. "Now why don't you go back to your tent and play with your pipes?"

The pipers hooted at that one. Megan certainly wasn't acting like the damsel-in-distress type, so I hung back and let her play it her way.

The punk with the sea urchin hair came up close to her and lifted his kilt. "I'd rather *you* play my pipes, sweetheart! How about it? Go on. Tickle my chanter!"

His friends thought he was the funniest thing since *Aqua Teen Hunger Force*. Megan didn't flinch.

"Is that all there is?" she asked. "I'm afraid my hands aren't small enough," she said.

The urchin's friends *oooohed* her comeback, and I saw something in his face get mean. He dropped his kilt and invaded her personal space. I looked around for help, but the whole vendor area was as dead as Duncan MacRae, and the loneliness seemed to embolden the urchin and his posse.

"You know what?" he said quietly. "I'm not leaving here until you give me a kiss. *None of us* are leaving here until you give me a kiss."

Megan put a hand to her lips. "Sorry," she told the urchin. "I think I just threw up a little in the back of my mouth."

The urchin's friends laughed again. He didn't. I didn't know what Megan was planning, but I wanted to be ready to step in when things went to Threat Level Orange. I slid into the tent near the cash register with my back to the pipers like I was a shopper browsing the jewelry and pretended to examine a leather bracelet.

Lucy's eyes flashed to mine, begging for help.

"Go get security," I whispered.

Lucy's eyes darted back to Megan like she was reluctant to leave her, then back to me. I nodded to tell her she could trust me. Lucy slipped off her stool and disappeared out the back of the booth.

"How's about it, ice queen?" the urchin said. "Are you gonna kiss it?"

I glanced over my shoulder. Megan's hands were balling into fists. We had skipped Threat Level Orange and gone straight to Threat Level Plaid. If she took a swing, things were going to get very ugly very fast.

"Pucker up, motherf—"

"Excuse me," I interrupted. "Is this Corinthian leather?"

Suddenly every eye in the booth was on me.

"Because that's what it feels like," I said. I petted the bracelet I held in my hand. "Rich, Corinthian leather."

For a second both Megan and the urchin looked like they might say something to me, then went back to their standoff.

"You were just saying something about puckering up?" the urchin said.

"Can you get these with sayings on them?" I asked. "Like 'Bagpipers do it with Amazing Grace'?"

The urchin turned on me.

"Hey, we're having a conversation here, bunghole!"

"Sorry. I was just wondering if these could be personalized."

"If you don't get out of here I'll personalize your face!"

I watched Megan. She was starting to get it now.

"I thought I'd get my name embossed on one," I told her. "'Horatio Wilkes.' Maybe in gold. Something sparkly."

To the urchin's surprise Megan stepped away from him and went behind the table where I stood. She took the bracelet from me and ran her finger along the Celtic knotwork there.

"No, see, you don't want to get your own name. That's too scene," she told me. "But you could do, say, your girlfriend's name."

"Alas, that position is currently vacant," I told her. "Besides, wearing a girl's name is a little too emo for my tastes."

The urchin yanked me around by my shoulder and got in my face. "Hey asswipe! Do you understand what I'm telling you?"

"Well, I see your mouth moving," I told him, "but the only thing coming out is crap."

The urchin gave me a two-handed shove that sent me

head over heels out of the tent. Something white and wheeled squeaked to a stop behind me and I rolled into it with a *thud*. When I opened my eyes I found myself wrapped around the front bumper of a golf cart. Lucy was hanging out of the front and staring at me.

I smiled. "Hiya kid. Good timing."

A security guard was already out of the golf cart and headed for the urchin. The punk stood his ground while the rest of the Hell's Pipers scattered like pigeons. I guess that's what made a Neanderthal like him their leader.

"Terry Scruggs!" the guard barked. He grabbed the urchin by the jacket. "You were warned about this kind of behavior last year. You want to get thrown out of the games for good?"

Terry the urchin glared back at him.

"Well, do you?" the security guy asked again.

"No," Terry said finally.

The security guy let him go. "Then I suggest you straighten up. One more incident like this and you're gone. Get me?"

"I get you," Terry said to the guard, but he was looking at me. I gave him a smile.

"You and your friends are banned from the vendor booths for the rest of the games," the security guy told him. "Any of your crew we see here gets the boot."

Terry turned to the security guy. "What about the IRN-BRU booth?" he asked.

"Banned from the *entire vendor area*," the guard told him. "Maybe next time you'll think before making trouble."

"Yeah," the urchin said. He turned his eyes back to me. "We'll do that."

The security guy put Terry into his golf cart and drove him away from Megan's booth. I waved to him as they left.

"Good-bye, Terrence," I called. "You stay classy!"

"You're just going to make him madder," Lucy told me.

"I'm good at that," I told her. "I have mad skills." I picked a piece of grass out of my hair. "Besides, he won't do anything stupid enough to get him kicked out of the games. This is the only place he has any real power."

Megan moved around the booth, resetting everything the pipers had displaced. Lucy, with the perfect grace of a practiced wingman, went to sit with the cash box and let us have some space.

"Don't worry about Terrence," I said to Megan. "He was just trying to break your crayons."

"I suppose I should say thank you," she said.

"Then I suppose I should say you're welcome."

Megan peered at me. "I saw you with my uncle."

I nodded. "General Sternwood. I like him. I hope someday I grow up to be a crotchety old bastard too."

"I wouldn't worry then," she told me. "Teenage bastards usually do."

I raised the eyebrows at that.

Megan crossed her arms. "So you like my uncle and thought maybe you'd like me too and came to say hello, is that it?"

"Something like that."

"Hello then," she told me. "And good-bye."

Megan turned her back on me and walked to the cash register. I raised my palms to ask Lucy what the deal was, but she only had time to shrug before Megan turned.

"You know, I don't believe in psychic powers or anything," I said, "but I'm sensing you don't like me."

Megan counted the money in the cash box without looking at me. "I don't like your friends."

"My friends?"

"You're here with Beth Weigel and her boyfriend, aren't you?"

I thought about pressing her on that, making her admit she'd been spying on Mac's campsite, but I didn't think it would help our diplomatic relations.

"I'm here with Mac, yeah. Joe Mackenzie. He's the one dating Beth. He and I grew up together."

Megan took a few dollars from the cash box and slapped it shut.

"Anybody who would date that arrogant bitch is a rat bastard in my book. And so are his friends." She turned to her sister. "I'm going to get some food. Do you want anything?"

Lucy said she didn't, and Megan left.

"That went well," I said.

"She likes you," Lucy told me. "I know it."

I watched Megan's pixie shape disappear into the crowd.

"If she does," I said, "she certainly has a strange way of showing it."

CHAPTER TWELVE

So Megan hated Beth and Beth hated Megan. That meant Megan hated Mac and Mac hated Megan, since he was apparently happy to let Beth do all his thinking for him. All this was going to prove pretty awkward ten years from now when Megan and I were living together and I wanted to invite Mac over for a game of Madden Football, but that was a bridge I'd burn when I got to it. First I had to convince Megan I was worth moving in with.

I knew better than to go looking for Mac again after Beth had dragged him away. They were probably off doing things that would have gotten them a million hits on YouTube before the video got taken down. The Highland Games decathlon would be starting soon anyway, and Mac was now on the team. I wouldn't be seeing much of him during the next couple of days unless I sat with the three other people who'd shown up to watch the competition.

I went looking for Banks at the music stages instead. If it was possible, there were even fewer people on the paths now than there had been that morning. Yesterday there had been so many people they had to run a fire truck around, spraying water on the dirt paths to keep down the dust kicked up by everyone's feet. Today was an exercise in "What if you threw a Scottish Highland Festival and nobody came?" and I wondered if the organizers had made the right call after all.

I spotted Mona snapping a picture of a kilted boy pulling a sword out of a plastic stone at the MacArthur clan tent. I waited until she had gotten the kid's name from his parents and went over to her.

"The once and future king?" I asked.

Mona consulted her notebook. "Duane Camacho, of Spruce Pine, North Carolina."

"Yeah," I said. "Maybe not. So what are you doing back? I thought you went down to Knoxville last night."

"I did. The newspaper sent me back. They're letting me stay on the story instead of giving it to someone else."

"Congratulations."

Mona tried to smile, but that haunted look was still in her eyes.

"You still need a place to stay? The newspaper's putting me up."

As much as I disdained the Hillbilly Haven, I dreaded sharing a bathroom with Mona again even more and declined the offer.

"Where'd you find a place?" I asked. "Everything was booked up last night."

"Not anymore. Nobody's coming to the games. It's like there's a—a black cloud hanging over the whole place. You can't see it, but you can feel it. I can't believe they're still having the festival."

I walked with Mona as she took pictures of empty booths.

"So I've been meaning to thank you," she said.

"For what, the scoop?"

"No," she told me. "For helping to send the first guy who's shown any real interest in me in a year to jail."

I stopped. "Mal MacRae is arrested for his father's *murder*, and the thing you're the most upset about is your love life?"

"Oh, come off it, Horatio. You know I have zero luck with guys."

"But seriously, *this* is what bothers you?"

Mona looked away. "They found my phone," she told me. "In Mal's things. In his tent. There was a text message in the outbox, telling him to meet me near the parking lot."

"Really? And it wasn't you that . . ."

"No! God, Horatio. I'm not *that* desperate." Mona walked off and I trotted up alongside her.

"Okay, okay," I said. "So you didn't text him. But there *is* a message on your phone."

"The sheriff thinks he took it out of my bag and used it to give himself an alibi. There weren't any fingerprints on it, not even mine, which means he wiped them off when he was done."

Mac had called it—Mal had sent the message to himself. But if he meant it as a real alibi, why would he delete the message off his own phone? It didn't make any sense.

"The sheriff thinks he was going to try and put my phone back in my purse sometime today. But *your* snooping around got him hustled off to jail."

"Okay, how is this my fault?" I asked her. "Did you not see the big 'Malcolm' written in blood on the wall of the tent?"

A couple of nearby clansmen gave me a curious look, and I dropped to a whisper.

"Besides, if he *is* a murderer, why would you want to go out with him anyway?"

Mona started to take a picture of an old man in the full kilt-and-waiter's-jacket getup, but she pulled the camera away from her eye before taking the shot like she couldn't summon the enthusiasm.

"He was just using me, wasn't he. That's the only reason he showed any real interest in me in the first place."

I closed my eyes and shook my head. Only Mona could make this about her.

"Come on, Mona—"

"No. Seriously." She teared up. "Is this what I'm reduced to? Jealous soldiers and homicidal maniacs?"

"Jealous soldiers?" I asked.

"My last boyfriend." Mona dried her eyes with her palms. "Oh Horatio," she whispered. "It was so horrible."

I knew she was talking about the murder now. Maybe she'd just been agonizing over her love life so she wouldn't have to deal with the real horror of it all. At least I hoped. Behind her I saw an empty clan tent, and with a cold shiver I realized it was the MacRae family's table, its lone metal folding chair knocked over on its side.

"All that blood, Horatio. Do you think he—do you think Mal really did that? To his own father?"

"The phone thing doesn't help," I told her. "I mean, it looks like it."

Mona nodded.

"Do you have it? Your phone I mean?"

Mona shook her head. "The sheriff said he had to keep it for evidence. Not like it worked up here anyway."

"What?"

"Can I borrow yours?" she asked, sniffling. "I need to check in with my editor."

I pulled out my phone and handed it to her, but my mind

was elsewhere. Mona flipped it open and shook her head.

"It's no use. You've got the same service I have."

She handed my phone back and I glanced at the bars. No reception. It made me remember how I hadn't had any reception when I tried to call the police after I'd discovered Duncan's body. I'd just thought it was the crazy weather.

"Nothing? Really?" I said. I held the phone up and moved it around, as though I might be standing next to a bubble of phone signal and just hadn't stumbled into it yet. I realized I was being ridiculous, snapped the phone shut and stared at it.

"I don't know, maybe nobody's phones work up here," Mona said.

"Yours did. Somewhere up here. Otherwise it couldn't have sent that text message. And there's somebody *else* whose phone works up here too."

"Oh yeah? Whose?"

"Mal's."

That reopened an industrial-sized can of worms, and I immediately wished I'd kept it to myself. Mona choked back a sob.

"I better—I better go find a phone that works," she said.

I tried to say I was sorry as Mona left, but I didn't get it out in time. I looked down again at the silver phone in my hand, then slid it back into the clip on my belt and headed for the groves.

The groves were secluded, wooded areas off the main meadow where small stages and sets of bleachers had been built onto natural outcroppings of rocks. The trees and the landscape made the place a kind of quiet, peaceful refuge, although at present the tranquility of the beautiful mountainside hideaway was being destroyed by an all-bagpipe Pink Floyd cover band called The Pipers at the Gates of Dawn.

It sounded like they were playing a Highland version of "Another Brick in the Wall," but it was hard to tell with my busted eardrums.

Beyond the groves was a line of tables where the bands went after their performances to regain their hearing and sell CDs. A few spaces down, Banks and his father played a duet at their booth. Banks's father sat strumming a guitar while Banks stood next to him, huffing and puffing away on his bagpipes. The pipes were absolutely deafening up close, and Banks couldn't even hear me when I yelled. I finally got his attention by waving my hands in his face, and Banks let up on the bag under his arm. The strangled cat sound suddenly stopped and left me yelling over nothing.

"If you don't eat your meat, you can't have any pudding!" I screamed. The other musicians around us stared at me and I waved hello at them to make them look away.

"If you don't eat your *what?*" Banks asked.

"Your meat, Wallace," Banks's dad told him. "If you don't eat your meat, you can't have any pudding. It's from a Pink Floyd song. I've told you you need to branch out musically, listen to those old records of mine." He turned back to me. "In honor of the band playing in the groves?" I nodded and he smiled. "How can you have any pudding if you don't eat yer meat?" he asked, finishing the line.

"That's a very good question," I told him. Banks's dad and I shook hands. He was a thicker, older version of Banks, kilt and all, only Mr. Banks had a balding spot on the back of his head and the missing hair had migrated down to a beard on his chin.

"How are you, Horatio?" he asked.

"Swell. If things get any better I'm going to have to hire someone to help me enjoy it."

Mr. Banks laughed. "I like that! Maybe I'll use it in a song."

"So how goes the Highland music racket?" I asked. I picked up one of Mr. Banks's CDs and scanned the back cover.

Wallace pulled the mouthpiece out of his bagpipe and put it in his pocket protector. "Well, with Great-Uncle Duncan's death . . ."

"I know I said we should go on with the games, try to recoup some of the money we've invested in getting here," Mr. Banks said, "but now I regret that. It feels wrong. And to add injury to insult, the groves have been empty all day long."

"We can usually sell enough CDs to at least pay our food and gas for the whole trip," Banks said, "but we'll be lucky to make enough to eat lunch today."

"How often do you do this kind of thing?"

Mr. Banks picked softly at his guitar. "After this we're in Minnesota, then Illinois, Virginia, and New York State," he told me.

"And that's just July," said Banks. "In August we hit a bunch of festivals on the West Coast."

"You ever get tired of it?" I asked.

"What, the travel or the festivals?"

"Both," I said.

"The travel can wear you down," Mr. Banks confessed. "And being on the road so much means I can't keep a regular job. When Wallace was little I had to leave him with my cousin's family a lot—Mac's mother, when she was alive—and in the off-seasons I still have to get by on guitar lessons and substitute teaching. But I wouldn't trade the festivals for all the money in the world. My only regret is that we've never been able to afford to go to the motherland, play some *real* Scottish festivals."

"You'll have to come hear Dad play," Banks told me. "He's on this afternoon. I won't be there. I need to practice."

He drew the mouthpiece for his bagpipes back out and licked it to prep it for playing again.

"You keep worrying about that bagpipe competition and you'll be too worked up to play," his father told him. "Just be cool, Wallace. You're going to ace it."

"That's what I keep telling him," I said.

Banks frowned at us. "You guys know I can't screw this up. This is like the only way I'll *ever* be able to afford to go to college."

Mr. Banks had probably asked himself a million times if he should quit the Highland Games gig and get a real job, if only to make sure Wallace had some kind of future. The way he was looking at his reflection in the shine on his guitar, I guessed he was up to a million and one times. Banks must have seen it too.

"No, Dad, I didn't mean it like that," he told his father. "You know I love this life. I wouldn't change a thing. Except maybe wish that Mom had loved it as much as we do."

I felt a very moving moment coming, which was my cue to be moving along.

"Time for me to exit stage left," I told Banks, "but before I go, I think I found a girl for you."

Banks blushed, but his dad looked hopeful.

"Here at the Highland Games?" Mr. Banks asked.

"Daaaad," Banks groaned.

I told Banks about Megan's sister, Lucy, and where to find her.

"She's a freshman, so she's just a year behind you. And she's smart."

Banks narrowed his eyes. "Which means—"

"Which means she's smart. She's cute too," I told him.

Banks blushed again. "I don't know—"

"Don't worry, sport. I already laid the groundwork for you."

"You mean she knows I'm coming!?"

"No," I told him. "But I did make sure she liked bagpipe music."

Banks smiled.

"One more thing," I said. I pulled the pocket protector from his shirt and put it on the table. "Leave this behind."

"But—" he started.

"Seriously, Banks. Now gird your loins, straighten your skirt, and go get yourself a girl."

Banks took a deep breath—then let it all back out with a slump of his shoulders. "Maybe later."

"Okay," I told him. "Just remember, if you don't eat your meat, you can't have any pudding. I gotta go."

I shook hands with Mr. Banks again and waved so long to his son. As I left, I saw Banks sit down to finish the heart-to-heart he'd begun with his dad. They were two peas in a pocket protector, those two.

Saying I had to go wasn't completely a lie. I did have some-where to go—I just didn't know where yet.

I pulled out my phone and checked the reception. No bars. Mona told me she had the exact same service I did, and that she hadn't gotten any kind of signal up here before her phone was used as Mal's alibi. So how exactly *did* he use it? Send-ing a text message was just like making a phone call—you couldn't do it if there wasn't a cell phone tower in range.

I swung the phone around trying to get a signal like I was one of those guys from *Star Trek*, scanning for alien life signs or something. I was focusing more on my phone than where

105

I was walking, though, and I almost tripped over something small, black, and red.

It was a black Scottish terrier, tethered to an old lady by a leash. The woman and the dog wore matching red and black kilts.

"Beam me up, Scotty," I told the dog. "There's no intelligent life down here."

CHAPTER THIRTEEN

—/—

I got no signal from the mothership in the groves, or by the meadow where Mac was running some kind of race in his kilt, or in the vendors area. That left the campground. I stumbled my way there, tripping over tree roots while I stared at the empty satellite bars on my phone. They never budged.

The campground was quiet this time of morning. Anybody who had stayed on was over at the field for the games, and a lonely bagpipe somewhere in the distance bleated out "Amazing Grace." There is nothing so lonely as a dead place that should be alive.

There were certainly some ghosts haunting the Mackenzie camper and tent. I don't mean rattle-the-chains "boo!" kind of ghosts, of course. Mac and Beth and Banks may have believed Madame Hecate's psychic mumbo jumbo about spirits and omens and portents, but all that stuff was just their imaginations playing tricks on them, like a horror movie where you never see the monster but picture something ten times scarier in your head. I mean the ghosts of sin and failure, the things that haunt us worse than anything Stephen King could ever dream up.

Yellow police tape formed a perimeter around the tent and the campfire. Sheriff Wood had been thorough—and smart. A place like this, the evidence might be trampled or trashed before you ever knew you needed it. Still, the whole place screamed "crime scene," and it gave the usually playful campground area a grisly feel. A man in a kilt and a T-shirt passed me on the road and quickened his step.

I held up my cell and did a sweep. Nothing. I suddenly felt self-conscious, worried somebody would think I was a morbid fetisher taking pictures with my camera phone to post on the interweb. I flipped it closed so it would fit in the palm of my hand and kept activating the little screen on the front to check the bars as I walked. I was most interested to see if there was any reception out behind the tent, where I thought Mal might have had time to work the trick after killing his father. But there was no signal there either.

Something *thunked* softly inside Mac's trailer and I froze. There was nothing for a minute more—I timed it on the phone in my hand—and then the springs on the RV squeaked softly, like your parents' bed upstairs when they're fooling around and don't want you to know.

Someone was inside Mac's RV.

I crept over to almost exactly the same spot where Megan had taken a peek inside. I caught a flash of tartan, but it wasn't a Mackenzie tartan.

It was pixie tartan with a Macduff crest pinned to it.

I moved quietly but quickly around to the front of the trailer, pulled the door open and jumped inside. Megan jumped four feet backward in two feet of space, slammed into the kitchen cabinets, and crumpled to the floor. And like every girl I'd ever met, she somehow managed to keep her skirt down while doing it.

"Jesus!" she cried.

I offered her a hand up, but she just glared at it as she pulled herself up on the fold-out breakfast nook.

"You gave me a heart attack," she said. She straightened her sweater. "Are you trying to kill me?"

"Sorry. I didn't expect anybody to be in here."

"Right. So I suppose you just go hopping into trailers like Superman on the off chance there's a bad guy to catch," she said, trying to push past me.

I put out a hand to stop her. We stood face-to-face.

"You do seem to be in trouble, Lois."

"Thanks, but I can look out for myself," she told me. She tried to shoulder past me again, but I wouldn't let her go. She took a step back and gave me an evil glare.

"That's a good look," I told her. "Do you practice that in front of a mirror?"

She practiced it on me some more and I leaned against the wall to block her way out of the narrow camper.

"I saw you here yesterday too," I told her. "Before Duncan MacRae was murdered."

"So, what, you've been spying on me?"

"It seemed only fair. After all, you were spying on Duncan and Mr. Mackenzie."

"What are you, some kind of perv?"

I shook my head. "My interest is purely professional," I lied. "Your uncle asked me to keep an eye on you."

That got her. "He *what*!?" she cried. She balled her fists and stamped her foot, then stalked the few feet to the back of the camper, fuming. I thought about telling her she was cute when she was mad, but I was afraid I'd be kissing one of those fists if I said it.

"Oooh! I told him I could handle this by myself!" she said.

"You what?" I said. I stood up straight. "You mean he knows you're here?"

Megan started opening and closing drawers again, like she was looking for something and like I wasn't there telling her to stop.

"Hey, wait a minute—" I said.

"If you're just one of Uncle Guy's trained dogs, make yourself useful and guard the front door," she told me.

"Whoa, whoa, whoa. I'm *not* here to help you do whatever it is you're doing. I'm here to stop you. And just what *are* you doing?"

She slammed another drawer shut and opened a cabinet above the stove.

"Looking for evidence," she said.

"Evidence of what?"

Megan lifted the lid on one of the benches in the breakfast nook. There among some old orange boating life vests was a roll of paper almost as long as the table.

"Aha," she said. Megan pulled out the roll and let the bench top fall back into place. There was a rubber band holding the pages together, and she yanked it off and spread the papers out on the table.

"Evidence of this," Megan said.

They were architectural drawings, blueprints. Dozens of little clusters of buildings and miles of snaking roads in between what looked like a golf course.

"What is it?" I asked her.

"Don't you recognize it? That's MacRae Meadow."

"It doesn't *look* anything like MacRae Meadow."

"Look at the big brain on you. This is what Beth's dad and your friend's dad planned to do with it after they bought the mountain from Duncan."

Looking at it more closely I could begin to make out land-marks. The groves were cleared to make room for row after row of rental chalets. The peak of Mount Birnam was a ski slope. MacRae Meadow was a fairway.

"They're business partners, your friend's dad and his girl-friend's dad—Mackenzie and Weigel. Land developers. They wanted to buy the whole mountain from Duncan, and this is what they were going to do with it: the Birnam Mountain Country Club and Ski Resort—A Gated Community."

I ran my hand along the cool, dark paper. There was a pool where the big rock in the parking lot would have been. I flipped the pages. There was more and more. Rental cabins, vacation homes, an ice skating rink—and farther down the mountain, commercial zones with strip malls and acres of paved parking.

"They're going to turn it into another Pigeon Forge," she told me. "Just another tourist wasteland."

"Why would he do it?" I asked.

"Your friend's father? Beth's father?"

"No." I stood. "Duncan. Why would he sell them the moun-tain?"

Megan shrugged. "I don't know. Not even my uncle under-stands. Mackenzie and Weigel have been after this land for years, but Duncan wouldn't sell. He loved this place. He loved these games. He founded them, for God's sake. Then Uncle Guy caught wind of what was going on, and he sent me to snoop."

"So you and the General take the evidence to the clan elders and what—they put a stop to it somehow?"

"Something like that," she told me.

She tried to leave again, and I grabbed the roll of blue-prints so that we both had hold of it.

"Why do you care?" I said. "Besides wanting the mountain to stay the way it is."

"Isn't that enough?" she asked.

"For the General, yes. For you, I'm guessing no. Not to go through with all of this."

"So maybe I've got my own reasons."

"Which are?"

"My own," she told me. She tried to work the blueprints from my hand, but I held on tight.

"What are you doing?" she asked.

"I can't let you take these," I told her.

"What are you, the Highland Guard?"

"They don't belong to you."

"Are you serious? Don't tell me you've never stolen anything."

"Only glances," I told her.

That wasn't true, of course. Most recently I had stolen a medical folder from the records room at a hospital, but it belonged to a dead man, so I'm not really sure it counted.

I yanked the blueprints from her hands and put them back under the seat.

"The papers stay here," I told her.

Megan went for the bench lid again and I moved to stop her, but we heard someone climbing the steps to the camper and we froze. The door swung open, and I did the first thing I could think of.

I took Megan in my arms and I kissed her.

At first it was good—it was really good—and I wasn't the only one doing the kissing. Then Megan remembered she hated me and she pulled away and gave me a slap that loosened a wisdom tooth.

"What are you doing here?"

I looked up and blinked my eyes, trying to focus. It wasn't Mac or Mr. Mackenzie, it was Beth. She was carrying a change of Highland dance clothes on a hanger.

"And what the hell is *she* doing here?" Beth asked. Maybe it was just the slap, but her voice suddenly sounded like one of those remixed voices they do in movies when somebody is possessed by the devil.

I nodded at Megan. "I brought her here thinking I could get someplace with her," I said. "I guess I was wrong."

Megan's eyes were still blazing from the stolen kiss, but I saw a change come over her when she realized I was giving her an out. She covered it well. She kept the fire in her eyes, but now I could see it was just an act.

"*Pig,*" she said. She gave me a shove into the breakfast nook and I fell on the bench where the blueprints were hidden. She marched past Beth, and they snarled at each other.

"Swamp Donkey," said Beth.

"Roundmouth," said Megan.

I would have been more amused if my brain hadn't been dislodged. I stood up and shook my head as Megan left the camper.

"Ooh. Cat fight," I said.

Beth poked a long fingernail in my chest.

"I don't know what that girl was doing in here—or why you're covering for her—but I'm going to find out."

"I'm telling you, I was just trying to—"

"Skip it, assclown. Whatever that girl is up to, I'm going to put a stop to it. *Permanently.* Now get out."

"Scary," I said. "And what are *you* doing in here? Don't you have a camper of your own?"

"There's a team of sheriff's deputies crawling around in it. Now *get out*."

I put my hands in the air and surrendered. "Fine, fine," I said on the way by. "I wouldn't want to catch a glimpse of you naked and turn to stone anyway."

Beth pushed me out and slammed the door behind me.

CHAPTER FOURTEEN

—🖋—

As I left the campground I tried to imagine myself walking the back nine, not the path to MacRae Meadow. Somewhere off to the right, where a forest now stood, would be the clubhouse and restaurant. To my left, past the fairways and the greens with their little red flags flapping in the cool mountain breeze, there would be a line of condominiums instead of a rhododendron thicket. All this—the woods, the meadow, the festival—all of it would be gone, replaced with a carbon copy of every other mountain resort in the area. The only constant would be the golf carts, but instead of festival officials and security guards they'd be piloted by overweight, beer-swilling men in polo shirts and khaki pants.

As if I was having a vision of that future coming about, I saw two men in work boots, jeans, and orange vests setting up surveying equipment near the unused picnic area where Mac had tripped over a root on our midnight run from MacRae Meadow. I stopped and blinked my eyes. It was no vision. There really *was* a surveying crew working here. One of the guys was standing a few yards away with a pole and the other was peering through a gizmo on top of a tripod and writing things down on a clipboard.

"There's somebody," the guy with the pole said, meaning me.

"Hey, do you know where we can find, uh . . ." He consulted his clipboard. "William Mackenzie?"

Something stank here. The plans I'd just seen in Mac's trailer were dated two years ago. From the looks of things, Mackenzie and Weigel had been trying to get Duncan to sell them the mountain for a long time now. So how did Mr. Mackenzie know Birnam Mountain would suddenly be his to survey this weekend?

"What, did he call you out here today?" I asked.

"No, he put in the work order last Tuesday," the guy said, showing me the date on the paper. "You know where he is?"

"Right there," I said. And there he was, Mr. Mackenzie in all his glory, hustling down the path toward us.

"No, no, no," he said to the work crew. "The woman in your office told me you were going to come out on Monday."

"We're backed up," the surveyor told him. "We're having to pull overtime."

"No. You can't be seen here. Not this weekend. You'll have to come back another time."

The surveyor looked put out. "We do that, it could be another couple weeks before we can get out here again."

Mr. Mackenzie didn't like it, but he told them to pack up and go home anyway.

"Not too crazy about the rest of the clans knowing you're about to build a ski resort on top of their Highland festival?" I asked.

He'd been trying to ignore me, but I wasn't going anywhere. And I wasn't pretending I hadn't just seen what I'd seen.

"I don't know what you think you know, Horatio, but you don't know the half of it."

"Wait a minute," I said, pretending to work that one out on an invisible chalkboard. "I only know half of what I think I know? Or I don't know half of—"

Mr. Mackenzie got in my face. "Listen, smart guy. I don't want it getting around that I had a work crew out here today, understand?"

"Yeah. I can see how that would be bad for you."

"So. We have an understanding, right?"

"Yeah. I understand you called in a surveying team three days ago, *before* you knew Mac was going to inherit the mountain."

"Let it go, Horatio."

"Or else what?"

Mr. Mackenzie glared at me, then broke away to see the survey team covertly back to their truck.

How *had* Mac's father known he was going to inherit the mountain this weekend? He couldn't have anticipated Mal's arrest—unless he and Mr. Weigel had some hand in Duncan MacRae's death. Had they decided Duncan was never going to sell them the mountain and killed him for it?

I stood at the top of the hill overlooking MacRae Meadow, watching the games below. There was still too much evidence against Mal, and not enough pointing to Mackenzie and Weigel. And yet, all this would be gone if Mac's and Beth's dads had their way, and that in and of itself was enough of a crime. On one side of the field, bagpipers marched back and forth in front of judges' tables. That's where Banks would be performing soon. On the other side, tent-covered stages played host to groups of dancing girls all dressed up like Scottish theme-park cast members. In the middle, in the largest part of the field, kilted athletes were busy chucking heavy weights over crossbars and tossing telephone poles end over end. I wondered if they really went around doing such silly things in Scotland. Somehow I doubted it.

I picked out Mac's blue and red tartan and his "MacGalla" T-shirt among the competitors. He was near the edge of the field talking to Beth, who had already changed and beaten me back to the competition area by using the secret passage between the lounge and the conservatory. She was no doubt giving Mac an earful about me and Megan in his camper and throwing in a few "man lessons" for good measure. I waited until Miss Scarlet clomped away and went down to talk to him. When I got there he was rubbing his hands with some kind of white talcum powder.

"If you're getting ready to rub that somewhere under your kilt, I can catch you later," I said.

"Ach. There's no chafing when you go regimental, laddie," Mac said. I assumed that was the Scottish equivalent of going commando and decided it was better not to ask.

"Just powdering up for Beth then?"

"Forty-two-pound weight throw," Mac told me. "The big guys'll beat me in this one, but I've got them beat in the kilted mile and the Highland wrestling. That one they do by weight class. I think I can also take the sheaf toss."

"The sheep toss?"

"*Sheaf*," Mac repeated. "It's a burlap sack of straw. You stick a pitchfork in it and see how high you can chuck it."

I glanced around at the empty grandstands. "I'm surprised they didn't stick a fork in these games. Nobody's here."

"I'm here," Mac said, "and I'm going to win." He slapped his powdered hands together, making a dust cloud. "What have you been up to?"

I hadn't decided yet whether or not to tell him about Megan snooping around in his trailer and I wasn't sure why. Instead I led with the news about Mona's cell phone showing up in Mal's tent.

"Looks like you were right. About him texting himself to create his own alibi."

Mac shrugged. "I guess he thought it would clear him. He just never figured on Duncan fingering him with his name on the wall."

"You know about that?" I asked him. "I didn't tell anybody but the sheriff and his deputy."

"Horatio, you think the gossip is bad with the kids at Wittenberg? Try keeping something secret from the clans at a Highland Games. Duncan's murder is all anybody can talk about."

"Yeah, I guess you're right."

"So this pretty much seals the deal," Mac said. "Your sister's phone, I mean."

"Yeah, except—"

A guy with a clipboard and a megaphone called Mac's name for his first throw.

"Except what?" Mac asked.

"They just called your name," I told him.

"I've got a second. What's wrong with the phone thing?"

"Mona's phone doesn't work up here. Same as mine. So how could Mal have sent a text from her phone?"

The games official made a second call for Mac. He glanced that way.

"You'd better go," I told him.

"Look, that's easy," Mac said. "The reception thing. There's only one place up here most phones work—on top of the BFR."

"The BFR?" I could guess what the F stood for, but I didn't know the rest.

"The big rock in the middle of the parking lot," Mac explained. "Me and Beth figured it out a few years back. Her phone works up here but mine doesn't. I've got a valley phone just like you and Mona, but you can get one bar if you climb up on top of the rock. Mal must have known the same thing. He went up there after killing Duncan, texted his phone, waited until he got it, and then ran to the bonfire. You said he was late coming—"

Mac's name was called for a third and final time.

"Wait here," Mac told me. "I'll be right back."

He ran over to a complicated wire and pole contraption, where an unhappy-looking games official signaled for him to take his turn. The weight was a small metal rectangle with a large iron ring attached to it. Mac took the thing by the ring, positioned himself under the high bar, and started to swing the weight back and forth between his legs like he was taking a granny shot in basketball. He worked up speed with it, then tossed it over his head with a "Rrrrrrrrrraaaaaaaaaa!" The weight hurtled skyward and looked like it might actually clear the thin rod strung between the wires, then dipped at the last second, clipping the bar and not crossing it.

Mac screamed a curse and clenched his shaking fists. The judge took a step back, and Mac cursed loudly again before stalking back over to where I stood.

"Why are you so upset?" I asked. "I thought you said you expected to lose this event."

"I'm so *weak*," he said. "I'm *pathetic*."

I'd never seen Mac so hard on himself, and I let him stew. He realized I was watching and he smiled, trying to show me he wasn't mental, but it was forced, and his clenched fists still gave him away. He shook his head, like he was trying to make himself focus.

"So, ah, listen—I've been thinking about that other thing you said too," Mac finally said.

"What other thing?"

"About Mal deleting the text message off his phone. I've been thinking that maybe he did it on purpose, you know? So it wouldn't *look* like he'd just done it for the alibi. Then when they found Mona's phone he could prove he got the message, but until then he could be like, 'How did I know I needed to save it?' See?"

"Maybe," I said. "It just seems awfully complicated."

"Trust me on this, chum. I'm a Mac and you're a PC."

"Then shouldn't this be simpler?"

The few people in the audience applauded another athletic effort and I turned to look at the hill. A familiar kilt and pixie haircut caught my eye, and I watched as Megan Sternwood sat down on the grandstand with her lunch.

When I turned back I saw Mac was looking at her too. He pretended he hadn't been.

"So, um, Beth says you were in my trailer today," Mac said. "With Megan Sternwood." It was about as subtle as Gollum saying, "So, Frodo, that's a nice ring you have there."

"I told you, man, she's bad news."

"She doesn't seem all that bad to me," I said. "A little *angry*, maybe—"

"That Macduff bitch has got it in for me, Horatio. She'll do anything she can to bring me down."

"Whoa, where is this hostility coming from? Beth?"

"I don't need Beth to tell me who my enemies are."

I had debated telling Mac why Megan was in his camper, but now I saw that would only fuel the flames. Instead I let my anger get the better of me and led with what was really bothering me.

"Mac, how long has your dad been trying to buy Birnam Mountain from Duncan MacRae?"

"Where'd you hear that? Megan Sternwood?"

"No," I lied. "Like you said, the world of the Highland Games is a small one."

"Well, for your information, *and hers*, Dad's been trying to buy the mountain for years, but Gramps would never sell. He just couldn't see the potential. How much bigger the Highland Games could be if there were more hotels, more restaurants—"

"More strip malls?"

"It wasn't going to be like that. It was going to be classy. Like Sugar Mountain or Beech Mountain. Dad wanted to do a golf course too. An exact replica of St. Andrews. Keep everything Scottish. Not like it mattered. Gramps was never going to sell."

"So you don't have any idea then why your dad would have known to call a work crew to come out and survey everything to start building?"

"What?"

"A survey crew. I just ran into them, over near the picnic grounds. Your dad called them three days ago. How did your dad know you were going to own the mountain this weekend after years of your granddad saying no?"

"I—I don't know," Mac said. He looked rattled. Maybe he could see where I was going with all of this.

Mac's name was called for his second throw.

"Sounds like you're up again," I told him.

"Look, just—just stay away from Megan Sternwood," Mac said again.

It was really delightful being told who I could and couldn't talk to, and I asked Mac if he would always be around to help me pick my friends.

"Just stay away from the whole Macduff clan, Horatio. And if you see Megan Sternwood again, tell her that if she keeps on sticking her neck where it doesn't belong she's liable to lose it."

That sounded suspiciously like a threat, but Mac walked away before I could challenge him on it. Partly to spite him, I went right up the hill to where Megan Sternwood was sitting. I hoped he was watching.

CHAPTER FIFTEEN

The "Macduff bitch" watched me get closer, her eyes cool like she was thinking about saying hello to my face with the palm of her hand again.

"This grass taken?" I asked.

Megan stared at me for a few seconds, then scooched over so I had room to join her. She had her lunch on her knees in a Styrofoam box—some kind of pastry turnover with a side of deep-fried hardboiled eggs. She kept eating and watching the games as I sat down.

"So," she said with a mouth full of food. "I suppose you were down there telling your friend all about our little adventure in his camper."

"He knows all about it—but not from me. Beth's already been by to poison him."

Megan shot me a sidelong glance, trying to decide if she believed me.

I nodded at her lunch. "Scotch eggs and—?"

Megan chewed a bite and swallowed, making me wait for it. "Meat bridies," she told me. She put down a half-eaten turnover, and I could see it was filled with a beef and onion paste. From her other side she produced a bottle of IRN-BRU and took a drink from it.

"Oh, not you too," I said.

She knew I meant the orange drink. "I couldn't help it," she told me. "The girls at the booth were really *hot*."

She smiled at me, and I knew I didn't have another slap coming.

"You covered for me with Beth, and you didn't tell your friend Mac what I was doing in his camper. So why didn't you rat me out?"

"Maybe I'm not a lapdog for your uncle *or* the Mackenzies. Maybe I'm my own man."

"Or maybe you're just hoping to cop another feel like you did in the camper."

"Hold on. I might have stolen a kiss, but there was zero gropage. *That* I would have remembered."

She grinned. "And you said you'd never stolen anything."

"Well, there's a first time for everything."

"You certainly didn't act like it was your first time."

"I said it was the first time I'd ever stolen it. Usually girls just give it to me."

She liked that. I could tell from the way her eyes smiled at me. This close I could see they were deep and clever and playful all at the same time.

She turned and watched the games. "So I'm sorry about the slap," she said.

I shrugged. "It helped sell it, whether that's how you meant it or not."

Megan took another bite of her lunch.

"So what is it with you and Beth, anyway?" I asked. "I mean, besides the fact that she bears a striking resemblance to Godzilla."

She chewed her food for a while.

"We have a history," she said.

"No kidding. I thought Beth hated me, but she hates you in a wicked witch kind of way. What did you do, kill Toto?"

Down on the field, Mac made his third throw. This time the weight cleared the bar.

"Your friend is doing very well," Megan said.

"Yeah. He's pretty good at throwing his weight around."

Mac got in his competitors' faces and taunted them.

"He seems very . . . intense."

Too intense, I thought. Nobody else on the field was taking the games as seriously, and even from where we sat I could see the confusion and disgust on their faces.

"Just wait until you see him toss sheep," I told her.

One of the contestants he was goading pushed him away, and Mac turned with his arms raised to the grandstand, demanding the meager audience's attention and praise. There were so few of us it was easy for Mac to pick me out of the crowd, and when he saw me disobeying his direct orders and sitting next to his mortal enemy he lowered his arms, stared at me for a few seconds, then walked off to his next event. I enjoyed the moment.

On the other side of the field the music started back up for the Highland dancers and a half a dozen of them began to twirl and jump around the stage.

"What is that they're hopping around on the ground?" I asked.

"Swords," Megan told me. "They lay two swords across each other in an X and they have to dance in the empty spaces."

"Better than dancing *on* the blades, I guess."

"You should see the dances they used to do with the weapons in hand, like the Highland Dirk Dance. They even had special songs for it, like 'Bualidh mi u an sa chean.'"

"Which means?"

"'I will break your head.'"

"Nice. So tell me, are the Scots related to the Klingons in some way?"

Megan raised her chin at the stage. "The fourth one from the right is good. She's going to move on."

"How in the world can you tell?"

"Watch her feet."

I watched her feet but it didn't make any difference. Not to me.

"So is this like some kind of Highland DDR?"

Megan laughed. "Yeah. Soon it's going to be all the rage in malls across the country. Girls in pleated skirts and velvet vests thumping away on Dance Dance Revolution machines to electronic bagpipe music."

"Good, lassie! Almost, lassie! Keep going, you're doing GREAT, lassie!" I said in my best DDR voice.

Megan cackled. "Ach, you need more practice!"

"What if everything in life was more like DDR?" I said. "Your credit card clears, and the little machine says 'Perfect!' You flunk a test and your teacher writes 'Boo!' on it."

Megan got it right away. "The signs on the security cameras at the mall say, 'Everybody is watching you!'"

"You pick what you want to order at a restaurant by scrolling through the menu with your foot."

"You kiss a guy," Megan said, laughing, "and he says, 'Almost! Keep going, you're doing GREAT!'"

"'Nice moves!'" I said. "'Your lips are amazing!'"

It was funny and we laughed, but the kissing thing suddenly made us both uncomfortable since we'd kissed in Mac's trailer and liked it. We downshifted into awkward chuckles and caught ourselves glancing at each other. We both looked away.

"See? She's moved on," Megan told me. I looked down at the dancing tent, where the girl Megan had picked out was being congratulated on stage.

"You seem to know an awful lot about Highland dancing," I said. "Just a fan?"

"I used to dance. Competitively."

"Used to?"

Megan popped the last bit of a Scottish egg into her mouth and wiped her hands on a napkin.

"See that girl who just won? How she's changing out of her dance slippers when she goes offstage? You do that so you don't ruin your dance shoes. They're made for the smooth surface of a dance floor. Sometimes the stage is too slick, though, and you have to spray water on your shoes."

"Spraying water on them makes them *less* slick?"

"I know, it's weird, but it works. The shoes absorb the water and grip better. So in the nationals in Seattle a few years back, me and Beth were two of the finalists. She went on in the group before mine, and when she came off she told me the stage was really slick and I should use more water. She was like an older sister to me. We'd come out to the West Coast together. We were even staying in the same hotel room. I trusted her."

She shook her head. "I don't know. Maybe I should have seen it coming. Like the way she used to make fun of me for always mending my dance costume myself instead of sending it out for repairs or just buying a new one. She never had to worry about money, you know? Her dad's worth nothing, but her mom is rich. That's where the family gets it. Beth could be really snotty about it, but she'd never been *mean* before. She'd never been vindictive.

"So I did what she said. I sprayed more water on my shoes. And the first time I do a turn-out on stage my legs go flying and I fall down on my ass and right out of the competition. Just like that. All those years of training and hard work and competitions at little rinky-dink Highland festivals to get there, and there I was sprawled out on the swords with my skirt over my head in the last stage of the nationals. I was done."

"Too much water?" I asked.

She shook her head. "I felt the bottom of my shoes. They were too slippery to just have water on them. When I got back to my stuff I unscrewed the cap of my spray bottle. There were bubbles inside. Someone had put soap in my spray bottle. Dishwashing detergent."

"Beth," I said.

Megan closed the lid of her Styrofoam box and set it aside. "I could never prove she did it, but I'm sure she did. She denied it, said she was sorry I'd crashed out, but that didn't stop her from enjoying her first-place finish. That was it for me. I loved dancing, but I quit. I couldn't be a part of something that Beth or anybody else would get so mental over to sabotage someone. All that training, all that discipline—it just wasn't worth it to have to play dirty too, you know?"

I nodded. I could see why she'd want to get back at Beth now too, why she cared enough to break into Mac's trailer and try to steal the blueprints for the project that would make Mac's and Beth's families wealthier than a Scottish king.

Megan sighed and held her hands out in her lap longingly. "Still, I love the Highland Games too much to stay away, you know? I can't bear not to be here. When I'm not minding the store, I'm usually up here watching the games, or off in the groves listening to the music. It gets under your skin, you know?"

I didn't know. Not personally. It hadn't gotten under my skin, but I could see where it had for her, and for Sternwood, and Banks and his dad, and for all of the people who had felt compelled to stay on, even after the greatest among them had been killed.

"That's why Lucy and I started the shop. My parents, they're into the genealogy thing, but Lucy and I wanted something to do and not just be tourists, you know? So now I do my own thing and don't have to worry about somebody trying to take me out." She showed me the bracelet she was wearing, a wide green leather one with Celtic knotwork stamped into the side. "See?" she said. "Now I'm into leather."

I felt the bracelet. "I think I'm getting into leather too."

Her hand turned and found mine, her fingers tracing the contour of my knuckles. I opened my palm and her hand fit inside.

"You know, a psychic read my palm and told me I was thinking too much with my heart," I told her. "What do you think?"

"I think you talk too much," Megan said, and she kissed me.

CHAPTER SIXTEEN

I felt light-headed as Megan and I walked toward the bag-pipe area where Banks was due to compete soon, and I wondered again at how quickly this girl had gotten to me. Things were moving fast—very fast—and the same part of me that liked to take ten minutes to plan my next Scrabble word wanted to slow things down, make sure I knew where we were going every step of the way. That was my head talking. My heart wanted to grab this girl and kiss her again right in the middle of the path, logic be damned. I didn't want to admit that Madame Hecate had been right, but if this is what she'd meant about listening with my heart, I was all ears.

I kept my hands and lips to myself and we passed the music groves, where this time somebody was actually doing justice to a Scottish tune. I looked at the schedule board: It was a duo named Jamie Laval and Ashley Broder.

"I like that, that sound," I told Megan. "The mandolin and the violin together."

"Fiddle," she said.

"What?"

"It's a fiddle, not a violin." She pulled away from me to look me in the face. "You're not a Yankee, are you?"

"Hey!" I said. "I've lived in Tennessee my entire life. I grew up in Knoxville."

"Sure you did," she said, leaning into me.

No one was on the bagpipe side of the field, perhaps because you didn't have to sit anywhere near it to hear the music. Megan and I picked the best spot on the grass and I waved to Banks, who was already checking in with another clipboarded official.

"That's your friend?" Megan asked. "I know him. He came by the booth today and hit it off with Lucy."

"The wingman shoots and scores," I said.

Megan eyed me warily. "You mean you had something to do with that?"

"I met your sister while you were off breaking into somebody's tent or something. I thought they'd make a cute couple, so I did a little nudging."

Megan crossed her arms. "Why do I get the feeling you knew what you were doing this whole time?"

"I always know what I'm doing," I told her. *Except when it comes to you,* I added in my head.

"Uh-huh. Well, if he breaks her heart I'll kill him," Megan said. "And then I'll kill you too."

I said a quiet prayer that Banks wouldn't screw this up for both of us and settled in to watch him squeeze the octopus under his arm. The judge gave him a minute or two to tune the drone things sticking out the top.

"Banks has got a lot riding on this competition," I told Megan. "He and his dad don't have a lot of money, but the winner gets a free ride to Lees-MacRae College over in Banner Elk."

"Cel-tech," Megan said. "That's what everybody calls it. Get it? Like 'Celtic'?"

"Cute," I told her. "Anyway, thanks for coming with me. Banks is pretty worked up over this, and I didn't want to miss it."

Megan squeezed my hand, and I felt punch-drunk all over again.

Banks took his place in front of the scorer's table and started his tune. I was happy to hear it wasn't "Amazing Grace." It sounded good, whatever it was, and Banks turned and began the pacing he used to keep time.

I knew something was wrong when he made his first turn and marched back our way. I didn't know enough about playing bagpipes to say what it was, but Banks didn't look right. He always got this look on his face when he played, like he was trying very hard to remember pi to sixteen digits—that was from having to constantly blow into a pipe to fill the bag under his arm that he squeezed to make the music—but now he looked like he was trying to pass a grapefruit. He huffed and puffed out of step with the rhythm of the music, and his face turned Alabama crimson.

"Something's not right," I told Megan.

Banks did his best to soldier through it, whatever it was, but he was laboring. And the longer he played the worse it got. Sweat poured out from under his tam, and his neck swelled to three sizes too big. He was hitting all the notes, as far as I could tell, but he looked like he was about to drop dead from the effort.

Then something else dropped dead: his bagpipes.

The thing he held down low, the pipe with the holes on it like a flute that he played with his fingers, shot straight down out of his hands and hit the ground. Without the reed stopper inside, all the air rushed out of his bag and the drones petered out with a sound like a carousel dying.

"Banks!" I cried. I jumped to my feet and scrambled down to the piping table. Megan was right behind me.

"Banks," I said when I got close. "Wallace—what happened?"

Banks didn't breathe. He didn't move. He just stared at his hands like he couldn't believe they were empty. Beside me, Megan picked up the piece of his bagpipe that had come unstuck.

"I'm sorry, son," the judge at the table said. "I've got to disqualify you."

"But he can go again, right?" Megan asked. "His bagpipes fell apart."

"I'm sorry," the judge said. "He should have checked his instrument more carefully."

"What? No!" I said, rounding on the judge. "You've got to give him another chance."

Banks shook his head, the first sign of life I'd seen from him since the whole thing fell apart. "No do-overs," Banks said to no one in particular. "Those are the rules."

The judge closed the big book of sheet music in front of him and left the table.

"Banks—Banks," I said, trying to get him to snap out of it. He finally raised his eyes to me. They were empty.

"Banks, I saw you adjust everything when you were tuning up," I said. "What happened?"

"You never check the chanter," Banks told me. "Not right before a competition." He focused vaguely on the thing in Megan's hands. "It just—popped out. It's never done that before."

"Horatio, look," Megan said. She pointed to the top of the

chanter. Banks had wound a thin yellow string around the top where it fit into the bag. I ran my fingers along it. It was waxy, probably to hold it snug in its hole. It was also sliced from top to bottom with a knife.

"Banks, is this something you did? Did you slice this for some reason?"

Banks frowned at what I was showing him, but somehow it got through. He shook his head. "No—no, it wouldn't hold like that . . ." He trailed off. "Must have been where all my air was going—"

"That means somebody did this to you, Banks. Who? Who wants you out of the competition that badly?"

"I don't—I don't—" Banks stammered.

I grabbed him by the shoulders. "Banks, I need you to think. When did you leave your pipes alone? When could someone have done this to you?"

Banks put a hand to his empty breast pocket and looked up at me. "I always keep my reeds in my pocket protector," he said. The reeds joined the chanter to the bagpipes. That's the part you'd want to mess with to make the chanter shoot off like a bottle rocket. "But I left the case at Dad's table when I went to talk to that girl."

And Mr. Banks had been away from the table while he played the groves. I felt sick. It was my fault. If I hadn't told Banks to lose the pocket protector—

"Banks, we've got to find that judge," I told him. "Someone's sabotaged your pipes. They've got to let you go again."

"No do-overs," Banks said again. He walked away without saying good-bye, his drones dragging on the ground behind him.

"Banks," I called. "Banks!"

It was like talking to a ghost.

Megan took the chanter back from me and ran her thumb over the yellow string, exposing the cut. "Who on earth would do this to him?"

It was too pretty a prank not to stay and watch. I scanned the hillside and saw them almost immediately—Banks's old friends Hell's Pipers. They were trying very hard not to look at me, but I could see them snickering and laughing. The redheaded ringleader was coolly smoking a cigarette, holding it between his two middle fingers so his hand covered his mouth when he took a drag. He turned his head to blow out a plume of smoke and we locked eyes, then he tossed his cigarette in my direction, said something to the rest of his sheep, and walked away.

"I think I might have an idea," I said.

Megan handed me the chanter. "Listen, I've got to get back to the booth and give Lucy a break."

I nodded, watching the punk with the spiky hair go off alone around the path.

"Hey," she said, bringing my face around to hers. "Will I see you later?"

"Yeah," I told her. "Count on it."

"I will," she said. We kissed again. When it was over she kept her hand on my face. "I'm sorry I can't stay."

"That's all right," I told her. "I've got to see a man about a sea urchin."

CHAPTER SEVENTEEN

—✐—

Terrence the sea urchin left his Hell's Pipers friends behind and went around the far side of the path that circled Mac-Rae Meadow. There wasn't much out that way except some auxiliary parking and a food vendor or two. Maybe he was going for food. Maybe he was looking for a Porta-John. Maybe he was walking to the clan tents farther along on the other side of the meadow. But no matter where he was headed, he was going to find me.

I skirted the ridge where the rest of the Hell's Pipers hung out so I didn't draw a crowd, then fell into step about fifteen yards behind Terry. He sauntered down the path like he owned the place, then darted up a little bank and into the woods. I didn't know what he was up to, but a few seconds later I followed him in.

The undergrowth was thick and it was hard to see too far ahead, but I could follow his trail well enough. I crept along quietly for another few yards until I saw a little clearing open up ahead of me. The sea urchin was easy to spot in his red tartan kilt, sleeveless black leather jacket, and ridiculous spiky red hair. He had his back turned to me, smoking a cigarette.

I came out into the clearing and he turned.

"Hello, Terrence," I said. "Surprised to see me?"

He grinned. "Not especially."

The rest of the Hell's Pipers came crashing out of the woods all around us, and I realized I'd been lured in. Half of them sipped on bottles of IRN-BRU, and a couple of them carried black cases covered with band stickers. They snickered like I was the biggest patsy since General Custer. And maybe I was.

"You guys come up here to play with each other's pipes?" I asked.

Terrence laughed, low down and mean. He nodded to a couple of goons behind me and they grabbed my arms and wrenched them behind my back. They knew what they were doing too; I couldn't budge.

Terrence came over close, but not close enough for me to kick him. "We saw you get all worked up over what happened to poor Banks," he told me, "and we just knew you'd come after us, thinking it was us that did it."

"You did do it," I told him. "And I want to know why."

Terrence took another drag off his cigarette and let the smoke come out of his open mouth like a cloudy breath in my face. His sheep tittered. I kept my eyes glued to his.

"This goes way beyond stupid prank," I told the urchin. "That competition was Banks's one chance at going to college. You didn't just ruin his day, you ruined his future."

"Awwwww," Terrence said, playing to his crowd. He put his hands to his chest. "You're breaking my heart, mate."

His crew laughed.

"Seriously," he told me. "I think I might cry. His *future?*" He faked wiping a tear from his eye, then turned on me quickly, pulling his little ceremonial dagger out of his boot and holding it under my chin.

"Very dramatic," I told him. "Did you get that move from an old episode of *Highlander*, or was it from one of the movies?"

"You don't seem very scared for a guy with a sgian dubh at his throat," Terrence said with all the menace he could muster.

"Well, see, I know you're not really going to cut me with that knife," I told him. "Not even you are that stupid. That's the kind of thing that would get you kicked out of the games for life. Besides, sticking anybody with a knife right now is a dumb play, considering the police—and I mean the *real* police—are still looking for whoever it was that stabbed Duncan MacRae."

Terrence kept the knife at my throat. "Mal did that. That's what everybody says."

I shrugged as much as I could with two goons pinning my arms back. "Great. Then you have nothing to worry about. Cut away, Terrence."

Drawing the sgian dubh had been stupid, and he saw that now. He couldn't stick me with it without getting in trouble, and he couldn't *not* stick me with it and save face with his gang. Terrence pulled the knife away and cracked me across the face with his left hand, the one with the cigarette. I could just feel the touch of hot ash on my skin before it gave way to the pounding sting of my cheek bruising up. First Megan, now Terrence. Suddenly my face was everybody's punching bag.

"Don't call me Terrence," he said. He'd had to pop me one not to lose points with his peeps, and me using his name again was good enough reason to do it. From the way he'd landed the fist I could tell Terrence didn't have much practice hitting people, and it was weak anyway because he had his sgian dubh in his good hand. It still hurt like a mother, and I knew I'd have a black eye.

"If Terrence is out, how about I call you MacGalla?" I asked him.

Terrence put his sgian dubh away. "You believe this guy?" he asked his gang. He reared back and punched me in the stomach. He wasn't much better with his right, but it did make my lunch think about coming back.

"That's it," I told him. "Now you're getting it. You have to hit me where people can't see it, so you don't get in trouble."

"Man, you are screwed up," Terrence told me. Even when he wasn't talking his mouth hung open like he was a hayseed.

"So what was it," I said. "You just got bored and needed somebody to pick on?"

"What, you mean this? You're just fun to mess with."

"No. Banks. Why the bagpipe competition? Did one of you want to win and needed him out of the way?"

"Fffff," Terrence said. "You think any of us cares about some scholarship?"

"Then why?" I struggled against the goons to make sure they hadn't fallen asleep. They hadn't. "Why knock Banks out if it didn't make any difference to you?"

Terrence smiled. "Why don't you ask your friend Mac?"

I stopped squirming. "What?"

Terrance grinned at his friends. "I don't think he saw that one coming." They laughed.

"What are you talking about?"

Terrence signaled to one of the others, and she tossed him a bottle of IRN-BRU. He uncapped it and took a long drink, making me wait.

"Ahhh. Refreshing," he said. He wanted me to ask again,

but I wouldn't do it. I didn't have to. I could tell from the look on his face he was dying to tell me. He was enjoying this too much not to.

"Your friend Mac?" he said. "He paid us to do it, mate." He held up the orange and blue soda bottle. "With three cases of IRN-BRU."

That brought a big laugh from the pipers, who raised their bottles in a toast with him and drank.

"See, maybe you haven't heard, but we've been banned from the vendor tents, so we can't procure our own. The hell of it is, we would have screwed with that dweeb for free! Just don't tell Mac."

"I don't believe you," I said.

Terrence came over and put an arm around my neck like we were old buddies. "I know you don't, mate. And I wish I had some way to prove it to you. I really do. Because I would love—*love*—to be there to see your face when you find out your pal was the one who crushed his cousin's dreams."

I really didn't believe him, but turning me against my friend seemed a little too clever for a guy who couldn't remember to close his mouth when he wasn't talking. A quick look around didn't reveal any other geniuses either. Something small and dark started eating away at me down deep in my gut and I couldn't make it go away.

"You keep hanging your mouth open like that you'll catch flies," I told Terrence.

He shut his piehole and stepped back from me.

"You know, you're pretty cocky for a guy who's about to get his ass handed to him."

"Oh, cut the crap," I told him. "We're ten yards from the path. The minute you really lay into me, I'm going to scream whatever the Gaelic word for 'rape' is and bring a fleet of those security guys in golf carts crashing down around us. Then you and your 'peeps' will be playing Warriors on the mean streets of Pigeon Forge the rest of the weekend."

Instead of grimacing, the sea urchin grinned, and the bad feeling in the pit of my stomach got worse.

"See, this buttsucker has forgotten who we are. We're Hell's *Pipers*, you retard. Johnny?"

A lanky kid with a face like a pizza set down his black stickered case, unlatched it, and pulled out a set of bagpipes. In just a few seconds he filled the bag with air and had a light drone going, then launched into "Amazing Grace." It was so loud I could barely hear the urchin, and he was right in my face.

"Let's see how tough you are when nobody can hear you scream, jackhole!"

"Mouthbreather!" I yelled.

"I have asthma, you dumbass!" he said, and he punched me in the nose.

CHAPTER EIGHTEEN

—⚔—

I must have looked like I'd gone ten rounds with a bear when I stumbled out of the woods a little while later, because a lost, lonely tourist took one look at me and screamed. Actually, I was kind of grateful. It saved me the trouble of remaining conscious.

When I came to I was being loaded onto a stretcher strapped to the back of a golf cart. I thought that was a bit much, as I was sure nothing was broken. Just a little bloody and a lot bruised. Still, the few tourists around liked it. One of them was even videotaping me, like I was all part of the show. I tried to tell them to go to hell but my mouth didn't seem to want to work. All that came out was "mmmo-tellll."

"You can go back to your motel once we get you patched up in the first aid tent," an earnest security woman told me. "Are you in any pain?"

I took that to be a rhetorical question and passed out again.

There was a great deal of fussing over me in the first aid tent, but somebody who knew what she was doing got me a couple of ice packs and some butterfly bandages. My head felt like it was swollen to twice its size and it probably was. It hurt, bad, but what hurt worse was that little pit in my stomach that hadn't gone away, the pit that kept nagging at me that something in what Terrence had told me about Mac was true. It just didn't make any sense.

Mr. Mackenzie and one of the event organizers I recognized from the announcer's booth ducked into the tent while I was getting some hydrogen peroxide dabbed on a cut on my lip. I didn't bother trying to say hello.

"Horatio Wilkes." It was disapproving, the way Mr. Mackenzie said it, with a hint of amusement. Like he knew this was coming. I suddenly wondered if he really did. "Why, I certainly never expected to find out *you'd* gotten into a fight."

"You just don't know me well enough, I guess," I told him.

The woman tending to me unsheathed a butterfly Band-Aid and sealed my split lip. That was going to be a lot of fun to pull off when the time came.

"You know this boy?" the official asked.

"He's a friend of my son's," Mr. Mackenzie said, as though that alone was enough to damn me. So he liked to pile it on his son even when he wasn't there to defend himself. Nice.

"Can you tell us what happened?" the official asked me.

"It was a bunch of idiots who call themselves Hell's Pi—"

"I don't much care who it was that did this to you," Mr. Mackenzie said, cutting me off. "The last thing we need at these games is some fool running around picking fights. I think there's already been far too much violence at these games, don't you agree, Horatio?"

I glared at him. "Yeah, I'll say."

"I still think we should get to the bottom of this," the official tried. "Find out who's responsible."

"Horatio is responsible for his own actions," Mr. Mackenzie said. "And I have half a mind to send him home."

So that's what this was all about. Mac's father had set the Hell's Pipers on me to get me sent home. Had I gotten too close to something when I stumbled on him with the surveying team? Were he and Beth's dad up to no good? Had Banks just been an innocent victim of Terrence and his sheep trying to bait me into a fight? And what did Mac have to do with any of this? I had a lot of questions I needed to answer, but first I had to tell Mr. Mackenzie I wasn't scared of him or his hired thugs.

"Does having half a mind mean you get one of those blue handicapped tags for your car?" I asked him.

Mr. Mackenzie stepped closer and talked low. "It's time for you to leave, Horatio. You're not welcome at these games anymore."

"Gee, and I'd been having such a great time up until now," I told him. "But you know what? I've got a good feeling about these games. Like everything's going to be kittens and butterflies from now on. I think I'll stay." I pulled my shirt on and thanked the nurse. "Am I all through?" I asked her.

"You're through all right," Mr. Mackenzie told me.

I stood up to leave the tent. After being ganked by a marching band I was hardly in the mood to be badgered by an overbearing prick.

"Save the material for someone who cares," I told him. "If you want to get rid of me, you're going to have to do better than bribing a bunch of kilted goons with bad haircuts."

Mr. Mackenzie kept his poker face on. "I don't know what you're talking about," he said.

"Sure you don't." I turned to the games official. "If you want to know who did this to me and kick out the real troublemakers, just let me know. Otherwise I want to get back to the games. I don't want to miss the kilted pole vault."

Mr. Mackenzie stopped me with a hand on my shoulder.

He was a big man and I was in no condition to resist. His fingers dug into my skin as he leaned close.

"Go home, Horatio. You don't belong here."

"The boy's with me," came a crotchety old voice from the entranceway. "He's a Macduff."

General Sternwood tried to wheel his way into the tent but had a hard time on the grass. I moved to help him and Mr. Mackenzie let go of my shoulder.

"What are you talking about?" Mac's dad asked.

Sternwood took in the beatdown I'd gotten as I went around behind his chair, but just as quick his hard eyes were back on Bill Mackenzie.

"His family is a sept of the Macduff clan, so he's a Macduff. He has as much right to be here as anyone else. And near as I can tell, he wasn't the one doing most of the hitting. What kind of fool would start something where he ends up looking like this?"

I winced a little at that but I let it go.

"Now, can the Macduff clan be assured he won't be hassled anymore?" the General asked.

"As—as long as he stays out of trouble," the official blustered.

Mr. Mackenzie said nothing.

"Good enough," Sternwood told them. "Take me away." That last bit was for me, and I was happy enough to get out of there. I pulled his chair back out through the tent flap, and that was the end of it.

"Take me back to the clan tents," the General ordered. I pushed him along the gravel path for a while in silence, trying to ignore the stares I was getting. I must have looked like a prizefighter—the one lying facedown on the mat when the bell rang.

"What the hell happened?" Sternwood finally asked me.

"Hell's Pipers," I told him. "A goth-punk bagpipe corps who messed with Wallace Banks."

"So you thought you'd mess back."

"Yeah. That part didn't work out so well."

General Sternwood put his hands to the wheels and brought his chair to a quick stop. He wheeled on me.

"You've got to be more careful, Horatio."

I frowned, which hurt.

"More careful? What are you talking about? I can handle the village idiots."

Sternwood scowled. "There's more to this than a bunch of young punks playing punching bag with your face."

"Yeah," I said, throwing a glance over my shoulder in the direction of Mr. Mackenzie. "I'm starting to get that."

"The time is coming when you're going to have to figure out which side you're on," Sternwood said.

"I didn't know there *were* sides."

"There are now," General Sternwood told me, and he turned and wheeled himself away.

I shook my head. It had already been a crazy weekend, and it was only Friday afternoon. How had I gotten myself mixed up in the petty politics of a Highland Games festival?

All I wanted to do was lie down and take a long nap that lasted until Monday, but that meant finding my car and driving back down to Pigeon Forge and crashing at my motel. It was too much trouble to go all that way only to come back for the parties tonight, where I hoped to hook up with Megan again. Instead I went for the food vendors, hoping some greasy curly fries and a root beer would put some energy back in my tank. Or at least stop up my arteries enough that I quit bleeding.

On the way I passed the IRN-BRU tent again and I stopped. The new girls on duty were just as busty and bouncy as the ones there before, and that same Scottish song blared from every speaker and television monitor in the booth. I went to pay another visit to the house of iron.

"Feasgar math!" a girl said when I walked up. "That means—"

"Yeah, I know."

"Oh," she said. "What happened to your face?"

"Plastic surgery gone wrong," I told her. "I told them I wanted to look like Patrick Dempsey and I came out looking like Jack Dempsey."

She didn't get it. I think she thought I was serious. While she was wondering if her boob job could leave her looking like this, a kid came up looking to get his fix.

"Can I have a bottle of IRN-BRU please?" he asked.

"Feasgar math!" the girl told him. "I'm sorry, we had a couple of big sales this morning and we're all out! We've already sent for more. Check back in a couple of hours, okay?"

"Somebody must have had a wad of cash on them to buy out your stock," I said.

"Oh, we take credit cards," the girl said. She pointed to one of those old *ca-chunk ca-chunk* imprint machines stores use when their network connection goes down. Another kid came up looking for some IRN-BRU, and I slipped back toward the credit card gadget while the girl greeted him in Valley Girl Gaelic. The receipts for the day were stacked in a shoe box next to the machine. I glanced around to make sure no one was watching and thumbed through them. There weren't many. I hoped I wouldn't find what I was looking for, but there it was: a receipt for a credit card in Mac's name for fifty dollars' worth of IRN-BRU.

The empty pit in my stomach got a little bigger, and I knew that curly fries and a root beer were not going to make it go away.

CHAPTER NINETEEN

—/—

There was plenty of IRN-BRU on hand that night at the campground. Every other Friday night party had been canceled with curt notices on the community dry erase board, but Mac and Beth had decided to forge ahead with theirs, Duncan's death be damned. Throwing a shindig on the same lot where the old man had died the night before was as awkward as Michael Vick at a PETA rally, and I put off my arrival as long as I could, walking the gravel paths in search of Megan.

It was cool again, though not nearly so cold as the night before, and the breeze brought the smell of roasting meat and mountain laurel, not blood and gore. I walked every path in the campground, but if Megan was around she was hidden in a tent or a trailer somewhere. Knowing how she felt about Mac and Beth, I didn't figure her showing up at their party, but that's where I ended up when I couldn't find her. After I put in an appearance I'd go looking for her again, but I didn't want to look too desperate. I wasn't Mona, after all.

Mac's tent was still cordoned off, but every teenager who remained at the games was gathered practically on top of it, standing around the Mackenzie and Weigel campfires with beer or IRN-BRU in hand and trying to force the small talk. The boys wore skirts and the girls wore shorter skirts, and despite the specter of death still haunting the tent next door, everyone was on the make for someone to snog in the woods. We're teenagers, after all. It's not like we can turn off the hormones.

"Horatio!" Mac called. Spot and Beth were by his side. Spot came running out to meet me. Beth didn't. I bent low and scratched the border collie behind his ears. "That'll do, Spot," I whispered, using some of Sternwood's dogtalk again. He wagged his tail but stopped fidgeting, and he was calm alongside me as we went over to Mac and Beth.

Mac held his arms out for a hug but I left him hanging.

"Where you been, chum? The party's already started!" He squinted through the darkness at me. "Jesus Horatio, what happened to your face?"

"I got run over by a bagpipe," I told him.

Beth spared me a glance and I waited for the smart remark, but it never came. I had never known Beth to miss a chance to put me down, and this was an easy one. Before I could ask why, she spied a friend across the campsite and went over to play hostess.

I looked at Mac's tent, the one with the yellow "POLICE LINE—DO NOT CROSS" tape strung all over it. "Don't you think this is all a bit . . . uncomfortable?" I asked.

"Everybody looks like they're having a good time."

"Mac, the smiles around here are so forced you'd think they were being paid to do it. We're partying at a crime scene."

"But that's just it. That tent is like a party magnet. Everybody wants to come by and see where the old man died, but it's too weird, right? So now we invite them to a party, and they can all come and check it out without looking like creeps."

"The 'old man' was your grandfather," I reminded him.

"Come on, Horatio. Like that isn't already eating me."

"Where's Banks? Is he here?"

"Yeah, but he's moping around like his mom just died."

"You do know what happened to him today, right?" I asked. I tried not to put too much into that, but it was hard. If Mac was really behind Banks's downfall, he knew *exactly* what had happened.

"The bagpipe thing, you mean? Yeah. But it's not like it's the end of the world or anything. Look, there he is. Come on."

Banks was standing by the fire, staring at it like he wanted to jump in. There were people around him talking, but he was alone. Mac and Spot and I went over to him. "Banks, man, come have a beer," Mac said.

Banks said nothing.

"Come on. You can't beat yourself up over this. Accidents happen, right?" Mac looked to me for backup, but I didn't say anything. I was too busy trying to read Mac's face in the firelight. There seemed to be genuine concern there. Or maybe it was guilt.

"Lot of pretty girls here tonight," Mac tried. "Let me introduce you to one."

Banks didn't bite.

"Damn it, Wallace, it was just a stupid bagpipe competition!" Mac erupted. "Let it go!"

When Banks still didn't respond, Mac stormed off. I hung back for a second, feeling the sting of Mac's outburst and wanting to say something to make Banks feel better, but I didn't have anything for him. A cold, damp wind blew, and

I looked up to see a dark cloud pass across the face of the moon.

"I think it might rain tonight," I told him.

"Let it," he said. He walked away from the fire, disappearing into the darkness.

Spot and I found Mac getting a beer from one of big lidded coolers near the RV.

"A little hard on Banks back there, weren't you?"

"He deserves it, you know? I mean, seriously. He acts like his whole life is ruined."

"It might as well be," I said. That creepy feeling in my stomach was at it again. I should have been surprised at how easy Mac was taking this—and yet I wasn't. "You know that was his only shot at going to college. They give out that scholarship like once every four years. When it comes back around he'll be too old to try for it."

"So he doesn't go to college and get some big job and get rich or whatever! His dad is happy with what he's got. Why can't Banks be happy with that too?"

Where was *this* coming from? Since when did going to a little high-country college that nobody ever heard of mean getting a big job and getting rich? And why did Mac feel so threatened by that? The pit in my stomach growled louder. Had the Hell's Pipers been jerking my chain, or did Mac really have something to do with all of this? What would possibly make him want to ruin his cousin's life?

"Mac, why did you buy an assload of IRN-BRU?"

"What?"

"I went by the IRN-BRU tent, and they said you bought fifty bucks' worth of the stuff. What'd you do with it?"

"Oh. Yeah. I, uh, I bought few cases," he told me. "For the party." He flipped open the next two coolers down the line.

They were filled to the top with ice and IRN-BRU. "You want one?" he asked.

"No," I said. The memory of the taste made me feel sick all over again. Still, that thing gnawing at my insides settled down a little. Mac had bought a few cases of IRN-BRU, and here it was. Maybe I was wrong. Maybe Terrence *was* that clever. Maybe a lifetime of being a bully had honed his skills at saying just the right thing to get under his victim's skin. I had known a guy like that back in fifth grade. Somehow he knew just the right buttons to push to drive kids to tears or make them take the first swing. The guidance counselor said he was secretly insecure and sad on the inside. I said he was just an ass.

"You want a beer then?" Mac asked.

I didn't dignify that with a response.

"You gotta lighten up," Mac told me. He popped the top on his beer with a bottle opener on his key chain. "You always walk around so high and mighty, like you're too good to drink."

"Seriously, Mac, I have been there, done that, and had my visa stamped. Can we just drop it?"

Mac shrugged and took a swig. Forget the dead guy in the tent—things were suddenly awkward enough between me and Mac. Besides the time when we were ten and didn't talk for three days because we disagreed on who would win a foot race between Superman and the Flash, Mac and I had never argued. About anything. Mac had *never* commented on my abstinence before, and I had never once thought him selfish or mean. I felt awful, like I had betrayed him somehow, and I decided to make a peace offering.

"I hear you're first place in the games after day one," I said.

"Yeah," Mac said. He didn't sound too thrilled, and I told him so.

"It's great being on top," he told me, "but it's cutthroat out there. Everybody else is gunning for me, trying to take me down. They'll do anything to win."

"It didn't look that way to me."

"Trust me. When you're king, you're always looking over your shoulder. All those other guys in the competition, they're out to get me. They want to knock me off the throne and take it all away from me. But they'll see. I'm not going to back down. I'm never going to back down again."

The "king" bit was kind of overkill for a guy who was just in first place in the tartan skirt Olympics, but it made me remember that nutty psychic in Pigeon Forge, the one who'd told Mac he'd be king of the mountain. Maybe he was taking what she said way too seriously.

"He's just wandering around not talking to people!" Mac said. It took me a minute for me to realize he was talking about Banks again. Mac couldn't take his eyes off of him.

What else was it the psychic had said? That Mac would be king but that Banks would own the mountain someday? I glanced back at Mac, who was scowling at Banks. If he was taking the first part of the prophecy seriously, did that mean he saw Banks as some kind of competition?

"What, um, what was it that fortune-teller said about him again?" I asked Mac, playing dumb.

That dragged Mac back to me. "What? The fortune-teller?"

"Yeah, what was it she said about Banks? She said you were going to be king of the mountain, but there was something else about Banks."

Mac's mouth hung open for a moment while he tried to

decide what to say. "I—I don't know. I can't remember," he said finally.

Which was a crock. Mac was pretending he'd forgotten, the same way you pretend you didn't see somebody you don't want to talk to in the crowd at a ball game or across the food court at the mall. You just keep your eyes moving past them like you didn't recognize them, but you both know you did. It was like that now, and I was the guy getting the glassy eye treatment.

"You don't remember," I said, calling him on it. Making him lie to me again, giving him one last chance to get out of it.

"No," he said.

So that was it then. The only reason he would lie about the prophecy was because he didn't want to admit that he'd been preoccupied by it, *consumed* by it—so much so that, what—he'd paid off Terry and the Pirates to sabotage Banks at the bagpipe competition? Or maybe his dad had come to him with the idea of running me out of the games and he had seen a way to kill two birds with one stone. And for what, because some two-bit hustler in a Gypsy costume convinced him that Banks was going to win a scholarship, go off to school, and get rich or clever enough to take the mountain from him?

Spot stood up and pointed his ears at me like he could sense my anger.

I looked at Mac again. Really looked at him. Joe Mackenzie, who was everybody's friend. Joe Mackenzie, who acted like he didn't have a care in the world. Joe Mackenzie, to whom so much was given and so little expected in return.

Beth called Mac over to where she was sitting with a group of girls, and I think Mac and I were both relieved to have something else to talk about. Beth's supermodel friends all wore leggings with their Highland dancing skirts on over them and had their hair and their butts up tight like Beth's. They sat at a picnic table covered with bags of chips and cookies, none of which they were eating, of course, because sticking your head down the hole of a Porta-John to purge was something even *they* wouldn't do to look thin.

"Come and sit down!" Beth said, squeezing in between two girls. "Horatio, you too!"

Now I *knew* something was up with her. The only place Beth would have ever invited me to sit was in an electric chair. Ordinarily I would have declined out of principle—or maybe spite—but I was too curious about this new and even scarier Beth. At her command, two of the girls made room for me and I climbed onto the bench.

Mac didn't follow me, which was even stranger. The Mac I knew would have already found a place between two of the girls, making some sort of off-color comment about the contents of his kilt in the process. Instead he stood where he was and shook his head.

"The table's full," he said.

Beth smiled, but it was tight and controlled, like she was forcing it. "Of course it's not, sweetie. Tiffany and Caroline can just scoot down."

Two of the girls on Beth's end of the big table wiggled their bottoms and inched away from somebody sitting at the back end of the bench. With a start, I realized who it was.

"Banks?" I said.

If Banks heard me, he ignored me. He had his back to us and was staring off into the darkness of the woods. I figured he had been there when the girls had descended on the table. If he'd been in his right mind he would have gotten up and left it to them, but Banks was hardly in his right mind.

Mac wasn't either.

"I—I can't," he said, taking a step back. "There's no room."

It was like Mac was actually scared of Banks. Beth glared at him. "Mac. *Sit. Down.*" She turned on the smile for her friends. "He's just being silly."

The girls looked like they wanted to believe her, but this was too weird for them. They stared at the snacks on the table instead, like the secrets of the universe lay in the packaging for potato chips if only they looked hard enough.

Mac lowered his voice and gestured at Banks. "But he's just *sitting* there and not *saying* anything."

Beth was up in an instant. Spot growled behind me as she marched over and pulled Mac away from the table.

"Will you get it together?" she told him, loud enough for all of us to hear. Then, more quietly, she said, "What's done is done, all right?"

"I—I just—why can't he let it go? It's not like he lost something he already had."

One of the girls at the table thought it would be polite to start up a conversation and pretend we weren't all listening to Mac and Beth. She cleared her throat and tried to smile at me.

"What, um, what happened to your face?" she asked.

"What, this?" I asked, knowing full well what she meant. "A bear attacked me. Right on the path."

The girls looked horrified.

"*You* need to let it go," Beth told Mac. "Everybody is *watching* you."

It was a DDR line, and I thought of Megan. She would have been amused. I would have been too if I could shake the ominous feeling this evening had.

Mac broke away from Beth. "Does nobody else see this?"

he said, moving toward Banks's spot at the table. He froze. Banks wasn't there anymore.

"See, there's room," the girl on the end said.

Mac blinked and looked around, trying to find Banks in the darkness. He was gone. But it was clear that Banks was haunting Mac, and it was just as clear why. The fortune-teller had been right—Mac had inherited the mountain when Mal killed Duncan—and now Mac was worried the other part would come true too, that Banks would some-how take it away from him. Mac had betrayed his cousin, pure and simple, and over nothing more than a twenty-dollar palm reading.

"This is a game Mac's played ever since I've known him," Beth said, forcing a smile. "A *stupid* game. But look, no rea-son to let it ruin the mood, right?"

Beth walked Mac over to the empty spot at the table. For a moment I thought he might refuse, but Banks's absence rallied him.

"Ladies, avert thine eyes," Mac announced to the girls at the table, "lest you catch a glimpse of the infamous Loch Ness Monster."

Which meant they were all looking, of course, when he lifted his kilt and flashed them. The girls tittered, and the old Mac was back just like that. I'd seen the new Mac, though, and I didn't like it.

"It's creepy, isn't it?" said one of the girls. At first I thought she meant Mac's reaction to Banks, but she was looking at the tent with the yellow police tape on it. "Duncan MacRae died right there."

"Was murdered right there," I corrected her. "I'm surprised Beth hasn't dared Mac to go inside. Or have you already?"

Beth blanched and started randomly rearranging the

snack bags on the table. That she didn't retaliate—or take up the dare—puzzled me.

"I can't believe what's-his-name did it either," one of the girls said. "Malcolm?" she tried.

"Mal," another girl said.

"He was so cute."

I smacked the table and made the girls jump. "That's it!" I said.

"That's what?" Beth asked.

"I couldn't figure out what it was that bothered me about his name, but now I've got it."

"About whose name?" said one of the girls.

"Mal's," I told them. "Did you know I was the one who found the body?"

The girls leaned in, babbling. No, they hadn't known. What had he looked like? Was he still alive when I found him? Was it really a dagger that killed him? I quieted them with a hand.

"There was blood. Lots of blood," I said. I was really playing it up. I didn't know why—maybe because I was mad as hell at Mac and in a nasty mood. "Blood covered everything. The floor squished when I walked, and I couldn't touch a thing without getting Duncan's blood all over my hands."

Beth inadvertently knocked over a cup of soda and there was a minor scramble for paper towels by the Airhead Corps of Engineers.

"Seriously, Horatio, do you really need to go into all this?" Mac asked.

"Hey, everybody wants to come by and find out how the old man died, right?" I said, throwing his own words back at him. That shut him up. "It was pitch-black inside the tent," I continued, the girls' eyes back on me, "and all I could see

159

was where my flashlight landed. I followed the trail of blood to a body in the corner—Duncan MacRae's body—and then up the tent wall behind him where there was a single word, written in blood: *Malcolm*."

The girls at the table gasped.

"He wrote out Mal's name with his own dying hand!" one of them said.

I pointed to her. "But that's just it. He didn't write 'Mal.' He wrote 'Mal*colm*.'"

"Well, that is his name," Mac said from the end of the table.

"Yeah, but Duncan was dying—dying fast," I told him. "So why did he write out the whole thing? Why not just write 'Mal'? That's what everybody calls him anyway. Even Duncan called him that, remember?"

That got them quiet.

"It's only four more letters," Beth said from the end of the table.

"Four more letters is a lot when you're dying," I told her.

"I wouldn't know," she said, a bit of the old Beth resurfacing. But why was she reining it in? And she'd been nervous all night, playing with the potato chip bags and spilling drinks. She was so worked up over something that she couldn't remember she hated me.

"And why didn't he crawl for help?" one of the girls asked. "I mean, if he had the time and energy left to prop himself up and write 'Malcolm,' why didn't he try crawling out of the tent to look for help?"

"Yes!" I said. I could have climbed across the table and kissed her. "You're dying—you're bleeding to death—and you crawl across the room *away* from the door to write your son's full name in blood?"

I stood up and traced the letters *M-a-l-c-o-l-m* large on the table, pushing food bags and plastic cups out of the way.

"That takes ten seconds to write, and I'm not bleeding through a slit in my throat."

Beth stood and started cleaning up the table like the party was over. Maybe it was. One or two of the girls turned white, and I worried I might have gone too far. But I couldn't help it. I was giddy from hanging an answer on that nagging question from the night before. Then, while I was standing there, the enormity of what I was saying hit me: If Duncan didn't write out his son's name, that meant someone else did.

Someone who *wasn't* Malcolm MacRae.

Mac broke my reverie. "Maybe he just wanted to be sure," he said. "He was dying. Mal—Malcolm—killed him. He wanted to make sure there was no mistake. Besides, why crawl out of the tent? Everybody was down on the meadow for the bonfire already."

"Your dad wasn't," I said.

I hadn't meant anything by it, hadn't been deliberately leading up to that point. I just said the first thing that popped into my head, like some dimwitted professional celebrity.

"What?" Mac said. He and Beth were paying a lot of attention to me.

"When they were looking for someone to light the bonfire he wasn't there," I said. "Neither was your dad," I told Beth. "He was in your trailer."

"He was *what*?" Beth said. This was clearly news to her. "He was supposed to be down at the bonfire with my mom."

"He wasn't. Neither of your dads were."

"But that doesn't mean anything," Mac said.

"Sure it does," I told everyone at the table. "If Mal didn't kill Duncan, then anybody who wasn't at the bonfire that night is a suspect."

"We're leaving," Beth said. She stood from the table but tripped over Spot when she turned. "Get out of my way, dog!" she screamed. "Out, out—damn Spot!"

And there was the real Beth, the one who'd been hiding out for some reason all night long. Spot growled and Beth took a kicking swipe at him, catching his tail end with her shoe. I was almost around the table to stop her when Spot sprinted away into the woods.

Beth pointed a finger my way. "You leave me the hell alone too, you ass-faced jerkoff."

"Nice to have you back," I told her.

She flipped me off and dragged Mac away.

The girls at the table stared at me standing there all by myself. I'm not sure any of them knew quite what to say.

I clapped my hands once. "Good. Okay. New topic for conversation: lather, rinse, but *don't* repeat. Hmm? Let's hear it now, lively debate."

Nothing.

"Right. I'll just go and see about Spot then while you talk amongst yourselves."

I walked off toward the woods. I had to admit, I was a bit overwhelmed myself. If Mal didn't kill Duncan, who did? And where *had* Mac's and Beth's dads been when Duncan died? They certainly had a motive. Was Mac helping his dad cover for it? Did Beth know too, and was that why she'd been so nervous all night?

I didn't want to think about it. I just wanted to find Spot and get in my car and drive back to my motel room and go to sleep.

"Here, Spot!" I called out. I tried to remember the command to bring him home. "Way to me! No—way back!"

Spot wasn't coming back, though. He had run pretty deep

into the woods. I followed him so far in I couldn't even see the lights of the campsite behind us. I worried Beth had hurt him worse than it looked, but then I heard something digging and scratching in the darkness ahead. I clicked my flashlight on and caught Spot burrowing in the leaves and dirt.

"There you are, Spot. Are you okay? I won't let that mean old witch hurt you anymore." Spot ignored me and kept digging. "What are you after, a rabbit?" I crouched down beside him. "Let me see, boy."

Spot finally got at what he'd been digging for and pulled it out.

It was a little dagger caked with blood.

CHAPTER TWENTY

If my campfire ghost story rendition of Duncan's death didn't kill the party, finding a bloody dagger buried out back sure did. Sheriff Wood and his deputies were called in again, and I went through the story three times with three different deputies, although there wasn't much to tell. Dog runs off; dog smells blood; dog digs up dagger. I made an effort not to get my prints on the thing when I took it from Spot, but he hadn't made much of an effort not to coat it in dog drool. I didn't know if that would foul up forensics or not. If they'd covered that on *CSI,* I'd missed the episode.

I checked the time on my phone when the cops finally released me: almost midnight. This was getting to be a habit. I was tired and cold and pissed. Not pissed at the police; they were just doing their job. I was mad at Mac for sabotaging Banks because of some stupid prophecy, I was mad at whoever had killed Duncan MacRae and set up his son to take the fall for it, and I was mad at myself for helping get Mal arrested.

Where was a hot IRN-BRU girl to make me feel better about myself when I needed one?

There were a few people headed for their cars in the parking lot, which I thought was strange for it being so late. One of them was Lucy, who was walking with adults I took to be her parents. I waved to her and she came over to say hello while her mom and dad chatted with another kilted couple. She told me they were staying in a motel this year; after spending one too many festivals in a tent, they'd finally upgraded.

"Horatio, what happened to your face?" she asked.

"Your friends from the booth decided they'd rearrange it for me." I nodded to her parents and the other people in the parking lot. "Why were you guys out so late?"

"The Ceilidh," she said. It sounded like "Kay-lee." "It's kind of like a Scottish dance party."

"Sounds thrilling. Where's your sister?"

"She skipped it. I thought she'd be with you. I told you she liked you," Lucy said.

"You're good," I told her. "You should start a service."

"So should you."

I pretended I didn't know what she meant.

"Wallace? Or are you going to say you had nothing to do with that."

"I plead the fifth," I told her. "Have you talked to him at all today?"

"Kind of. I ran into him this afternoon, but he seemed pretty depressed."

"Yeah," I said. I was ready to talk about it, tell Lucy some of my suspicions about that, when I caught sight of somebody who shouldn't have been in the parking lot.

"What is it?" Lucy asked, following my gaze.

"That guy. Doesn't that look like Beth's dad?"

"Yeah. So?"

"So why is he heading for a car in the parking lot? He's staying in a trailer."

"Going down to Pigeon Forge for Krispy Kreme doughnuts?" Lucy ventured.

I watched Mr. Weigel look around for his car. One near the back of the lot flashed its lights, and he went to it and climbed into the backseat.

"Curiouser and curiouser," I said. "Come on."

Mr. Weigel was already on my list of people to replace Mal in his prison cell, and this was too suspicious not to investigate. What *had* he been doing last night in his trailer? And had there been somebody else with him? Mr. Mackenzie, maybe? Had they just come from killing Duncan MacRae?

I suddenly worried for Lucy's safety.

"Um, why don't you stay back. Let me handle this," I said.

"Not a chance," she said, darting ahead of me. "I know what's going on!"

"Lucy no, wait," I whispered, but she was already up to the side of the car. She snickered and pointed through the window at what was clearly two people in the process of ripping each other's clothes off.

"Oh. Hey," I said. "Well, that's something you don't see every day."

The woman in the backseat equation caught sight of us through the window and squealed. There was a flailing of arms and legs inside the car, and the two people became hopelessly tangled in half-removed shirts, pants, and underwear.

"Help!" the woman cried, impossibly wedged between the seat, the ceiling, and the door. Being the helpful kind of guy I am, I opened the door. She couldn't decide if she wanted to cover her nakedness or brace herself for the fall, and she did neither well. She glared up at me from the ground. I'm not sure she thought I'd been much help.

Looking at her upside down, I couldn't place the face but I certainly remembered the breasts.

"Feasgar math!" I said. "It's one of those IRN-BRU girls."

"Lucy, what on earth are you doing all the way up—oh," her mother said. She and Lucy's father came walking up and found more than they were bargaining for. "Oh, good heavens!" her mother said. Her father gallantly offered the IRN-BRU girl his coat, which she accepted before crawling back inside the car behind Mr. Weigel to get dressed.

"This isn't what it looks like!" Mr. Weigel cried from the backseat of the car. "We were just—we were just—"

"You were just trying to put more iron in your diet," I told him. "We get it. Was this who you had in the trailer with you the night of the murder?"

"Yes. We'd been fooling around, all right? When you ran off to get security I sent her home. Satisfied? I had nothing to do with Duncan's death!"

A few of the other families who'd been lingering in the parking lot came over to see what was happening. It must have been terribly embarrassing for him. I stepped aside so everyone could get a better look.

"You know what? Fine," Mr. Weigel told everyone. "I'm glad you've seen us. I'm tired of hiding it. We're in love, all right? Is that so wrong?"

"Well, it's kind of a problem if you're already married to someone else," I said. "And has he told you that all his money belongs to his wife?" I told the IRN-BRU girl. "When she divorces him over this, he won't have a shilling to his name."

"What!? Ach!" the girl said. She pushed Mr. Weigel out of the door and locked the car so he couldn't get in. In moments she crawled into the front seat and started the ignition.

"Fiona, wait!" Mr. Weigel called, chasing after the car as the IRN-BRU girl drove away.

Lucy giggled. "Does this sort of thing happen to you all the time?"

"Surprisingly, yes," I said.

"Hey," Lucy's father said. "She drove off with my jacket."

When the excitement died down everyone went to their cars, but the story of Mr. Weigel and the IRN-BRU girl in the parking lot was already the stuff of legend. There was no escaping it: By morning every last person on the mountain would know. Including Beth's mother. I felt a twinge of regret for Mr. Weigel, but he had made his own backseat and now he had to lie in it.

I said good night to Lucy and told her to say hey to Megan when she got back to their motel room, then found my car. The drive back down the mountain was lonely, with just one car close enough behind to occasionally show up in my rear-view mirror. Unlike the beautiful views during the day, in the dark I saw nothing ahead of me but the crooked shadows of trees and rocks and brooks, and maybe the occasional possum or deer, eyes blazing yellow in my high beams. Then the road flattened out at Pigeon Forge and my headlights sliced open the surface of the night like a medieval surgeon's blade lancing a boil, revealing strip mall after strip mall of tattoo parlors and T-shirt shops and pancake huts. The main drag itself was a full-blown plague, but that I could see from the neon and the strobes and the spotlights alone.

There was a lot more traffic here in the valley. The music mansions were just letting out and there were still funnel cakes to be consumed and go-carts to be ridden. I worked my way over through six lanes of traffic and had to wait until the light turned yellow to make the left onto the little road that would take me to my mountain motel hideaway. I heard honking and looked up into my rearview mirror. The car in line behind me ran the red light. It was a dark blue hybrid four-door—a Prius, maybe—with a Scottish clan crest vanity plate on it. The car zoomed up close to my antique Volvo like it was making sure who I was and then dropped back a few car lengths and settled in at the exact same speed I was traveling.

I had a tail, and a not very subtle one at that.

Farther down the road the giant fiberglass hick and his cornpone wife welcomed me back to the late-night wonderland of the Hillbilly Haven Motel and Wedding Chapel. I put my blinker on early and took the turn nice and slow so my shadow wouldn't kill anybody trying to keep up. I watched in the rearview mirror as I parked. The Prius cruised on by and took the next available space a few cars down.

I collected my things and walked down the row of doors to my room. Nobody got out of the environmentally friendly stalker-mobile. The Hillbilly Haven office showed no signs of life, but a few of the motel guests sat in white plastic patio chairs outside their rooms sipping Pabst Blue Ribbon and watching the traffic go by. I said howdy to each as I passed. One of them offered me a seat and a beer, both of which I politely declined.

I glanced over my shoulder as I dug out my room key, but nobody was following me. My room now had the added scents of drier lint and lemon cleaning agent, which meant there'd been some form of room service while I was gone. I opened the window to get some "air-conditioning" coming in and checked my things. Everything was still where I'd left it except for the crunchy blanket. Someone had thoughtfully put that back on the bed.

I brushed my teeth and splashed water on my beat-up mug, then went for a bucket of ice. The Prius was still there, and I stole a peek at the driver with my peripheral vision. On the way back, I made a point of fiddling with the lock at my door so my stalker had plenty of time to see where I was staying and pay me a visit if she wanted to.

With the crusty bedcover safely hidden in the corner I stretched out on the white sheets with an ice pack on my face and tried not to sweat. Cold on the mountain, hot in the valley. It had taken me two painful days to learn my lesson, and tomorrow I would be prepared. For the weather *and* for the investigation. Because that's what it was now. What it should have been from the beginning. I hadn't seen it—or maybe hadn't wanted to see it—but there were high crimes afoot at the Highland Games, and it was high time I got my head out of my ass and started answering all my questions.

There was a knock at my door. My stalker had finally decided to pay me a visit. I glanced at the digital alarm clock on the dresser: 12:41 A.M. I set the ice pack on the bedside table and pulled my T-shirt back on, but I didn't cover my boxers. It's my policy that callers after 12:30 in the morning don't rate pants.

The door didn't have a peephole in it, but I knew who it was and opened it.

Megan Sternwood stood on the other side.

CHAPTER TWENTY-ONE

"I don't remember ordering any women," I told Megan.

She smiled. She was still wearing her skirt and sweater number, and she held something behind her back and wasn't showing me what it was. "Do you always open your door to strangers in the middle of the night, Horatio Wilkes?"

"Only when there are beautiful girls on the other side. It rarely happens, but it's a decision that generally pays off."

"But I could have been a mugger."

"A mugger who followed me all the way down the mountain in a blue Toyota Prius with North Carolina tags?"

"How did you—?"

"You stayed too far back. That's why you missed that light. And for future stalking reference, you might want to take the vanity plate with the Macduff family crest off the front of your car if you're trying to be inconspicuous."

"Ooh," Megan said. "You am smart."

"Me know."

I leaned on the door frame trying to look cooler than I felt. For all my bravado, girls *never* came knocking on my door late at night. I'd had my fair share of girlfriends and we'd fooled around, but I'd be lying if I said it happened as frequently for me as it did for Mac. It was like comparing dog years to human years.

"You know, you could have just found me at the games," I told her.

"What, and ruin the surprise?"

Megan looked down at my stilts.

"Nice legs," she said. "You should take them out once in a while and let them play in the sun."

"I like my programmer's tan just fine," I told her. "Besides, they like playing in the dark."

"Is that so?" she asked. She took her eyes off my legs long enough to see what had become of my face. "Oh my God, Horatio." She put a hand to it. "Uncle Guy said you'd been in a fight, but I didn't know it was this bad. Does it hurt?"

"Only when I think about it."

"Maybe I can help you not think about it then," she said. She stood on her toes and kissed me. It was a good kiss, filled with magic and wonder and strawberry lip balm, but I needed to ask her something before we made it a double.

"Did you kill Duncan MacRae?"

Megan's nose nuzzled mine.

"I thought Mal killed Duncan," she said. She bit off another kiss.

"I think it was somebody else," I told her. "Somebody who framed Mal."

"Why would I kill Duncan MacRae?" she asked.

"Because maybe he was about to sell the mountain to Mac's and Beth's families and you didn't want to see that happen."

Megan stared at my lips like she was going to devour them. One of her hands found my chest. "Do you really believe that?" she asked.

I was having a hard time believing much of anything beyond what was right in front of me. "No," I told her. "But I'm beginning to like the alternative even less."

Megan's hand found my neck, then my chin, then my ear. "What's the alternative?"

I didn't say anything, but I kept my hands to myself. Under the circumstances, I thought I deserved a medal.

Megan finally looked me in the eyes.

"Look," she said quietly, "you know I didn't do it. If I did it to keep Duncan from selling out to Mac's family, why would I point the finger at Mal? With him in jail, Mac's family will inherit the mountain without even having to buy it. Now there's no chance of stopping them."

"Yeah. Yeah, you're right," I said.

"You sound disappointed."

"No, it's not that," I told her. "It's just—my head hasn't been in the game and I've fallen behind."

"So get back in there, player."

I smiled. "All right, Coach." I tried to glance around her. "So what's in the other hand?"

Megan produced a CD case. "A little motivational music," she said. "That violin and mandolin duo you liked."

"Fiddle," I corrected her.

"If you insist," she said, playing with my hair.

I wanted to invite Megan in, and I knew she wanted me to invite her, but I was nervous, and when I'm nervous I talk. It keeps me from actually having to do anything.

"Thanks," I said. "I'll give it a play."

Her empty hand found its way to my chest again.

"I thought maybe if you're not too busy accusing people of murder we could play it together," she said. "Unless you like playing solo."

"Oh, no—I definitely prefer company," I told her.

She waited and I waited, knowing the moment was about to slip away but still afraid of making the first move.

"But what would we do while we listened to it?" I asked.

"There's always the Highland fling," she said.

I prepared my next line of banter, then caught myself. Megan was right; I did talk too much.

"What, can't think of anything smart to say?" she asked.

"I don't want to talk anymore," I told her, and I opened the door wide and let her inside.

Someone knocked at my motel room, and this time I didn't know who it was. I rolled out of bed, tried to make my eyes work, and pulled on a pair of khakis. Morning visitors rated pants. I answered the door, leaving it mostly closed behind me.

Mac stood outside in the early Saturday sunshine. Along with his big smile he was wearing his blue tartan kilt and a black T-shirt that said: "Got Haggis?"

"I haven't got any," I told him.

"Any what?"

I pointed at his T-shirt. "I haven't got any haggis."

Mac shook his head. "You *look* like yesterday's haggis, chum. Your face, your eyes—"

I gave my peepers a rub. "I was up most of the night," I told him.

"Doing what?"

The door swung open and Megan Sternwood glided out past me. She was bright and chipper and put together like she'd just stepped off the angel assembly line. Compared to her I was a dung beetle, but then I always felt that way before I'd had my morning coffee.

"I better run," she told me, ignoring Mac completely. She stood on her toes and kissed me again, and I thought maybe I wouldn't need that coffee after all. "You're not an ordinary fella," she whispered, copping another line from DDR.

"You're a pretty super dancer yourself," I told her.

Megan untied the leather bracelet on her left wrist, took my hand, and tied it on me. It was smooth and green and stamped with intricate Celtic knotwork.

"I bind thee with a lover's knot, Horatio Wilkes."

"Should I be reserving the Hillbilly Haven Shotgun Wedding Chapel?" I asked.

Megan smiled. "Let's not go that far."

I turned it over to see the back. Megan had signed her name there as the artist.

"What do you know," I said. "I ended up with a bracelet with my girlfriend's name on it after all."

She liked that and she kissed me for it, then pirouetted off toward her car.

"Wait, I've got something for you too," I told her. I put a hand in my pocket and pulled out my motel room door key and flipped it to her. "Consider this a temporary gift, until I can get you something nicer."

She waggled the large rhomboid keychain. "Diamonds are a girl's best friend," she said. "But I will see you at the games, won't I? At least at the Celtic rock concert tonight."

"It's a date," I told her. "And hey, what about your CD?"

"I'll come back for it," she said.

I watched her drive away in her car. When I turned back, Mac was watching me with cold eyes.

"I thought I told you that girl was bad news."

"Right. I'll tell you what," I said. "The minute you start to listen to *my* relationship advice, I'll start listening to yours."

"I think you need to remember who your *real* friends are, Horatio."

"Oh, you mean you? You mean, like the kind of guy who would sabotage a friend just because some idiotic roadside psychic who knows as much about ESPN as ESP told you he was going to own the mountain someday?"

"What are you talking about?"

"You know *exactly* what I'm talking about, Mac. I'm talking about you ruining any hope Wallace Banks ever had of going to college because that fortune-teller told you he was a threat. Or did somebody else put you up to it?"

"Is that what that Macduff whore told you?"

I grabbed Mac by the T-shirt and slammed him against the wall of the Hillbilly Haven Motel. "Watch your mouth, Mac."

When the shock wore off, Mac knocked my arms off and pushed me back. I stumbled into somebody's parked car and their alarm went off, deafening us.

"What *is* it with you and this 'me against the world' attitude!?" I yelled. "Why does somebody always have to be out to get you? Who's next, me? What if that fortune-teller told you *I* was a threat. Would you come after me next?"

Mac shook, the way he had when he got in the faces of the other Highland Games contestants. "Look," he yelled back, "I don't care what Madame Hecate says about you or Banks or anybody else! She told me I was going to make my clan team, and I did. She told me I was going to win, and I'm in first place heading into the final rounds. I'm going to be *king of the mountain*. She was right about everything, Horatio. You may not believe all that stuff, but I do. She *knows* things, Horatio. She can see the future!"

Somebody finally came out of their room and turned

the car alarm off, giving us both an it's-nine-o'clock-on-a-Saturday-morning shut-the-hell-up look. The look and the sudden silence sobered us.

"Damn it, Horatio. I didn't come down here to fight with you."

"Then what did you come down here for?"

Mac rubbed the back of his neck and avoided my eyes.

"The psychic," I said. "You came down here to see Madame Hecate again, didn't you?"

"What if I did?"

"Great. Let's hear it then. What did she say? Who's standing in your way this time?"

"She was busy."

"What, wake her up, did you?"

"She was recharging her aura. I had to get an appointment for when the competition is over this afternoon."

"Well, let's just hope she doesn't say *I'm* going to own the mountain someday."

Mac softened. "Look, Horatio. I know you think I messed with Banks somehow, but you gotta believe me. I had nothing to do with that. I mean, I've known Wallace longer than I've known you, man. Me and Banks used to be those kids you see running all over the campground playing with wooden swords. He's family."

Mac made me doubt myself all over again. In all the time I had known him and been his friend, how many times had I seen him be unkind to any other person, let alone a friend? But it wasn't just the Hell's Pipers who'd convinced me, it was Mac himself. The way he'd been preoccupied with Banks all night, the way he'd faked remembering what Madame Hecate told Banks about his future. If all that was true, if I'd read him right, then Mac was lying to me right now, still playing me.

It all came down to whether I should listen to my head or my heart. In the end, I knew which way I had to go.

"You're right," I told him. "I'm sorry. I just got really upset for Banks, and I guess I was looking for someone to blame."

"Get dressed, chum," Mac said, brightening. "I'll give you a ride up the mountain. You can tell me all about catching Beth's dad in the parking lot with an IRN-BRU girl. It's all over the games. Mrs. Weigel has already left Mr. Weigel. Beth is pretty much hating you right now."

"And that's different how?"

"Come on. After that you can tell me all about Megan giving you Sternwood."

"Not going to happen," I said. "Besides, I want to check in with the police department before I come back up to the games for the day."

"Oh. Right. Yeah. The dagger. Did they figure out whose it was?"

"Not last night. I'm going to see if Sheriff Wood's made any progress. But Mal had his dagger on him when he was arrested."

"Well, he could own a second dagger, right? I mean, he could have bought one at a vendor booth any time that afternoon."

"Sure," I said. "And if he did, somebody'll have a receipt, or maybe even remember him. Then it's over."

"Oh, yeah," Mac said. "Or—or he could have bought a second one somewhere else and brought it with him, right?"

"I guess," I said. "The sheriff's probably already pulled his credit card bills."

"Yeah, of course," Mac said. He looked away like he was thinking. "What if he bought it with cash?"

"Well, then they're going to have a hard time tracing the

sgian dubh back to Mal, I guess," I told him. Mac seemed awfully concerned about Mal's connection to that dagger, only I couldn't figure out if he did or didn't want the thing traced back to him.

"Well, just let me know what the sheriff says, will you?" Mac said. "Mal's my uncle, you know."

"And Duncan was your grandfather," I reminded him.

"Yeah. Okay. I'm headed back up the hill. Come by and say hey while I'm competing, all right? And let me know what they say."

"Yeah," I told him. "See you then." I shut the door and leaned against it, fingering the bracelet on my wrist while I thought things through. It wasn't my heart I had decided to trust, it was my head, and my head told me Mac was lying, pure and simple. He'd lied to me last night, and he was lying to me this morning. And if he was lying to me about Banks, there was no telling what else he might be lying about.

CHAPTER TWENTY-TWO

This is how I added it up:

Mac's father arranges to buy Birnam Mountain from Duncan MacRae. Duncan gets cold feet at the last minute and backs out, leaving Mac's father holding a very expensive golf bag. Mac's father kills Duncan MacRae and blames it on Mal, leaving the inheritance to fall to his son Mac. Mac's dad owns the mountain (through Mac), makes a fortune, and in the process kills an old man and his fifty-year-old dream easier than knocking down a forest for the eighteenth green. And Mal, like the trees, is just a mildly regrettable casualty.

I had two questions as I pulled into the parking lot of the Inverness County Sheriff's Department: How much did Mac know, and how much was he helping to cover it up?

The sheriff's department was more like a sheriff's shed. It was a yellow and green steel truss building, one of those jobs they advertise on TV that you can assemble in a weekend with three friends, a cargo-lifter, and a great deal of profanity. The front looked exactly like a five-year-old draws a house, with a door in the middle and a window on each side. I expected a curlicue of smoke to be rising from the chimney and a bright yellow sun overhead with rays that reached the treetops. Instead a light morning mist obscured the sky. Or maybe it was a cloud. The sheriff's department was all the way up the other side of Birnam Mountain, somewhere around five thousand feet in the sky.

The rusty door on my old Volvo 240 screeched as I closed it, echoing down the steep incline as I made my way to the front door of the building. Flower boxes along the gravel path to the door popped with red begonias. The mood I was in, they put me in the mind of blood.

The office was a large front room with a door that led to a smaller space in back. There were three tables in the room, one that looked like a reception desk, one that looked like the sheriff's desk, and another filled with CB radios and walkie-talkies and fax machines.

Nobody was around, so I called out. There was a springy sound from the back room, and a head poked out through the open doorway.

"*Mal!?*" I said.

"Horatio?" Mal came all the way into the doorway. The open, unlocked, unguarded doorway. "What are you doing here?" he asked.

"What am *I* doing here—what are *you* doing here? I mean there. Out of jail."

"I'm still in jail," he told me. He nodded in the direction he'd come from, beyond the doorway. "Sheriff Wood keeps the door to my cell open when he's here."

A toilet flushed behind a door on the other side of the room and Sheriff Wood emerged. Mal disappeared back into his cell and the sheriff raised his chin at me by way of greeting.

"Horatio, wasn't it? Glad to see they haven't talked you into wearing a skirt yet."

He motioned to his desk, and I joined him there.

"You do know Mal's jail cell is *open*," I said.

"Well, it's not really a jail," he told me. "We're too small an operation to have a proper cell. Most any time we have to apprehend anybody, they get taken down to the Pigeon Forge Police Department until they can be arraigned. We couldn't arrange a transfer on Friday, so he'll have to spend the weekend with us."

"If you don't have a jail cell, what's he in now?"

"Storage closet. It's got a steel door and good ventilation."

"A storage closet?"

"There's a cot."

"And that's why you leave the door open during the day."

The sheriff shrugged. "Not like he's much of a flight risk." Wood raised his voice. "You ain't gonna run out on me, are you, Mal?"

Mal's voice came back low and sad. "No sir."

"See there? Besides," Sheriff Wood said quietly now, "we're not altogether sure he really did it now are we?"

I opened my mouth and closed it without words coming out—a notable event.

The sheriff leaned back in his chair. "That's what you're here about, ain't it?"

"Yes," I said. I was no longer going to be surprised by this man.

Wood nodded. "I knew you was smart. Can't let it go, can you?"

I shook my head. "And I'm guessing you didn't find any prints on that dagger Spot dug up," I said.

"Nope. Might as well give back all of them daggers we took up and cataloged now. Fat lot of wasted work, that was. Didn't figure a killer would stick his knife back in his sock after he done it, but you never can figure on what a person won't do in the heat of the moment."

"And nobody remembers selling Mal a dagger that day," I guessed.

"No receipts for one either. Checked his cards too. Nothing."

"Unless he bought one with cash," I said, borrowing Mac's line.

The sheriff raised his palms to show how much good that would do him. So Mac had found the one loophole that let the circumstantial evidence still point to Mal—just as he had with the cell phone, and as he'd tried to do with the bloody name on the wall. It certainly seemed like he wanted Mal to take the fall.

"I figured out what you didn't like about Mal's name written in blood," I told him.

"Too much time," the sheriff said. He'd already thought it out himself. "If he had that much gumption left in him, why not head for the door? Or if he was so desperate to point the finger, why not leave it at 'Mal' and then make for the door? Doesn't make any sense."

"Problem is it's all just ifs and buts," I told him.

He put a finger to the side of his nose. I leaned back in my chair and let out air through my lips.

"What about somebody using their dagger and then ditching the sheath?" I asked.

Sheriff Wood nodded. "Most likely what happened. Bonfire night's a big one with the tourists—just as many folks there without daggers as with," he said, "and no way to tell if they had one before we got to 'em or not."

"Can I see the list? The list of people you took daggers up from?"

Sheriff Wood looked interested enough to pull a file folder from a stack on his desk and toss it to me. There was a half an inch of papers inside, but mercifully the names had been typed up on the computer and alphabetized. I thumbed ahead to the section I needed and ran my finger down the page. I'd thought Mr. Mackenzie and Mr. Weigel had been in it together—until last night in the parking lot. Now Mac's father was my number one and *only* suspect. He had the most to gain from Duncan's murder and Mal's arrest, and sure enough his name wasn't on the list. Maybe he'd killed Duncan with his own knife and buried it in the woods before the bonfire.

Something else registered with me, slowly. If this list was truly alphabetical, there was another name missing, a name that should have been there. My stomach tossed like a sheaf. I ran through the page again just in case there'd been a typo, but there wasn't. I checked the pages in front and in back of that one too. Nothing. The name wasn't there.

"You got something?" the sheriff asked.

I closed the file folder. "Can I talk to Mal?" I asked.

"Sure. Don't know how much you're gonna get out of him, though. He's pretty far sunk."

The sheriff led me back to the storage room, where Mal sat on a cot. He still wore his kilt, puffy shirt, and coat, as neat and formal as the night of the bonfire. If I'd been in jail for two nights—even a storage room cell like this one—I think I'd at least have untucked my shirt by now.

Mal lifted his head from his hands as we shuffled in.

"Hey Mal," I said.

He put his head back in his hands. I sat down on the cot next to him.

"Listen, I'm sorry about, you know—"

"What, putting me in here?" he said. "It's not your fault. It's nobody's fault but my own. I swear to God I didn't steal your sister's phone and send a text message to myself. But it doesn't matter now. None of it matters now. I mean, my dad is *dead*. Whatever happens to me is pretty pointless. I *deserve* to be in here."

I glanced at Sheriff Wood, who was leaning against the wall. He just shrugged.

I tried again. "Mal, why would your dad have been talking about selling Birnam Mountain after all these years?"

Mal lifted his head. "You mean besides the back taxes?"

Sheriff Wood stood up straight. "How's that?"

"The Highland Games don't bring in nearly enough even to cover the taxes he owed every year," Mal explained. "Back in the day it did. Fifty years ago the taxes were nothing. Now, with all the development on the other mountaintops, Birnam Mountain is worth a lot of money. A lot of tax money."

I looked to Sheriff Wood. He was much more interested now, but he seemed content to let me keep going with it.

"Why didn't Duncan go to the other clans for help?" I asked.

"He was too proud to go begging."

"So nobody else knew this? Nobody but you and your dad?"

He nodded.

"But if someone brought him an offer for the mountain," I said, "it would be hard to refuse?"

"Hard? It would have been impossible. Another year or so and the county was going to foreclose. But who has the money to buy a whole mountain anymore?"

"Mr. Mackenzie and Mr. Weigel."

I watched Mal's face. He hadn't known.

"You mean Mac's dad?"

"And Beth's," I told him. "Your father never told you?"

"No. I mean, they wanted to buy the *whole* mountain from him? What for?"

"To turn it into a private golf course and ski resort."

Mal jumped to his feet.

"No *way*! No way would Dad have ever sold the mountain for something like that!"

"But you said money'd be hard to pass up," Sheriff Wood said, finally chiming in.

"Yeah, but Dad loved the games! He *never* would have sold their home out from under them. Never! He at least would have made sure there was some kind of provision in the contract, some guarantee that the Birnam Mountain Highland Games would go on forever."

"Unless there was no other choice," I told him.

"Not even then," he said. "But now they'll get it, won't they?" He ran his hands through his hair. "If I go to jail, Mac'll inherit the whole thing, and his dad and his partners will do whatever they want!"

Sheriff Wood nodded. "Sad to say."

"You gotta let me out of here," Mal told him. He moved toward the doorway and the sheriff put out a hand to stop him.

"Whoa now, son. I can certainly appreciate your new-found gumption, but you're under arrest for the murder of your father. Now, I've been pretty lenient up until now with the arrangements—"

"But I didn't do it!" Mal protested.

"I'll bring you a phone book and you can call that lawyer I told you to get, but you're staying put. You understand?"

Mal eyed the open door, then his body visibly slumped. "Yes, sir," he said.

I started to leave with Sheriff Wood, then stopped in the doorway.

"Mal," I said, "what's the best place to get phone reception up on the mountain?"

"What?"

"Up at the games. I can't get my phone to work. Is there some special place I should go?"

He frowned. Now that he knew what was going to happen to the mountain he didn't want to be bothered with insignificant things like phone reception. "No. I mean, I never had trouble getting a signal up there. My phone works all over."

"Yeah? What service do you use?"

"Same as everybody up here. Mountain Cellular."

"Right. Thanks."

Sheriff Wood brought Mal a phone book and a cordless phone and we walked back to his desk together—although this time I noticed he kept one of those hunter's eyes on the door to Mal's storage closet.

"What was all that phone business about?" he asked me.

"Just another angle that bothered me." I told him about having no signal except for maybe one place—one place Mal hadn't known about, because he had never needed to know. His phone worked all over the mountain.

"And all that in there kind of ruins his motive, don't it?" Sheriff Wood asked.

"Yes," I said. "If Mal and his father couldn't afford to keep the mountain, killing Duncan for it wouldn't do him much good. The state would just foreclose and take it away from *him* instead."

"Unless Mal was for selling and his pa wasn't," said the sheriff.

"It doesn't sound like it," I told him.

He nodded. "That boy was deader than the Confederacy in there until you told him somebody planned on carving up that mountaintop. I'm going to have to really keep an eye on him now."

"You add it all up—the mystery text message, the name written out in blood, the shirt conveniently thrown in the campfire, the dagger buried so far off in the woods, the lack of a motive—and it's sounding less and less like Mal really did it."

The sheriff leaned back and chewed on his beard. "That's the way it looks, all right," he said finally. "Problem is, until we got proof to the contrary, Mal's our man."

I told the sheriff I'd see what I could do about that and got up to leave. He stopped me on the way out.

"You're a smart boy, Horatio, and I know enough not to bother to tell you to stay away from this one. But if we're right and we've got the wrong man sitting back there in that room, that means the real killer's out there somewhere, probably still at those games." He handed me a card with his cell number on it. "I want to hear from you *before* you get into trouble, not after, you understand?"

"Okay," I told him. "But I don't think there's anything to worry about anymore. He's already got what he wants. He doesn't have anything left to kill for."

"Sure he does," Sheriff Wood told me. "Now he'll kill not to get caught."

CHAPTER TWENTY-THREE

On the drive back up the mountain I focused on Mac's father even though it was hard to keep from thinking about the other name that should have been on that list. First things first, though: Mac's father had a motive (the mountain), the means (a missing dagger), and the opportunity (he'd been late to the bonfire). I liked him for it—a lot more than my new, next-best candidate. Now I just had to figure out what angle to come at him with.

Some people are born talkers. You want to know what cards they're holding, you just get them started and they'll come around to it eventually. My sister Mona was that way. People like my sister Viola were just the opposite, though. She played things close to her chest and knew how to keep a secret. With her, you had to back her into a corner before she'd confess, and that was tough to do. My sister Juliet, she was a daydreamer, likely enough to start mooning about a rose when you were asking where she left the car keys. Each of my six sisters had her own way about her, and each had taught me a little something about getting what I wanted.

I didn't know Mac's father too well, but my guess was he

was going to be like my sister Kate. She could see you coming a mile away and have you arguing about something else before you even realized she'd changed the subject. That's if she didn't just kick you first. While I'd only twice been stupid enough to pick a fight with Kate, I sure wasn't going to be dumb enough to go toe-to-toe with big Bill Mackenzie. He was the kind of guy who'd stick a claymore in your chest and then have you kicked out of the games for carrying a weapon that wasn't peace-bonded.

I'd just settled on something that would put Mr. Mackenzie on the defensive from the get-go when I reached the campground and realized I wouldn't have to. Guy Sternwood had already gotten him riled up for me.

"You don't know what you're talking about, grandpa," Mr. Mackenzie said. He was already red in the face. "Now why don't you just turn that little chair of yours around, Sternwood, and wheel yourself out of here."

"I'm not going anywhere until you admit you killed Duncan MacRae and framed his son for the murder!"

It was a bit more blunt than the angle I'd planned on taking, but probably more effective. I suppose the General had figured on Bill Mackenzie not laying into a man in a wheelchair, but I wasn't so sure that would stop him. I came up beside Sternwood's chair in a show of support.

"Is that what this is all about?" asked Mr. Mackenzie. "You think I stuck a toy knife in the old man? For what?"

"So your boy would inherit Birnam Mountain and you could turn it into some kind of amusement park for a bunch of polo-wearing Yankees."

Mr. Mackenzie laughed like a donkey, which was actually scarier than if he'd come charging at us. "Let me show you something, 'General.' You're gonna get an absolute kick outta this."

Mr. Mackenzie climbed up into his RV and disappeared.

"If he comes back with a gun, you'll have to tackle him," Sternwood told me, and I didn't think he was kidding.

It wasn't a gun Mr. Mackenzie came back with, though, it was a piece of paper. He thrust it out to Sternwood, who took it like it might be poison. I looked at it over his shoulder. It *was* poison, of a kind.

"That's a contract," Mr. Mackenzie said. "A contract for the purchase of Birnam Mountain, effective the end of this month, and signed by Duncan MacRae himself. See? I didn't have to kill Duncan MacRae to own his mountain. It was easier to buy it!"

Sternwood skimmed the thing twice.

"A forgery. Duncan MacRae would never have signed this."

"He signed it all right. And all I had to do was promise him the Highland Games would have a home here forever."

I was stunned that Mr. Mackenzie would have promised that. Clearly the General was too.

"You—you would have done that?" Sternwood asked.

"Sure," Mr. Mackenzie said. "As long as he was alive. After that, how would he know?"

The General took the chunk of paper in his knobbly hands and tore it in two with a strength I didn't know he had. I got ready for Mr. Mackenzie to charge him, but instead he laughed again.

"Go ahead! Tear it up. Duncan was going to sell us the mountain and Weigel and I had the money to pay for it—as long as he didn't mess things up by screwing that little soda pop girl."

Of course. That's why he'd been worried about what Mr. Weigel was up to. "Because if Mrs. Weigel divorced him," I said, "the two of you wouldn't have enough *money*."

"That's all it was ever about. And it turns out Weigel couldn't keep it in his pants after all. I hear you caught him 'hanging out' in the parking lot last night!"

Mr. Mackenzie laughed again and my skin crawled.

"We would have lost everything, but now that Mac's inheriting, none of it matters. The mountain is mine."

"Mac's, you mean."

"Same thing," Mr. Mackenzie said.

Sternwood kept tearing up that contract until it was in little pieces. It must have made him feel better, but it wasn't helping anything.

"So where were you during the bonfire?" I asked Mr. Mackenzie.

"Having a beer with the Campbells," he said. "There were just about a dozen of them there, so I think *someone* can vouch for me."

"And what happened to your sgian dubh?"

"One of those little pretend daggers? I've never worn one. I hate all this crap, the kilts and the funny hats and the bellhop coats. I only got into all this because I wanted the old man to sell me the mountain."

Sternwood was shaking now. "That 'old man' was your wife's father," he told him. "And she loved this place and these games as much as he did."

"Yeah," Mr. Mackenzie said, sobering up a little. "Yeah, well, we all die of something, even if it wasn't her time to go. Now get the hell out of here. Both of you. You're trespassing on my property." He turned and stalked back into his RV.

Sternwood lowered his head. "Take me away," he told me, and I did.

The General's dogs were waiting for him at the Macduff clan tent, and he called for one of them to follow us and pointed to where he wanted to go: a field with little white obstacle fences set about. I wheeled him to a stop on a hill with a view of Mount Birnam's summit ahead of us. He whistled a command to the dog, who took off running happily around the field. Sternwood watched his border collie, but it seemed like he was thinking the whole Duncan thing through, so I gave him some time.

"Bring him back," Sternwood said.

"What?"

"Lennox," he said. "Call him back."

"Way back!" I called. "Lennox, way back!"

Lennox broke off his circling and made a beeline for where we stood.

"Good," Sternwood told me. He handed me some treats and I fed one to the dog, who was my new best friend. "Now send him around the right fence."

I tried to remember the commands. "Lennox . . . Lennox, way to me! Go boy, way to me!"

Lennox shot away like a bullet.

"Now the left," Sternwood said. "Come by."

"Lennox, come by! Come by!"

Lennox reversed course.

"Walk up!" I yelled, getting into it. Lennox slowed to a walk and stalked one of the obstacles. "Steady, steady," I told him, "now way back! Way back, Lennox!"

Lennox came running and I fed him another treat.

"That'll do, Lennox," I told him. "That'll do."

"I don't believe that contract," Sternwood said, finally getting down to business.

I bent down to scratch Lennox's muzzle. "You're a lawyer. Was there anything wrong with it?"

Sternwood shook his head. "No. I just don't believe Duncan would have ever signed it."

"I think he did," I said. I told the General about the taxes and the foreclosure.

"I never heard anything about that," Sternwood said. He turned his chair toward me. "If that's true, why wouldn't Duncan have said something? Why didn't he come to the rest of us for help?"

"Mal says he was too proud to beg."

"Beg!? Fah. That man gave this festival a free ride for fifty years. We owed him."

"Well, whatever the reason, he wouldn't ask. And I suppose he thought if he had to sell, he'd at least keep it in the family."

Sternwood snorted. "If you can call that oaf family."

The General sent Lennox out for another run and we watched him do rings around the meadow.

"You asked me to look after your niece so I'd figure all this out, didn't you?" I asked him.

"Yes," Sternwood said. He kept his eyes on Lennox. "I knew Bill Mackenzie was after Duncan to sell the mountain. For years he'd put him off, but now suddenly there were rumors it was going to happen. I didn't know why Duncan would sell, and he wouldn't say, but I knew something was happening. Megan kept her eyes and ears open, but I needed someone on the inside, somebody close to the Mackenzies who knew what was really going on."

I shook my head. "I should have seen it. If ever there was a girl who didn't need looking after, it was Megan."

Sternwood laughed. "Don't be too hard on yourself. I chased a few skirts in my day."

"Wait, you didn't tell her to—"

Sternwood glared at me. "What kind of a man do you take me for?" He sent Lennox to his right. "Any feelings she has for you are her own affair. And for your sake, I don't want to hear anything more about that."

"So it was you who sent Megan to steal the blueprints from the Mackenzie trailer, wasn't it? You were what, going to take them to the rest of the clan leaders to scare them? Try to put together some kind of competing bid?"

"That was the idea," Sternwood told me. "Now I want them as evidence. Evidence that Bill Mackenzie *killed* Duncan Mac-Rae."

I let that one go for the moment. The General called Lennox back.

"Why didn't you just ask me straight out to investigate Mac's father?" I asked.

"You were too loyal to your friend back then." He said it like it had been years ago, but it just seemed that way. "I hoped that tagging along with Megan would make you change your mind, see things the way she did."

Somewhere in the distance, "Amazing Grace" was playing again. "I was blind, but now I see," I said, the lyrics finally meaning something to me. "I see that, and a lot of other things."

"Yes," Sternwood said. He fed Lennox another treat and made him lie down. "It's those 'other things' that have made this all very messy. I'm sorry, Horatio. I never guessed it would come to this—that Duncan would be killed. I meant to pull you into our petty little land dispute, not drag you into a murder investigation. Now you're in deep." He looked up at me. "Can you handle it?"

"Yeah," I told him.

Sternwood nodded, and I lost him for a minute while he stared off longingly at the summit.

"The Mackenzie clan cannot have this mountain," he told

me. "The Smokies need one last place untouched by a developer's hands, and the Highland Games need a home."

"I'll do whatever I can to keep it that way," I told him. "I promise."

"I knew if I set you on the right path you would sniff out Bill Mackenzie," Sternwood said. "I saw it in you from the start. You're like my border collies. You were born to work. Even when nobody's telling you what to do, you're doing it."

"Trouble is," I said, "I think we're barking up the wrong tree. I don't think Mr. Mackenzie had anything to do with it."

Sternwood frowned. "What? Then who?"

Now it was my turn to stare at the mountaintop. What I was about to say hurt worse than being dumped. It was like learning you'd been dumped two weeks ago and were just now finding out.

"There's a list in the sheriff's office," I said. "A list of all the people they've taken up daggers from. Mr. Mackenzie wasn't on it because he doesn't wear one. Mac wears one, though, but his name wasn't on there either."

"Your friend? Bill Mackenzie's boy?"

"Yeah," I said. "My friend."

"Does that mean something? Not being on this list?"

It meant something all right. It meant Mac had lied when he said the police confiscated his old sgian dubh. It meant he'd ditched it sometime between the afternoon and that night.

It meant that Mac had murdered his grandfather.

CHAPTER TWENTY-FOUR

—✦—

Sternwood offered to help before I left him, but I wasn't really sure what I was going to do. For all my promises about trying to keep the mountain out of Mackenzie hands, I didn't have a plan. What I needed was a place to sit and think, and the place that called out to me was the music groves. A band called BarleyJuice was rocking out with a song called "Tartan is the Color of My True Love's Hair" in the first grove, and on another day I would have stopped to listen. But right then I didn't want distraction. I needed to focus, and the softer Celtic tunes lilting from the second grove were just the thing.

I caught Banks leaving the grove as I was entering, and I had to step in front of him to make him see me.

"Hey, Banks—I haven't seen you around. How are you holding up?"

He looked at the ground.

"You, uh, you talked to Lucy again? I think she's really into you."

Nothing. I almost told him what I knew about Mac torpedoing his chance at winning the bagpipe competition just to see if I could bring him back with some good old-fashioned righteous fury, but I worried it might do just the opposite and bit it off.

"Okay, well, I'll let you go then," I told him.

I moved aside, and it was as if my standing there was all that had been keeping Banks from going on his way.

When I went into the grove I understood why Banks had been there. His dad was the one responsible for the good music, and I settled in among the sparse crowd to listen. It was good that I had seen Banks on the way in, even if he was as talkative as the big rock in the parking lot. I needed to remember Mac's betrayal of Banks, his lies to me, his murder of Duncan MacRae. Just thinking about it all gave me shivers—that a person I knew, had grown up with, was friends with at school, that somebody like that would be capable of what I saw in the tent that night. Even now it seemed impossible, but there was too much stacked up against Mac to disbelieve it.

Had Mac been planning this well before the games? Had he come here—brought me with him—prepared to kill his grandfather? No, it seemed too spontaneous for that, like one of Beth's dares. If that really *was* Mac's dagger Spot had dug up in the woods, he hadn't even thought far enough ahead to buy a second knife, one that couldn't possibly be traced to him. It had to be something he'd done on the spur of the moment, an opportunity seized and then hastily covered.

The psychic. That's when it all began. Mac had to have already wanted it, already dreamed of power and riches and respect, but that was the first time he'd ever considered doing anything he could to acquire them. What was it he had said by the fire that first night? It was all there in front of him if only he would just reach out and take it. And he took it all right. He took it with the blood of Duncan MacRae.

Banks's father finished playing his song to a smattering of applause. It was strange—more and more people were filtering in, like they were drawn to the music, but they didn't look like Mr. Banks's kind of crowd. The newcomers were sort of Scottish grunge, with long unwashed hair, gray plaid tartans, and tattoos up and down their arms and legs.

"I'll play one more tune before I give the stage over to the band most of you are here to see," Mr. Banks said with a smile. "This is a song I wrote many years ago to sound like a classic Scottish ballad. It even got a little play on some Scottish radio stations. It's about a man named Angus MacIron, a Scottish warrior with a peculiar affliction. I hope you like it."

Mr. Banks launched into it on his guitar, and whether the crowd was just there to see the next band or not they clearly dug this song. It was easy to like. The melody was catchy, the lyrics were funny, and the chorus—

I knew this song from somewhere. I'd never heard Mr. Banks play before, so that wasn't it. And I didn't catch a lot of Scottish radio either. So where had I heard it?

By the end of the song the crowd was singing along with him. I knew if I didn't get it before he finished I wouldn't be able to remember, the way you're watching a show on television and you know you've seen an actress before, you know you recognize that voice, but if you don't figure out who she is before the end of the episode you'll end up having to go search for her on IMDb. And there wasn't an Internet movie database for homegrown Scottish ballad knock-offs.

"Angus MacIron, Angus MacIron," the crowd sang, "the man with the iron up under his kilt!"

Then I had it. I knew exactly where I had heard it before.

Mr. Banks left the stage to a roar from the crowd. It was as if everyone who had stayed for the games was here, now, in this grove. Survivors clinging to the last lifeboat of a sinking ship. Even though most of them had come for the next group, many people clustered around Mr. Banks's booth to buy his CDs. It looked like the Banks boys would have gas money to get home after all.

I worked my way to the booth and picked up a CD to read the back. There it was: "Angus MacIron," with Mr. Banks's name after it in parentheses.

"Thanks so much," Mr. Banks said, trading another CD for cash. He saw me and smiled. "Horatio! Did you catch the show?"

"Just the end," I said. "Great number. You brought the mountain down."

"'Angus MacIron' is always a crowd-pleaser."

I pointed to the back of the CD. "Does your name here mean you wrote the song? It's not just an arrangement of a classic ballad?"

"That's right," he said, selling another CD to someone. "Some of the others there are traditional, but that one's all original."

I found my wallet and pulled out a twenty.

"Horatio, put that away. If you want one, you can have it."

"Nobody ever made America's top forty giving away CDs," I told him. I put the twenty in his hand.

"I'm not even going to make Scotland's top forty," Mr. Banks said. "But thanks."

"You may do one better with this song," I said. "Do you know where Wallace went to?"

"Did you see him? He's hardly been around. He's off sulking about, I suspect. Losing the bagpipe competition that way really hit him hard."

"Yeah, I know. If you see him, tell him I'm looking for him, all right?"

More people were coming up to buy CDs, and I let Mr. Banks get back to plying the plastic discs. The next group had just taken the stage, and the crowd cheered. I went back to the grove to see what all the fuss was about, but my space near the front was long gone. Through the nappy heads and black T-shirts I could see the band—five men and one woman who all looked like they'd just stepped out of a scene from *Braveheart*. They wore pale red and brown tartans that wrapped around their waists like kilts and then up over their shoulders like togas. One man had long hair down past his shoulders, the kind of mane girls swoon over; another had a shaved head and a look on his face like he'd kill the first man he got his hands on. Four of them held some form of drum, each a giant tribal-looking thing meant for beating on. The last of them, a thin, wiry guy you wouldn't like to meet in a back alley, was ferociously filling up his bagpipes with air.

"Lads and lassies," the announcer cried, *"Albannach!"*

The bagpipes droned, then rose into a frenzied nonstop melody, like some kind of manic goblin tune that magically compelled you to dance. The people around me began to bounce.

Then the drums began. Deep, pounding drums you felt in your chest before you heard them in your ears. The lead drummer screamed like he was getting ready to charge the English with nothing but a kilt and a claymore, and the audience answered his cry with one of their own. *I* felt ready to follow them into battle, and I found myself nodding along with the rest of the Scottish headbangers.

For the first time all weekend, I thought I might actually want—or even *have*—some Scottish blood in me. Sternwood had said I was a Macduff, and I began to believe it, to embrace it. I was Horatio Wilkes of the Clan Macduff, and this mountain was ours, our home. It had been taken from us with Duncan's death, but there was still time to fight, to reclaim it, to take it back from the man who had stolen it. There was time enough, if only there was a way.

The drums hammered and the bagpipes wailed and my Scottish blood rose. I closed my eyes and heard the music, felt it. The pipe and drums spoke to me. They gave me the answer.

They told me how to take down Joe Mackenzie once and for all.

CHAPTER TWENTY-FIVE

I stayed through the whole Albannach concert, even though I had a head full of ideas and things to do. The crowd mobbed their booth when it was over, but I would have to wait and get a CD later. There was something else I needed to get first.

Megan and Lucy were both at their booth in the vendor area. It was Saturday, the biggest day of the games for tourists, but there were still very few people around. I slipped up behind Megan, turned her around, and kissed her. I was taking the reins now, and it felt good. From the look in her eyes when we separated, Megan was liking it too.

I pointed at her skirt. "Where can I get one of those?"

She looked at me suggestively. "Well, I was going to take a break in about a half an hour if you can wait—"

"Well, don't *we* have a dirty mind," I said. "I meant your *pin*." Where her skirt wrapped around in the front she wore her family crest: a lion holding a sword with the words "DEUS JUVAT" written above it.

"A Macduff pin?" she said. "Here, you can have mine."

"No, I want my own. I'm joining your clan."

"Ooh," said Megan. "Does this mean we can't date?"

"It better not."

"You can get one at most of these shops then," she said, and she pointed me to a likely source.

"Thanks," I said. "Listen, your uncle asked me if there was anything he could do to help, and there is something. Mal needs a lawyer—and someone to bail him out of jail. Can you ask him to do that?"

"Sure."

"There's one other thing. The schedule says there's a 'Parade of Tartans' tomorrow with all the clans. I want to march with the Macduffs."

Megan smiled. "That shouldn't be a problem. I'll even help you pick out a kilt."

"I'm not wearing a kilt," I told her.

She grabbed my belt at the buckle and gave it a tug. "Well then you won't be marching with the Macduffs, will you? They don't call it a Parade of Tartans for nothing."

"We'll discuss this in a half hour, when you go on break."

"It's a date," she told me. We kissed again and I went to buy a clan pin. I didn't put it on yet, though. I was waiting for the most dramatic moment.

After that I headed down to MacRae Meadow. The final round of athletic competition had started bright and early that morning, and Mac was across the way with the other contestants limbering up for the caber toss.

The caber was essentially a long stripped-down log like a telephone pole. From what I could tell, the object was to pick the thing up, balance it against your shoulder, and then try to flip it end over end.

This was the kind of thing people did for entertainment before there was television.

Mac was practicing his technique with a half-sized log when I flagged him down. He met me near his gym bag and pulled out a bottle of water to drink.

"Hello, chum," he said. "Come to watch me win the caber toss?"

It was going to be hard, pretending Mac wasn't a killer. I had to swallow my fury and play the fool. It was the only way I was going to catch him.

"You can actually do this?" I asked.

"I get a smaller-sized caber because of my weight," he told me. "Gives me an advantage."

"And see, in Highland gym class they always told us fatter was better," I said.

"You know where the caber toss came from?" Mac asked as he limbered up.

"You throw a telephone pole to honor Alexander Graham Bell, inventor of the telephone?"

Mac laughed. "No—but he *was* Scottish. The Scots invented everything, you know. The telephone, the steam engine, penicillin . . . golf . . ." He tried to think of something else.

"Scotch tape?" I tried.

"Look, I'll give Edison the lightbulb, but the rest was the Scots."

"So you're still in first?" I asked.

"So far. I just wish I'd been able to talk to Madame Hecate this morning."

"Right. Because one vague and meaningless prophecy wasn't enough." I had to stop myself there. For the sake of my plan, I needed to lay off the insults. "What time's your appointment?"

"Six o'clock, right after the games end for the day. Look, it's almost my time," he said, starting to go.

"You know, there's this other thing that's been bothering me about Duncan's death," I said.

Mac stopped. Ever since that first night, whenever I'd brought up some problem I'd had with Duncan MacRae's murder, Mac had been always been very interested. Too interested. I hadn't seen it from the start, but I saw it now. He always had a quick answer to make me feel better and I wanted to see what he had to say about this one.

"You remember Mal's shirt, in the fire?"

"Yeah, of course. I was there when you found it."

"It had blood on it all the way down to the shirttail."

"Well, yeah. I mean, do you have any idea how much blood there is when you stab somebody?"

"I think I have an idea," I told him, "seeing as I was pretty much swimming in it the night I found Duncan in his tent. How would *you* know?"

"Dude, did you never watch *The Sopranos*?"

"All right. Then how did blood get on Mal's shirttails?"

"What?"

"Mal always wore his shirttails tucked in. I saw him at the police station today. He even had them tucked in after two days in a jail cell." Or storage closet, but it was much the same thing.

Mac looked over his shoulder. It was almost his turn to toss his log, but he wouldn't go. He couldn't. He had to think of some way to explain it so that Mal could still be guilty.

"Maybe he . . . maybe he *un*tucked his shirttail to keep the blood off his kilt. These things cost a fortune, you know. Real kilts do, anyway. That way all he would have to throw out is his shirt, and he's got more of those."

"So you think he used it like some kind of blood-splatter apron," I translated.

"Yeah!" Mac said, happy that he'd come up with something that worked. His name was called by one of the games officials.

"I like that," I told him. "Or how about this? What if someone wanted to make it look like Mal did it, so they put one of his shirts on over *their* clothes. Kind of kill two birds with one stone. So to speak."

Mac came back. "What do you mean make it *look like* Mal did it?"

The games official saw Mac talking to me and called out to him again to take his turn.

"You'd better go," I told him. "I wouldn't want to mess up your chance to be king of the mountain."

Mac went, but he looked over his shoulder at me as he walked away. He still wasn't convinced I was any kind of threat, but I was going to change his mind about that. He lined up for the caber toss and started the awkward, hunch-backed dance the tossers do to get the thing balanced first. While all eyes were on Mac, I dove into his bag and fished out his cell phone. When I stood, Mac was just running up to toss the caber. He stopped and launched it end over end, but it didn't quite flip and fell back toward him with a *thud*. Mac screamed and kicked over a stand of cabers, sending the contestants scattering. He looked back at me and I waved. Maybe I was getting to him after all.

I flipped Mac's phone open as I walked away, looking to see if I had any kind of signal. It was out of range, just as he said it was. I walked past the clan tents and the genealogy society booths and the food stalls until I came to the parking lot on the other side of the games. Still no reception. The big boulder was still presiding over its flock of SUVs and 4x4s, and I put Mac's phone away while I climbed to the top. The view from the crest, high above the hoi polloi and their gas-guzzlers, was fairly impressive. I could even see beyond the mountain to the next ridge, where dark clouds were gathering.

I brought Mac's phone back out and checked the reception: one bar. I checked mine too: one bar.

So Mac had known about the only place Mona's phone would get reception. Who else had known it too? I typed up a text message on Mac's phone and hit SEND, then lay down and enjoyed the warm sun and the cool mountain breeze while I waited. In the distance I heard the deep roll of thunder.

At last I got a bite on my line.

"Mac?" Beth called. "Mac, what's this all about?"

I stood. Beth had her cell phone open in her hand. She looked like she wanted to cry when she saw me.

"You," she said. "You *ruined* my life."

"*I* ruined your life? I wasn't the one drinking IRN-BRU from a jug in the backseat of a car last night."

"Where's Mac?" Beth demanded.

"What, did you think he'd be here for some reason?"

Beth started to walk away.

"You didn't get a text message from him?" I called to her. "One that said, 'Horatio knows. Meet me at the BFR RN. LYKYAMY.' You must know what the BFR is. You're here and I'm standing on it. The long one is 'Love you, kiss you, already miss you.' Was that too much? I thought about asking RUMorF, but I figured, you know, as intimate as you two are, Mac would already know that by now."

"GFY," Beth said.

"That's a good one! How about ITICSMHFH—'I think I can see my house from here.'"

It was wasted on Beth. My old sparring partner was gone,

replaced by a hollow shell. She had bags under her eyes and her arms shook so much she had to hold them to her stomach to keep them still.

"Is he here?" Beth asked. "Mac? I need to—I need to talk to him."

"No. He's down on the meadow playing Scottish Poohsticks."

Beth's eyes wandered crazily, like tracking a mosquito.

"If you're wondering why I texted you," I said, "it's because I'm testing a theory. See, I think somebody stole my sister's phone and texted Mal to lure him away from the games, but this is the only place on the mountain where they could do it."

Beth's eyes found me again and she blinked.

"Mal's phone works all over the mountain, just like yours," I told her. "But Mac's and mine and Mona's, they only work when you're sitting on top of this big rock. Funny thing is, Mal and Mona didn't know anything about this place."

"What—what makes you think I did?" Beth asked.

"Did I say you did? No, I was just testing this, and I knew your phone worked up here. But you do know about it, don't you? I mean, there have to be a dozen big-ass rocks around here, but you knew this was the BFR I was talking about right off."

"Why are you doing this to me?" Beth asked.

"It's just, you know, now that Mal's been released, I thought you'd want to hear about the new investigation."

"Investigation?"

"Into Duncan's death, of course. You haven't heard? The police don't think Mal did it. They're letting him go."

Beth wrung her hands.

"I—I have to go sew up my dance costume," she said, but she didn't leave.

I sat down on the rock. "Can't afford to pay somebody to do that?" I asked. "I heard you used to give the other girls crap for doing their own repair jobs. Money tight around the Weigel house these days? Oh, sure, I guess what with your parents about to split up there'll be legal fees, alimony payments—or was there a prenup? And your dad, he'll have that new expensive trophy wife to take care of."

That snapped Beth back into RL, at least long enough to tell me to eat my own excrement and expire, though not exactly in those words.

"Love you, mean it!" I called, but Beth was already too far gone.

CHAPTER TWENTY-SIX

I followed Beth back to the games, but for safety's sake I stayed well out of fire-breathing distance. Once past the parking lot she took the path to the field and I took the path to the vendor area. The storm clouds I'd seen rolling in before were now on top of the games, and I ducked under the Sternwood sisters' tent just as it started to pour.

"You're with me, leather," I told Megan. She came around the table and gave me a kiss.

"Thanks for bringing the rain," she said.

"I only wear Kmart underwear. Kmart underwear. I'm a very good driver."

Megan stared at me.

"*Rain Man*? Dustin Hoffman?" I said. I got more of the blank stare and told her to forget it.

"So what now, Rain Man?" she asked.

I watched the water streaming from the roof of the tent.

"Well, I had wanted to catch the Highland dancing. I think Beth's about to go on."

"Why would you want to watch that?"

"You know how some people go to NASCAR races just to

see the wrecks? I think she's due for a pileup, and I want to be there to see it. I figured you could tell me if she misses a step or two."

Megan brightened. "Ooh. My pleasure. So, do we walk or run?" she asked.

"I knew this really smart kid in middle school who did his science fair project on that," I told her. "Tried to figure out whether you get more wet walking or running through a rainstorm. You walk, you get drenched slowly. You run, the rain pounds into you and soaks your clothes."

"So what's the answer?" Megan asked.

"Always bring an umbrella," I told her. I pulled a collapsible job from my backpack and popped it open.

Megan took my arm. "My hero," she said.

The few tourists ducked into tents and hid under trees all along the path to MacRae Meadow. No one else had thought to bring umbrellas or Windbreakers, and had it rained like this the first couple of days of the games I would have been running for the shelter of a Porta-John with them. I'd made myself a promise though. I wasn't going to get caught unprepared again. Not for anything.

The Highland dancing events went on through the rain, covered by party rental tents. Most of the casual viewers had run for the trees, but the diehard moms who'd been camped in their lawn chairs since the first day of competition didn't budge. These people were prepared: big golf umbrellas sheltered them, their coolers, and their piles of dance gear. If we sat behind them we'd never be able to see, so I led Megan to the front of the crowd and spread out a motel towel I'd brought with me. We were just in time too—Beth was up on stage, stretching for the next round of competition. *Her* mom wasn't here, but I suspected she was doing her best to stay out of the public eye.

"Hey!" an old crone behind us crowed. "Down in front! You can't just waltz in here and block my view. I've been here all day!"

"Oh, I'm sorry. It's just, that's my sister up there," I said. I pointed to Beth. "And she's carrying my baby."

The lady started to say something, then shut it.

"You're awful," Megan whispered as we sat down.

"Keep it in the family, that's what Mom always used to say."

Beth took her position onstage. The other two dancers with her stood at the ready position with their hands on their hips, but Beth was wringing her hands like she was rubbing in lotion.

"This stage is slippery!" Beth yelled. "What, am I following Betsy Wetsy!? Somebody get out here and dry this off!"

A woman jumped up on the stage and wiped it down with a towel, the way the ball boys do under the rim at basketball games when somebody's taken a spill.

"No, you idiot! Are you blind? There, there, and *there*!" Beth cried, and the woman scrambled to clean where Beth had pointed.

"Well, she *seems* normal," Megan said.

The woman finished up, and Beth took her position. "Are we going to dance sometime today or what?" she demanded. The other two girls rolled their eyes, probably wondering the same thing.

The dancing was done to live bagpipes, and at a signal from the dance judge the piper started to squeeze out the familiar drone. The notes of a tune kicked in—thankfully not "Amazing Grace"—and the dancers bowed to the judge.

"All right," I said to Megan. "Just watch Beth for me, and tell me if you think she's distracted."

But I didn't need Megan to tell me something was wrong. The other two girls raised their hands in different poses with the steps, but Beth did nothing but dance with her feet. Her hands she held out in front of her chest, working them like an OCD kid washing her hands for the fifty-first time that day.

Megan laughed. "The wicked witch is going to get points deducted," she told me. "Her footwork is perfect, but she's going to lose on technique and interpretation."

A murmur ran through the crowd as Beth danced. I heard a laugh or two, but the chuckles died down fast. Even Megan wasn't smiling by the end. Beth danced like a DDR zombie, her video game face twisted into a fierce knot of concentration like she was all alone in the world with nothing but the arrows scrolling up the screen. Step, step, step, step, step, step, step— she never stopped, not even when the music did.

At first, no one was quite sure what to do. They were probably too scared of the old Beth, and too frightened by the new one. The woman who had wiped the stage down tried to say something to her, but Beth was gone, lost in her own world where she could not stop dancing, could not stop squeezing her hands.

"We've got to help her," Megan said. She was already standing and moving before I could get my umbrella closed and run after her. We crossed the track and jumped the rope to the field, bypassing the bewildered judge and the other contestants.

"Beth, Beth!" Megan called. I hopped up onstage with her. Beth kept dancing. This close, I could see she was muttering something, although with her feet pounding on the wooden stage I couldn't hear what it was. While Megan tried to talk her down, I went up behind Beth and grabbed her around the waist, catching her flailing arms up in the hug.

"Beth, snap out of it!" Megan told her. "Come on now!"

Beth went limp in my arms, and it was all I could do to keep us both from falling.

"Somebody get a doctor!" Megan cried, and the person closest to us dashed away.

I let Beth down to the ground as gently as I could.

"Hurry, hurry," Beth mumbled. "Before someone comes. I'll hide it."

Megan and I were the only ones who could hear her, and we shared a confused look.

"Hide what, Beth?" I asked. "What is it you have to hide?"

"No one will know," she said, oblivious. She wrung her hands. "Only, I can't get them clean."

Megan snapped her fingers in front of Beth. "Her eyes are open, but there's nobody home."

"Beth—"

"What are you, afraid?" Beth screamed at me. "Be a man!"

"And do what, Beth? Be a man and do what?"

She wilted, whispering again. "Who would have thought the old man would have so much blood in him?"

Megan gasped. Someone from the medical tent rushed onstage with a security guard, and we backed away to give them some room. Beth wriggled as they strapped her to a gurney, but she didn't say anything more. Megan pulled me aside, out of earshot.

"Did she—was she saying what I think she was saying?"

I nodded. I was sure of it now. Mac and Beth had killed Duncan MacRae.

"It's funny," Megan said. "I've hated that girl for years. I hoped and prayed I'd see Beth Weigel go down in flames, but not like this. Not so . . . sad."

"She brought it on herself."

"Still," Megan said. "Nobody deserves this."

Beth's eyes rolled up in her head and she started to twitch.

"She's catatonic," the medic said. "We need to get this girl down the mountain to a hospital."

Beth was quickly loaded onto the back of a modified golf cart while the security guard got on his walkie-talkie for the event organizers to try and find her family.

"I'll go with her to the hospital," Megan said. "She needs to have somebody there. I'll see you tonight at the concert if I can."

I gave her a kiss and said good-bye, and Megan jumped on the cart and took Beth's hand as they drove away.

The rain had subsided a bit, but the Highland wrestling out on MacRae Meadow still looked more like mud wrestling. I found Mac standing apart from the other decathlon competitors while two of the others grappled away wearing nothing but kilts and muck.

Mac spied me coming and intercepted me halfway there. "You're not supposed to be out here, Horatio," Mac told me. "And I don't have time to talk about anything."

"Not even Duncan? You always seem to have time to talk about his murder."

Mac showed me his hand and tried to move away.

"Beth's in the hospital, Mac."

He stopped.

"She had a breakdown," I told him. "On the dance stage. She's out of her mind, Mac."

I'm not sure how I expected Mac to react, but I did expect *some* kind of reaction. Instead he looked at me as though I had just told him what time it was. One of the wrestlers in the pit was pinned, and the other athletes applauded. Mac turned to watch.

"Mac, did you hear what I'm telling you? Beth's lost it. She's catatonic."

Mac nodded, distracted by the wrestling.

"It figures," he told me. "She hasn't slept in two nights, and she's been taking stim pills to stay awake during the day."

"The doctors need to know all this, Mac. You should be at the hospital with her."

Mac didn't seem to want to do anything but watch the wrestlers.

"Mac—"

"She was having bad dreams," he said. He laughed, low and soft. "Sometimes I think the dead sleep better than we do."

"Mac, Beth said things when she collapsed. Things only Megan and I heard," I told him. "It's over, Mac. It's time to come clean. About everything."

Mac cut his eyes toward me, maybe at what we might have heard, maybe that Megan was there to hear it with me. The rain kept falling, the big fat drops playing percussion on my umbrella.

"It's a shame about Beth," Mac finally said.

"'It's a shame'? That's all you have to say? Beth's worst enemy in the world is sitting next to her in an ambulance right now holding her hand, and all her boyfriend can say is 'It's a shame'?"

"I was going to break up with her soon anyway."

"You—you *what*?"

"The sex was great, but she was always nagging me. I don't need her anymore."

Beth had finally done it. She'd made Mac into a man. And then he'd done the same thing Beth's dad had done to her mom—thrown her away like an empty wrapper.

I couldn't believe I was about to defend Beth, but someone had to.

"Mac, you owe her more than that. You really should be with her right now."

"I'll go see her later. I have to get ready to wrestle."

"I suppose it would be better if she just died," I said, smarting. "Then you wouldn't have to take time away from your busy Highland Games schedule at all."

Mac shrugged. "We all die of something, even if it's not her time to go."

I'd heard the same thing from Mac's father, only this time it gave me the shivers. I wanted to call the police right then and tell them Mac was a killer. I still had Sheriff Wood's card in my wallet if I could just find a working phone. But I had a plan to get proof. Real proof. *Then* I would call in Sheriff Wood and watch Mac get carted off to jail.

For now, though, I could only watch Mac turn his back on Beth and resume his relentless quest to be king of the Highland Games.

When it was his turn to wrestle, he won by breaking the other guy's arm.

CHAPTER TWENTY-SEVEN

he rain and thunder set the perfect mood at Madame Hecate's. The room was dark and candlelit, the flames sputter-
ing in the wind from the half-opened windows. An atmospheric
CD played something with harps and synthesizers that was
supposed to give the place an air of mystery while the "Palms
Read While You Wait" sign flickered in the window.

The bell on the door tinkled, and Mac entered Madame
Hecate's parlor.

"Mac, is it not?" Madame Hecate sat at the little card table
with the tarot deck in front of her. She flipped a card dramati-
cally. "I've been expecting you."

Mac sat down in the chair across from her, handed her a
twenty, and leaned forward.

"Madame Hecate, it's all come true. Everything you said. I
made the clan team, I'm winning the decathlon, and now . . ."
He looked around, as though there might be somebody else
in the room listening to him. "Now I'm king of the mountain
too. Just like you said."

"Of course," Madame Hecate said. She pocketed the
twenty. "Your future, it was strong and clear."

"But I need to see more," Mac told her. "I need to know what happens next. You have to help me."

Madame Hecate held up a hand. "Patience, young one. Madame Hecate sees all."

Mac held out his hand for his palm reading, but she shook him off. "For this," she said, "we turn to the tarot."

Madame Hecate began dealing cards out onto the table and making little noises in the back of her throat.

"What?" Mac begged. "What is it?"

"The Soldier," she said. "A threat. Macduff? This name, it means something to you?"

Mac frowned. "It's—it's one of the other clans. At the games."

"Beware Macduff!" Madame Hecate said. As though she'd timed it, thunder boomed outside.

"Beware Macduff? But which one?"

"There is more," Madame Hecate said. She laid another card across the Soldier. "The Musician. No harm shall come to you so long as—" She laid another card. The Priest. "So long as the pipers still play 'Amazing Grace.'"

"You mean like, as long as *all* bagpipers play that song, or like specific pipers?"

Madame Hecate started to say something more, then caught herself. "I—I know only what the cards tell me."

"What else?"

She uncovered another card. The Ranger. "Ah. Never vanquished will you be until great Birnam Wood comes for you."

"You mean the forest on Birnam Mountain? When would a forest ever—"

"Is all I see." Madame Hecate pushed away the rest of her deck.

"No, those are great," Mac said. He stood. "Beware Macduff,

can't be hurt until the pipers stop playing 'Amazing Grace,' and won't be caught until Birnam Wood comes after me." He grinned. "I'm set!"

"Good fortune to you then, Mac. You will come back and see me again, yes?"

"You bet," Mac said. The bell tinkled as he went out into the rain.

"Well? How'd I do?" Madame Hecate asked the empty room, her heavy Slavic accent replaced by a Southern one.

I waited until I heard Mac's SUV start up and pull away before I came out from behind the curtain at the back of the room. Graymalkin purred in my arms.

"You give great prophecy," I told her.

"I said everything you wanted me to say. I even stacked the deck. You know, to make it look good."

"It looked as real as a fake thing can," I said.

"I hated doing that. Giving false prophecies. It perverts the truth and purity of the psychic arts."

"What, is the Better Fake Business Bureau going to take away your license?" I said. Madame Hecate stuck out her tongue at me and took back her cat.

"So, who's this Macduff he's supposed to beware of?"

"Me," I told her. "He just doesn't know it yet."

"I should have known," she said.

"Yeah. Especially in your line of work."

"Make fun all you want, but I *do* have a reputation to uphold."

"Look," I told her, "if it's your record you're worried about, don't be. I'm going to make it all come true." I picked up the Ranger card. "All of it except that bit about 'never vanquished until Birnam Wood comes for you.' What was that? That wasn't part of the script."

"You gotta do things in threes, kid. Haven't you ever read any fairy tales?" She lit a cigarette with a lighter that looked like a genie lamp. "No, I forgot—your parents read you bedtime stories from Raymond Chandler."

I tossed the card back on the table and she raised her hands in self-defense.

"Hey, you didn't give me much to work with, you know? There's such a thing as creative license. Now, as to the small matter of my fee . . ."

I pulled out the forty bucks I'd promised her but I didn't hand it over. "I don't know why I'm paying you when you made Mac pay you too."

"You think he'd believe me if I did it for free? Besides, he paid me to tell his future. *You* paid me to tell me what to tell him."

I conceded the point and forked over the forty.

"I told you you'd be back," she said, counting the money. "And if I remember correctly, I told you you'd pay me too."

"Wow. You must be psychic."

"Tell you your fortune, Horatio? On the house."

"Don't waste your 'psychic arts,'" I said.

She started to turn over tarot cards anyway.

"Your signatory is the Knight of Swords, I would think. Frank, intelligent, forceful."

"You know, divination fails every scientific test because it's *bunk*."

"Yes, definitely the Knight of Swords," she said. She took cards off the top of the deck, arranging them in a kind of cross on the table. "I see you . . . in the woods. At night. Surrounded by . . . fools and fairies."

"'Fairies'? Isn't that a little un-PC?"

She ignored me, lost in her performance. "There you

will have to come to terms with the consequences of your actions . . ." She turned over another card. "And you will confront your doppelgänger. Your twin. Your other you."

"I know what a doppelgänger is."

She played more cards. "Later again . . . I see you . . . someplace hot."

"Like hell?" I asked.

"Like . . . Florida." She played the Lovers card, and then the Magician turned upside down. "There you will meet a beautiful girl and fall in love. But beware her father, who commands beings mysterious and magical."

"Magical beings. Right. I'll introduce them to the fairies. And you've guessed wrong," I told her. "I've already fallen in love, and I think this one's going to stick for a while."

"As for the near future," she said, pushing on. "Ah, the Chariot. Victory." She played another card. The Hanged Man. "But victory with a sacrifice."

"Everything has its price," I told her. "You don't have to be a psychic to know that."

"But for this one you will pay the ultimate price," she said. She played a final card: Death.

More thunder rolled outside, and I laughed.

"Oooh. Double, double, toil and trouble," I said. "Now who's getting the stacked deck?"

"Take heed, Horatio," Madame Hecate warned. "The Knight of Swords is clever and courageous, but often heedless of danger, even when he knows it is coming."

"Skip it. I make my own fortune," I told her. I picked up the deck and thumbed through the cards until I found one I liked. "Here, this is the only one I need."

I flipped the card onto the table.

Justice.

CHAPTER TWENTY-EIGHT

—✦—

Madame Hecate's ominous prophecies aside, the only thing I saw in my future was a Mellow Mushroom pizza. Unfortunately, what should have been a five-minute drive took me almost half an hour. Cars, trucks, tour buses, campers—we all shambled along at ten miles an hour through the asphalt graveyard of Pigeon Forge, our only view the brake lights and back windows of the living dead in front of us. Without a map you wouldn't know you were just a few miles from the entrance to the Great Smoky Mountains National Park. You certainly couldn't *see* the mountains. With the smog, you could only see as far as the next outlet mall.

One medium Kosmic Karma pizza later and both my appetite and my aura were satisfied. I checked my phone for the time: 6:14 P.M. Just enough time—even with the traffic—to get back up the mountain and see if Megan was going to make it for the Celtic rock concert.

On the way out of town I thought about what kind of place Pigeon Forge must have been once, back when the only traps around these parts were for raccoons and beavers, not tourists. The Pigeon was a river that allegedly ran through the town, though I'd never seen it. It was probably now banished to covered drains and underground pipes, quietly exiled from Pigeon Forge like the rest of Mother Nature. The Forge part of the name came from a real, long-lost forge, if the modest little welcome signs with a picture of a hammering blacksmith were to be believed. And I believed them. This was the mountains, after all. Appalachia. The first American frontier. At one time there would have been a real town here, with real people working real farms with real animals and real tools. Now the only thing real was the traffic.

As I passed The Beef Jerky Outlet Store I swore I would do everything in my power to make sure Birnam Mountain never lost its soul the way this place had.

The rain had stopped at the top of the mountain, but the ground was a soggy mess and the dark clouds overhead looked like they were thinking about making things worse. A few diehards had already pitched camp in front of the concert stage, but the first band, Mother Grove, still had their equipment covered with tarps and trash bags and were watching the skies. I scanned the small crowd for Megan but she wasn't there. I was looking for somebody else too, somebody I needed for the grand scheme foretold to Mac by Madame Hecate, but he wasn't there either. I hung out and waited.

First came the rains and then came the boos as the organizers called off the concert. I hadn't been looking forward to standing under an umbrella for four hours anyway unless it had been with Megan, and I could think of more comfortable locations and positions. Regardless, she was a no-show. There was a chance that if she was back from the hospital she might have stopped by her booth to make sure it was sealed up from the rain, so I detoured through the vendor area on my way to my car.

All the booths were closed and covered, including Megan's. I lifted one of the canvas flaps on the side of her stall and ducked underneath. It was dark in there, dark like the night I had gone poking around in Duncan's tent and tripped over a dead body. I shivered at the memory. Or maybe it was the cold water wicking through my gym socks.

"Megan?" I called. "Lucy?"

The booth wasn't very big, and a few seconds with my flashlight confirmed that the girls had closed up shop for the night and were long gone.

Footsteps splashed in the muck outside.

"I'll stand lookout, mate," said a familiar voice. "You slip inside and steal us a couple of cases."

I waited until the splashing moved on and slipped out of the canvas tent with my flashlight off. Two shadowy figures ran ahead in the driving rain. I followed them to the IRN-BRU tent, where one of them held up the edge of the canvas for the other to wallow underneath.

I slipped up behind the one left outside, the rain splatter masking the *thwuck-thwuck* of my shoes in the mud.

"Why do I think you're not here to ask out one of the IRN-BRU girls?" I said.

Terrence the sea urchin wheeled on me. His once spiky red hair lay plastered on his wet head like a washed-up jelly-fish and his mouth hung open like a sea bass.

"Well, if it isn't Scarface," he said. "I'm glad they were able to save your nose."

"Blow it out your bagpipes, Terrence. Your pal comes out of there with a case of IRN-BRU and I'm dragging the both of you to the nearest security guard."

Terrence laughed. "Is that so?"

"That's so," I told him.

He looked around, but there wasn't anybody to help him. At first I thought he might bolt, leaving me to grab the guy actually doing the pilfering, but instead he shrugged his shoulders and nodded toward the IRN-BRU tent.

"Why don't we step inside," he said. "Discuss this out of the rain so I can have a proper smoke."

I grinned. If he was hoping to have a better chance with two against one, he had another thing coming. Especially after the last time I'd let them gang up on me.

"Lead on, MacNugget."

Terrence lifted the canvas and I bobbed inside the darkened tent, wary that his friend might be lying in wait. Nobody had a go at me, though, and Terrence worked his way inside and shook himself off beside me. I heard the metallic *ping* of a Zippo lighter opening, then watched as an orange flame lit a cigarette hanging in Terrence's smiling mouth.

"Doesn't matter to me whether we do this outside in the rain or here under the tent," I told him.

"Eh, let's do it here," he said. "We don't like to get messy." A second later a dozen flashlight beams hit me in the face, blinding me. I was surrounded by Hell's Pipers. Again.

Terrence shook his head. "Mate, for a clever boy you sure are stupid sometimes. They lock away the liquids at night for fear some punks like us might come along and nick them."

A quick look around confirmed it—there was nothing inside the big IRN-BRU tent but tables and canvas banners. That meant the whole skit outside Megan's tent had been meant for me.

I vaguely remembered something Madame Hecate had said about me rushing into things and I slumped wearily. "We're not going to do this again, are we?"

"If it's any consolation," Terrence said, "we'll stay away

from your face this time, give it a chance to heal." He took a step closer.

"Whoa, whoa, whoa—did somebody put you up to this again, or are you freelancing?"

Terrence shrugged. "My crew's got to have their soda."

"That's it? You're doing all this for a case of IRN-BRU? Is that seriously all it takes to buy your services?"

"We're a simple folk, mate." He nodded to one of his gang. "All right, Johnny. Let's have 'Scotland the Brave' this time. We gotta have a *little* variety around here."

Johnny's bagpipes began to drone. One of the burlier pipers stepped up behind me.

"Wait," I said. "You say you're a simple folk? Then I have a simple proposition for you."

Terrence signaled for Johnny to lay off the pipes and blew a puff of smoke out the side of his mouth.

"What kind of proposition?"

I slid behind the seat of my Volvo a few minutes later and started it just to get some heat going. My pant legs were soaked up to the knees, and my shirt was as damp as a Mississippi summer, but at least I hadn't taken another pounding. Score one for the clever and courageous Knight of Swords, or whatever I was supposed to be. I was tempted to try and find out what hospital Beth was in and go sit with Megan, but I needed to get back to my room and get some sleep. Bringing Mac down was all that mattered right now, and Megan and I would have the rest of our blissful adolescent lives to sow wild oats together. Where was it she said she lived? While I drove back down the mountain I tried to figure out how long a trip it would be to go see her, and if my mom would notice if I just moved.

I was almost glad to see the Hillbilly Haven emerge out of the rain and darkness. Rather than go straight to my room I tied the Volvo up to the dock in front of the motel office and swam inside.

"No refunds," the clerk said as I entered.

"And a fine evening to you too, my good porter." I patted my hands on the counter. "I am in need of a second key."

"What happened to the first one?"

"I loaned it to a friend."

The desk clerk frowned. "You only paid for a single."

"That's okay," I told him. "She's only using it while I'm away, so there's only one person in the room at a time."

Somehow I don't think he believed me.

"Checkout's at eleven a.m. sharp," he said. He slapped a new diamond-shaped keychain on the counter. "And tell your 'friend' to keep the music down. We've had complaints."

I almost asked what he was talking about, then shut it. The mystery of the missing Megan had been solved. Case closed.

"Sweet dreams," I told the clerk, and I left the office whistling.

I was alone on the short walk to my room. The rain kept the locals inside. Either that or they were all still staring at the two-headed calf in the Ripley's Believe It or Not Museum. My whistling seemed a little forced, so I switched over to humming something by the Barenaked Ladies. I'm sure Freud would have had a field day.

My humming was overcome by the sound of Celtic music blaring through the thin walls of my room. It was the CD Megan had brought with her the first time.

I knocked at the door as I put my key in.

"Megan? It's Horatio. I hope you're not decent."

The room was dark but for a dim table lamp lit in the far corner of the room. Megan lay fully clothed on the made-up bed, her back to the front door.

"You better watch out," I warned her. "There's a UFS on that blanket—an Unidentified Funky Stain." I crossed to the portable boom box I'd brought with me and turned the volume down to something resembling ambience. "You had this music up so loud the desk clerk was getting complaints all the way from Knoxville."

I leaned against the table and stuck my hands in my pockets, trying to look cool.

"You know, you're saving me from a night of reading *The Sound and the Fury*. It's supposed to be all full of symbolism and stuff, but frankly, I think it signifies nothing."

I didn't get a laugh—or any kind of reaction, for that matter. Megan didn't speak, and she didn't move.

"Hey, Megan, you fall asleep on me or what?"

Even as I said it, I knew she couldn't have fallen asleep. Not this early, and not with the music that loud. She was either fooling around, or—

A sinking feeling threatened to suck me down into the dog-hair carpet. My Chucks weighed a hundred pounds each as I crossed the room to the bed.

"Megan?"

I nudged her, but she didn't move. I rolled her over.

Megan's eyes stared up at me, but they were empty. I shook her. I called her name. I couldn't see anything wrong with her, but she wasn't breathing. I did my best imitation of CPR, pushing on her chest and trying to blow air into her mouth, but nothing worked, nothing, and slowly I understood.

Megan was dead.

It was like I was at the end of a long, blurry tunnel. I staggered backward, falling off the bed and crashing into the table. I backpedaled away until I hit the wall. I kept kicking, trying to get farther and farther from the bed. I wanted to slither off into the night and crawl into a hole in the ground and close my eyes and never come out.

But I couldn't. The wall wouldn't give and my eyes wouldn't close and the tunnel was endless, and all I could see was Megan dead on my bed, the crusty brown stain on the blanket spread beneath her like a pool of phantom blood and the Macduff pin on her skirt glinting in the pallid light of a dead-end motel.

CHAPTER TWENTY-NINE

—✦—

Questioning me was beginning to become a routine event for the Inverness County Sheriff's Department, but Sheriff Wood let me go after taking my statement personally. I told him everything—even who did it. Because I knew who had murdered Megan Sternwood. I'd sent him to do it.

I stood outside in the rain with my hat in my hands until Megan's body came out of the motel room in a big black plastic bag.

Distantly, I felt Mona put her arm around me. I didn't even know she had come. Sheriff Wood must have called her to come get me.

The heavy door of the coroner's station wagon slammed shut.

"Go," Sheriff Wood told me. "We'll find whoever did this."

Mona steered me to her car and put me in the passenger seat.

"Stay here," she said. "I'll be right back."

A few years later Mona came back with a plastic bag.

"They let me have some of your things. Your toothbrush, a change of clothes. I can take you back to my motel room, let you get dried off and cleaned up, and then I'll drive you home."

"No."

"Horatio—"

"I'm not leaving. Not until I make him pay for this."

"Who?"

Water from my soaked hair ran down my eyes and into the corners of my mouth like tears. Mona backed out of the parking lot and didn't try to argue with me. She understood my silence and my anger and my pain like nobody else. She was my sister.

A few minutes later I sat in the corner of Mona's motel room with a towel over my head.

"You're going to catch your death if you don't change out of those wet clothes," she said.

"That's a myth," I muttered.

"What?"

I whipped the towel off of my head. "It's a myth! You can't die from being cold and wet. You know how you catch your death? You really want to know? I'll tell you. You come to the Birnam Mountain Highland Games and you meet a boy, a smart, funny, reasonably good-looking boy you share a laugh and a meat bridie and your heart's desires with before spending one glorious night in his bed."

"Horatio, I don't—"

"Then," I said, standing, "*then* this smart and oh-so-clever boy plays cards with a killer, only you don't know he's bet your life on a pair of twos in the hole. This boy you fell in love with, who loved you back and just maybe *possibly* thought you were the best thing to ever happen to him, he sends a psychotic *murderer* after you. And *that's* how you die, suffocated to death in a dark, filthy motel room in Pigeon Forge with a two-story-tall hillbilly couple leering at you from the parking lot and your favorite CD turned up to eleven so the neighbors can't hear you scream."

Mona crossed her arms. "Are you finished?"

I slumped into a chair by the window.

"Horatio, this isn't your fault."

"Yes, it is."

"No, it's the fault of whoever it was who killed her."

"Mac," I said. "It was Mac who killed her."

Mona sat on the edge of her bed. "What? *Mac?* How do you know?"

I told her how I figured Mac and Beth had killed Duncan and pinned the thing on Mal, and how Mac had sabotaged Banks because he was afraid his cousin would take the mountain away from him—all because of a hocus-pocus job by a fat lady with a crystal ball and a funny accent. Then I told her about my stunt this afternoon at Madame Hecate's.

"I meant me," I explained. "*I'm* the Macduff he's supposed to beware. He just doesn't know it yet. I was going to march in the Parade of Tartans tomorrow as a Macduff, try to lure him into taking me out. Catch him in the act."

"I don't understand, how does that make you—"

"Megan's a Sternwood. She and her family belong to the Macduff clan. She wears a Macduff pin, for Christ's sake. Why didn't I see that?" I took a deep breath. "Mac and Beth already hated her, knew she was out to get them. Mac tried to warn me away from her more than once. He said she was dangerous and I laughed him off. But when Mac heard 'Beware Macduff' from Madame Hecate . . ."

"He went after Macduff Enemy Number One," Mona finished.

"Just like he took Banks out of the way, only this time he made sure it was permanent. How could I be so *stupid*!?"

I couldn't sit still so I stood up and paced the room.

"And the sheriff, he knows all this?"

"I told him everything. But there's no way any of this will help him catch Mac. Not for Duncan's death, and not for Megan's. Sheriff Wood will talk to him, but I don't think there's enough evidence to even arrest him. He was sloppy the first time with Duncan, but this time he thought things out. There weren't any marks on her body. He either used a pillow or pushed her face into the bedding, playing that CD loud so nobody could—"

I pictured it all too clearly, and I wanted to rip my eyeballs out so I couldn't see it anymore.

"You're sure it's Mac? I mean, seriously, *Mac?*"

"He's not the guy you knew. He's not the guy any of us knew. Not anymore. Ever since that first day at the fortune-teller's it's like something's taken hold of him, some kind of monster has been awakened. Every single thing he's done from that moment on has been cold and calculating, and he's not going to let anybody stand in his way." I slammed my fist on the top of the television set. "It took me too long to see it. If only I'd been paying attention—"

"That's not it, and you know it," Mona said. "You trusted him because he's your friend. You didn't see the terrible things he was doing because you couldn't believe Mac was capable of them. If what you say is true, then he betrayed you just as much as he betrayed Duncan or Banks."

She was right. It was just like the General had said—he couldn't have asked me to spy on Mac and his family from the start because I was too loyal. But that didn't mean I couldn't have seen what he was up to sooner. Maybe then

235

Banks wouldn't be walking around like a ghost. Maybe then Megan would still be walking around.

"Stop it," Mona said. She leaned over to look up into my eyes. "I know what you're doing. You're beating yourself up over all this. I should know—I'm the expert at beating myself up. Like when I found out that boy I got engaged to, Gerard, had two other fiancées."

I gave Mona a tired look and she waved Gerard away.

"Never mind that," she said. "Look, are you going to pace around here all night banging my deposit out of the furniture, or are you going to figure out how to catch this bastard?"

"I thought you wanted me to go home."

"I do. You should. You need to talk to Mom. Maybe Viola. But we both know you're not going to do that, are you? Not until you've done whatever you can to fix this. Jesus, how long did we live in the same house? I think I know you well enough by now. Remember when you were eight and you went and told that wife-beater at the end of the street you were taking his dog away because he kept it chained to a post in the front yard all day? And you did, all by yourself!"

She meant my basset hound, Marlowe.

"Now come on. Let's see a little of the old Horatio magic."

"Expelliarmus," I said.

"Okay. Fine. Get your stuff. We're going."

"All right. All right. I . . . let me see the pictures you took Thursday night—for Megan's sake, if nothing else."

"You mean the ones of crime scene?"

"No, the bonfire. I think maybe the torches spell out the name of the murderer. Yes, of *course* the pictures of the crime scene."

Mona went for her laptop. "There's the old Horatio I know

and love. Here. I already downloaded them. It's in the folder labeled 'Kittens.'"

"Kittens?"

"Well, I still had some pictures of my new kittens on the camera, and I didn't want to forget where they were."

I sat on the bed beside Mona and flipped through the pictures she'd taken, skipping the ones with the cats. In the full light of a kerosene lantern, the crime scene looked eerily bright and warm. When I'd worked my way through all the shots I started over again, this time viewing them more slowly.

Mona went to the mini-fridge and brought me a Coke. "Here. Sorry I don't have any root beer." She watched the pictures scroll by. "What are you looking for?"

I shook my head. "I don't know. Something to tie Mac and Beth to the first murder. Maybe something I missed the first time around."

Mona sat patiently by my side while I went through the pictures again and again.

"Wait a minute," I said, clicking back to one. I caught a tiny little inkling and slapped handcuffs on it. "Do you still have those pictures you took of us clowning around at the campsite earlier that day? The one where Mac flashed the camera?"

Mona looked surprised, but she leaned across me and tried to find the folder where she'd put those pictures. To say that Mona was not born with the same anal gene as me was an understatement. I rubbed my temples while I waited.

"Here. I knew I put them somewhere I'd remember."

The folder was labeled "Cheese." I didn't ask.

Disregarding Mac's ass, which was fairly hard to do, it was a pretty good photograph. I tapped the wrist rest on Mona's laptop.

"What?" she asked.

"Look." I called up the first photograph. "See in this picture? Don't look at the shirt in the fire. That's what you were taking a picture of, but look here, on the edge of the shot. See? Mac's boots."

Two pairs of shoes were visible in the photograph—my Converse and Mac's hiking boots.

Mona shrugged. "So?"

I pointed to his sock. "No sgian dubh."

"That's . . . one of those little daggers, right? Like the kind used to kill Duncan."

"Yes." I pulled up the other picture of Mac mooning the camera. "Look here. Earlier that day he's wearing one." I clicked back. "Here he's not."

"So you're saying he used his own dagger to kill Duncan, then buried it in the woods."

"Or handed it off to Beth to bury, so he could get back to the bonfire in time to stand in for Duncan."

"There could be a hundred reasons he had his knife then and not later. It's just circumstantial, Horatio."

I was starting to reexamine every little thing Mac had said and done since that afternoon at Madame Hecate's, and something more about that night came to me then. Something I hadn't thought anything of at the time.

"Wait, do you *have* those pictures of the bonfire that you took?"

"Oh, now you really want to see them, huh?" said Mona. She double-clicked a folder mercifully named "Bonfire." It was dark that night, but Mona had been using a flash, so everything was lit up like a Hollywood movie set in her pictures. I tabbed through them, looking for the ones where Mac stood in for Duncan at the bonfire. What I'd taken then for assertiveness and initiative I now saw as nothing more than bald-faced ambition and arrogance. I cursed at myself. I'd even complimented him while we ran back to the tent where he'd murdered his grandfather

"There," I said. It was a good close-up of Mac giving his little speech about Duncan. It gave me a shiver, thinking about what kind of person it took to stab a man to death and then rush out onto a field in front of thousands of people and deliver his eulogy. And I was the one who'd put Megan in his path.

"Horatio?" Mona asked. She could see I'd slipped away again. I cleared my throat and zoomed in on Mac's boot. The picture was more pixilated this big, but one thing was clear.

"He's wearing a sheath but no dagger," Mona said.

"He ditched the dagger after he killed Duncan, but he forgot to get rid of the sheath." My circumstantial evidence had just gotten a little less circumstantial.

"Does the sheath match the dagger or something?" Mona asked.

"No. I doubt it. But the fact that the dagger is missing but the sheath isn't means he didn't just take the whole thing off. It means he lost his dagger—or got rid of it—sometime between the moon shot at the campground and his speech on MacRae Meadow. And sometime between the bonfire and the crime scene he lost his sheath too."

"So where is the sheath now?" Mona asked.

I wanted to smile, but I couldn't find it in me—not even at the thought of a way to finally bust Mac. The best I could muster was a grunt.

"Only one person knows that," I told Mona. "The man who killed Duncan MacRae and Megan Sternwood. Can you make sure and keep these pictures safe? Maybe put them in a folder that means something?"

"I'll do one better," she said. She took the computer from me and opened up her web browser. "I'll upload them to the newspaper's server. That way we'll have a backup."

I stood and resumed my pacing.

"You're not beating yourself up again, are you?" Mona asked.

"No, we're in between rounds."

"There. All three pictures are loaded onto the *Sentinel*'s server. Should we go to the police with this tonight?"

"No. Not yet. It still wouldn't do any good. Not really. We need more direct proof. We need that sheath."

"How do you propose to do that?"

"If the mountain will not come to Mohammed," I said, "Mohammed will go to the mountain."

"What's that supposed to mean?"

"It means that tomorrow Mac is going to show me where he tossed that sheath."

CHAPTER THIRTY

—🗡—

Birnam Mountain had an even more somber air to it Sunday morning than it had the day after Duncan died, if that was possible. The last half day of the Highland Games wasn't really for tourists—not that any would have shown up now anyway. Megan's death had seen to that. It still hadn't officially been declared a murder. If it had, I suspect they'd have just called the whole thing off, said "see you next year," or maybe "see you never." As it was, I suppose the organizers figured if they had come this far they would see things through to the bitter end. The only thing left was for the few remaining campers to honor their colors, get their awards, and say good-bye.

That morning they were saying a particularly solemn good-bye to two of their own—Duncan MacRae and Megan Sternwood. The traditional Sunday "Kirkin' o' the Tartans"— a church service where Scots sang and bagpipes played and the clan tartans were blessed by a chaplain—became an impromptu memorial service with candles and flowers and tokens of remembrance. I thought about contributing the bracelet Megan had given me, but I knew I wasn't leaving her behind today, and I wanted that bracelet so I would never forget. Instead I left the Scottish fiddle CD that had been the soundtrack to our one wonderful night together and to Megan's last night on Earth. I once had thought I never wanted to hear anything else; now I never wanted to hear it again.

Churches and services have never held any meaning for me, and even though I was there to join the others in remembering Megan I ducked out early, knowing I would say good-bye to her in my own time and place. I could still hear the pipers at the ceremony as they began playing "Amazing Grace," and I thought about what Madame Hecate had said yesterday, about everything ending in death, about there being consequences for my actions. I certainly didn't believe in her hocus-pocus, even though everything she'd said had come eerily true. But worse than the bad mood lighting and the dry ice machine and the amped-up air-conditioning, what I hated more was the idea that everything we do is scripted, written in the stars. That we're not the masters of our own fate.

I get why people want to believe that. Believing everything that happens was always *going* to happen means all your mistakes weren't really your fault. It means you can lay the blame elsewhere—on the stars, the cards, a crystal ball. I couldn't believe that, and that's what was eating me. Megan didn't die because some psychic with a deck of cards told me it was going to happen. Megan died because I *made* it happen.

For that, I would never forgive myself.

Back at MacRae Meadow a few of the folks who'd skipped the service were collecting at their clan tents for the Parade of Tartans. It didn't feel like they were gathering for a parade, though. It felt like they were preparing for a funeral march. Mac was already with the Mackenzies, but I noticed he was wearing a different color kilt. His new attire was red and black stripes, not the blue and red of the Mackenzie clan, and today's

T-shirt was black with "Kiss My Thistle" written across the front in white letters. Mac had drawn a small crowd of angry Highlanders, General Sternwood among them, and I found a place near the back and listened in.

"Frankly, I don't care what you want or what you think," Mac was telling them. "In five years' time, this whole meadow will be a golf course, and you'll be trespassing on private property."

There were grumbles and challenges from the assembled protestors, and Mac's father pulled him aside.

"What the hell do you think you're pulling?" Mr. Mackenzie asked him.

Mac yanked free of his father but stayed up in his face. "What? It's the truth, isn't it? And it doesn't matter if they like it or not."

"There's no reason to get everybody upset like this," Mac's father whispered. "Not here. Not now."

"Who cares? What can they do about it? What can anybody do about it?"

"There is such a thing as a public relations *nightmare*. We want to sell chalets to these people, not get them writing protest letters to the newspaper. Now go to the trailer. I'll take care of this."

"No," Mac said. He stood his ground. "No, *I* own the mountain. Not you. Gramps left it to *me*. I call the shots here. In fact, I won't let you go ahead with the building unless I have final approval on all the development up here."

Mr. Mackenzie's face turned tartan and his neck swelled like a bagpipe.

"See how many shots you're calling when I tell a court you're a minor and can't be expected to handle your own business interests."

"I turn eighteen next May," Mac told him. "You can't pos-

sibly get anything like what you planned moving that fast."
He hitched his thumbs in the top of his red kilt and appraised
his mountain. "Besides, I've got some ideas of my own. Like a
half-pipe. Maybe a whole slope for snowboarding."

"That—that is not the kind of element I want to attract!"
Mr. Mackenzie bellowed.

"Too bad," Mac told him. He walked away from his
father, and right into me. It was all I could do not to put my
hands around his throat and strangle him right there, but
besides landing me in Sheriff Wood's storage room, killing Mac would ruin the elaborate trap I'd set for him.

I'd have to wait to murder Mac.

"Horatio," Mac said.

"Mac."

"I didn't know you were there."

"I only caught the third act," I told him.

"You're wearing a kilt," Mac said, acknowledging my special
attire for the day. If I wasn't so preoccupied with Megan's death
I'd feel ridiculous in the thing. It was the first time in my life I'd
had to actually coordinate my underwear with my outfit, because
I certainly wasn't going "regimental" like Mac. It was weird; three
days ago, Mac would have laughed his ass off and given me a hard
time about it. Today, neither of us thought it was very funny.

"Whose colors are those?" he asked.

"Macduff," I told him.

I could practically smell his brain processing that one.

"I see you're wearing new colors too," I said. "Is that a
MacRae tartan?"

"What? Yeah. My mom was a MacRae, so I can wear
whichever tartan I want. Now that Gramps is dead and I own
the mountain—"

"The king is dead, long live the king, huh?"

"Something like that."

Mac was practically radiating hatred, and it was all I could do not to reciprocate. He was finally seeing me like I saw him: armor-clad and ready for battle. From here on out we were enemies, and he knew it.

"Oh, did you hear?" I said. "They're going to comb the forest today for the missing sheath. The sheriff and his men."

"The what?"

"Well, you know they found the sgian dubh the killer used on Duncan, but they never found the sheath, assuming there was one. Sheriff Wood's bringing a bunch of Boy Scouts up here after the closing ceremonies. It's a shot in the dark, but if he finds it, it might give them some clue to the killer's identity. You know, hairs or fingerprints or something."

"You mean Mal's hair or fingerprints."

"If you say so," I said. My kilt stirred in the breeze and I worried about my pale legs—which only made me think of Megan again. "Oh, hey," I said. "I never asked you. How did things go at Madame Hecate's? She give you any brilliant advice?"

"Beware Macduff," Mac deadpanned.

I dropped my fake smile. "Well, you don't have to worry about Megan Sternwood now, do you?"

"Oh yeah. I heard about that," Mac said. "That was a real shame. You guys were close, weren't you?"

I had walked right into that one, but I refused to give Mac the satisfaction of rising to the bait. I forced another smile.

"Good luck at the award ceremony today. I hope nobody gets in your way."

Mac popped his neck. "Not a chance, chum."

On my way to the Macduff clan tent Banks called my name and rushed over to me.

"Horatio! Oh my God. I heard about Megan. I'm so sorry."

Banks hugged me, and it felt nice for a moment to be around somebody human again.

"What happened? I heard it was natural causes, but some people are saying—"

"It's, they—they're not sure right now. How's her sister? Have you spoken to her?"

"I called Lucy as soon as I heard. She was devastated, Horatio. They've already gone home, everybody but the General, but I'm going to see her again this week, help her get through it."

I put a hand on his shoulder. "It's good to have you back among the living, Banks."

"I feel so stupid about that."

"Why? That competition meant everything to you. I understood."

"Yeah, but when I heard about Megan last night it put everything into perspective," he said. "I'd been walking around the games like my life was over, but it *wasn't*. I might have missed out on a scholarship, but . . ." He paused, worried about hurting me. "Megan is *dead,* Horatio. Her life is over, but mine isn't. Compared to that, I don't have anything to feel sorry about."

I nodded, and Banks frowned.

"What?" I asked.

"You're—you're wearing a kilt!"

"Yeah, look. Let's not—"

"We need to get you some kilt hose and garter flashes, and—"

"No, no, no. I'm not going for the whole Highland experience. I just wanted Mac to see me as a Macduff and get riled up and come after me."

"Why?"

Banks had been so far gone after the bagpipe competition he didn't even know what Mac had done. I debated how much to tell him. If everything went as planned, it would all come out in the open soon enough. Still, Banks deserved to know part of it.

"Listen Banks, about the bagpipe competition. Mac sabotaged your bagpipes. Or, well, he paid the Hell's Pipers to do it."

"What?"

"It was that psychic, the one we went to the first day of the games. Mac got it into his head that he was going to be king of the mountain but that you were going to *own* it. He figured the only way that was going to happen was if you went to college and made enough money to buy it, so he paid the Hell's Pipers to bollocks your bagpipes."

"But—but that doesn't make any sense!"

"Mac's been doing a lot of things that don't make any sense lately."

"He can't have—I don't believe it. Not Mac. That's crazy."

"I know. There's more too. I meant to tell you before, but I could never find you—"

"Clan members to their tents, please. Clan members to their tents," Douglas McGowan announced from the press box. "The Parade of Tartans is about to begin."

Mac had already seen me in the Macduff kilt, but I wanted to march as a Macduff. Both for Megan, and to drive the point home with Mac.

"Just find me when everything's over," I told Banks. He tried to stop me, a thousand questions on the tip of his tongue, but I waved him off. "Find me later, and let *me* take care of Mac."

Sternwood was the only one in the Macduff tent when I got there for the Parade of Tartans. He wore his usual Macduff tartan kilt and lap blanket, but his dress shirt was black in memory of Megan. He nodded hello and I did the same.

"Just you and me today," he said. "My brother's family didn't think—"

"I know," I told him. "It's all right. Look, I want to apologize—"

"Nonsense." Sternwood wheeled himself out onto the gravel path. His border collies Ross and Lennox followed on either side. "You're not going to say you're responsible for her death, are you? Because you can stop right now. Unless you're the one who suffocated her."

So Sternwood knew the score. "No. Of course not," I said.

"Then stop it. There's a madman on the loose at these games—a serial killer I'd call him by now. Megan was just in the right place at the wrong time."

There wouldn't have been a wrong time if I hadn't gotten Mac worked up over the Macduff clan too soon, but I didn't say any more. I fingered the green leather bracelet on my wrist. Megan's death was my burden to carry, and my burden alone.

"I didn't see you at the memorial service," I said.

"Don't ken much to churches and ministers," Sternwood said.

"Yeah. Me either."

With the General in a wheelchair we didn't have enough hands to carry the Macduff banner between us. We let our kilts be our standard instead, me pushing him along in place between the MacDougalls and the MacFarlanes. When we passed by the grandstand we got a respectful silence rather than applause, and the same courtesy was afforded the Mac-Raes when they passed a few lengths back. At the end of the circuit we turned onto the athletic field to gather with the rest of the clans for the award ceremony that followed. I looked back over my shoulder at the Mackenzie clan as they passed the audience. Mr. Mackenzie was waving to the crowd. Mac was staring straight at me.

Many of the people who had won bagpiping and dancing and declaiming honors had already bailed on the games and weren't there to collect their awards. The second- and third-place finishers in the decathlon were, though, and there was light applause as they went up and got their medals.

"And in his first year of pro level competition," Douglas McGowan announced, "first place in this year's Highland Games decathlon goes to Joseph Mackenzie of the Clan Mackenzie! Come on up here, Joe."

Mac bounced up onstage with his arms raised high. He tried to lead the small crowd in a whoop, but no one answered back. Mac frowned at us like we were no fun, and we weren't.

"Congratulations, Joe," McGowan said. "I now pronounce you king of the mountain."

Mac bent low and the president of the games crowned him king.

"And as victor in the Highland decathlon, Joseph has put the combined clan team of MacRae and Mackenzie into the points lead for Clan of the Games. Congratulations to Clan Mackenzie and Clan MacRae."

McGowan handed Mac a gleaming silver sword with the Mackenzie and MacRae clans' accomplishment etched onto the blade, and Mac held it up like a conquering hero.

"It's a fine tribute to your grandfather," McGowan told him.

"I didn't do this for the old man," Mac told him. "I did it for me."

What little enthusiasm the audience had been willing to

show trickled to a stop, and Mac's father quickly mounted the stage to commandeer the microphone, launching into a eulogy for Duncan MacRae that had probably been prepared by a PR flak. With all eyes on Mr. Mackenzie, Mac slipped off the back of the podium stand and disappeared.

"That's my cue," I told Sternwood, and I was gone before he could wish me good luck.

CHAPTER THIRTY-ONE

The bagpipes kicked in behind me as I ran away from the meadow. There would be a long musical session while the assembled piping corps played on the field and then paraded around the track once more with the clans. That gave Mac plenty of time to find the sheath before the close of the ceremonies—and me plenty of time to catch him in the act. I didn't know exactly where it was—I needed Mac for that—but I had a general idea.

The kilt was surprisingly easy to run in, though I did worry I was showing a little too much of my underwear had anyone been there to see me. I sprinted back down the shortcut Mac and I had taken in the darkness the night Duncan had died. It wasn't quite as harrowing this time, but I was running in the daylight now and Mother Nature hadn't sent a hurricane into the highlands. The opening for the picnic area loomed ahead and I slowed to listen. The bagpipes from the meadow still carried all the way up here like the background music to the build-up of the final scene in a movie. Even with the drone of the pipes I could hear someone stomping around in the underbrush along the edge of the field, and I caught sight of Mac's new red kilt through the greenery.

"Come on boy, hurry up," Mac said. "What have you got, huh? Is that it?"

I took a second to get everything ready, then stepped out of the woods and into the clearing. Mac was a few yards away near the edge of the picnic area bent over in the undergrowth, the big claymore he'd been given for winning the decathlon stuck in the ground beside him. Mac didn't see me at first, but Spot did. He came bounding over and barked.

"That'll do, Spot," I said.

Mac stood, the missing sheath in his hand.

"Looks like we can call off the search," I said. "You found the sheath. That why you brought Spot along?" I bent over and scratched the border collie behind the ears.

Mac's expression went from shock to sneer in half a second. He wasn't afraid of me and he wanted me to know it. We weren't pretending anymore.

"Figured if he found the dagger he'd be able to find this in no time," Mac said. He stuck the sheath in his pocket and yanked the claymore from the ground. "I should have come back for it before now, but I had the competition."

"Can't let a little thing like murder get in the way of winning the Highland Games," I said.

Mac stepped closer, and I was well aware of that big-ass sword now in his right hand. When I had thought all this through in my head I hadn't figured that tiny little detail into the equation.

"How did you know?" Mac asked.

"How did I know you did it, or how did I know you'd be here?" The bagpipes still droned on in the background. "That night we ran back to your tent, the night Duncan died—you said you tripped on something, and when I swung back with the flashlight you were holding your ankle. But you didn't trip on anything. You realized you hadn't ditched your sheath, and you had to do it before we got back to the campsite with all those police."

"Banks was right. You really don't miss a thing, do you, Horatio?"

"Oh, I missed a lot of things, Mac. At least the first time around. All those mistakes you made: the impossible text messaging, using Mal's full name, the bloody shirt you planted, sabotaging Banks." I paused. "Killing Megan."

"I know you must hate me for that, Horatio."

I laughed. *Hate* wasn't nearly strong enough a word for how I felt right then.

"You betrayed me, Mac. I was your friend, and you lied to me. *That* was the worst thing you did to me. You used me."

Mac swung the blade. It made a heavy *whhht* sound as it sliced the air between us.

"I had to do it, Horatio. You don't understand. The mountain, the prophecy. Once we started, it just got worse and worse."

"We? You mean Beth? What did she get out of all this?"

"The thrill of it, Horatio. The excitement. You have no idea how she got off on that. I wanted the mountain, but I didn't have the balls to take it. Not without Beth. She kept pushing me and pushing me, telling me to be a man." Mac looked away, like he still couldn't bear the humiliation. When he looked back, his eyes were as cold and sharp as the sword he held. "In the end, though, who was the only one who could take it? *Me,* that's who. She's the one who couldn't handle it. I did what had to be done, and I'll *keep* doing what has to be done, all the way to the bitter end."

"You don't have to," I told him. "Come back with me right now and turn yourself in. It doesn't have to go any further."

"And lose everything I've fought for until now? No. You know I can't do that, Horatio. And I don't have to. I can't lose; it's preordained. I *own* this mountain now, just like the psychic said I would. All it took was being man enough to go after it and *stay* after it, even if that meant getting blood on my hands. Did you see the way I talked to my dad today? That's power, Horatio, real power, and it's all because of this dirt we're standing on. It's mine now, and I'm not going to let anybody take it away from me." He raised his sword, a crazed look in his eyes. "Even if I have to kill more people to keep it."

I took a step back. Bagpipes still played on MacRae Meadow in the distance. My kilt fluttered in the breeze.

"And you think you're what—going to get away scot-free?"

"Mal's going to take the fall for the first murder, just like we planned it. As for Megan, well, I'll have to pin her murder on you. Tell the sheriff you came up here to blackmail me, then we fought, and I accidentally killed you in self-defense." He swung the sword. "A claymore's kind of a hard thing to control, you know?"

"You're insane. There's no way anybody's going to believe that."

Mac took the sword in both hands. "Everything will work out. It has to. It's fate. I'm sorry, Horatio, but this is the only way."

He launched at me with the sword and it was all I could do not to end up haggis on a stick. The claymore was heavy and hard to maneuver, though, and while Mac was angling for another stab I slipped in a right hook and caught the bottom of his jaw. He staggered back and put a hand to his lip to see the blood he could already taste.

Spot ran back and forth between us, barking like he was hounding a bear.

"Beware Macduff," Mac whispered, like he had to keep reminding himself why he was doing this. He really was insane, I could see that now. He'd completely lost his head. Now I just had to make sure I didn't lose mine. He took the sword in both hands again and we circled, me feeling a bit like a one-legged man at an ass-kicking contest.

"Don't bother to run, Macduff," Mac told me. "If you haven't heard, I just won the kilted mile in the decathlon." He wasn't smiling, but there was a merry glint in his eyes that made me remember what Sternwood had said about all this being the work of a serial killer.

"I wouldn't think of running," I said. I lunged for him, figuring it was better not to wait for that sword again. Even in a fair fight Mac could have taken me, but the claymore was something else altogether. Mac shunted me off with an elbow to my sternum and then slammed the butt of the thing down into the crown of my head. I fell to my hands and knees. Mac spun around, building up speed with the claymore. I scrambled to my feet to try and get out of the way.

I couldn't. The sword caught me on my left arm, right below my shoulder. I heard a crack and felt an explosion of pain and I knew in an instant my upper arm bone was broken. I fell and rolled a few feet away, trying to favor the side that wasn't screaming bloody murder. Without thinking, I clutched at the wound, bringing me all new worlds of hurt. The arm was still there, but there was blood, lots of it. The sword must have caught me mostly flat, which was the only reason I had an arm left at all. Even so, I wouldn't be catching fastballs anytime soon.

Mac walked over and stood in front of me. I stared at his

boots, trying to stay angry and not pass out. From the woods behind us, "Amazing Grace" began to play.

"You hear that, Horatio? They're playing my song. Madame Hecate told me I couldn't lose while the pipes still play 'Amazing Grace,' and they're *never* going to stop playing that song. They play it so much you'd think it was the god-damned Scottish National Anthem."

"You can't—kill me," I said, panting. "My sister—Mona—in the woods—"

"You really expect me to believe that? Horatio Wilkes, who takes care of things by himself? Horatio Wilkes, who's better than all his friends and doesn't need help from anybody?" He spread his arms wide. "Mona! Mona, are you there? Come on out and save your brother!"

Nothing. In the distance, the bagpipes still played.

"Nice try, chum." Mac held the claymore low so I could see it. My blood was splashed across his family name. "You know what 'claymore' means in Celtic, Horatio? 'Sword-big.' Nice and simple. You want to know how those Scottish High-landers did the most damage with it?"

I didn't particularly, no. I focused all my energy on stay-ing conscious as Mac stepped back and started to swing the claymore over his head like a helicopter blade. If there was a way out of this, I didn't see it.

"There can be only one," Mac said. I closed my eyes. Of all the things I thought I'd hear before I snuffed it, I hadn't figured it'd be a cornball line from *Highlander*.

"Mac, no!" someone cried.

The bagpipes stopped abruptly and Mac suddenly lost his will, letting the claymore spin down. The point slammed to the ground and tore up divots as it came to a stop, but he still held the hilt in his hands.

"Dad?"

Mac's father ran across the field with Mona and a security guard in tow. In seconds Spot had joined Mr. Mackenzie, both of them barking at Mac.

"What in the name of God are you doing!?" Mr. Mackenzie cried. He took the claymore from his son and tossed it a few yards away. "Have you gone mad!?"

"'Amazing Grace'! What happened to 'Amazing Grace'!?" Mac cried, casting his eyes around wildly.

All around us, Terrence and the rest of the Hell's Pipers stepped out of the woods with their bagpipes in hand. Mona rushed to my side to help me up and the security guy grabbed Mac by the arm.

"No grace for the wicked," I told Mac. "They were the ones playing in the end. The ceremonies have been over for a while now. Long enough for Mona to go get help. She was taking pictures the whole time too. And I recorded everything—on this." With my one good arm I pulled Mona's little digital voice recorder out of my shirt pocket and held it up for him to see. But Mac wasn't listening. All he cared about was "Amazing Grace."

"They were playing just for us?" Mac said, trying to understand.

"You'd be surprised what these guys will do for a case of IRN-BRU," I said. "Or maybe you wouldn't. Turns out they weren't real happy about being accessories to murder either. It's over, Mac."

Mac tried to back away, but the security guard held his grip. "No—no! Madame Hecate said I couldn't be stopped until Birnam Wood came for me—"

I started to tell Mac the prophecy was all mumbo jumbo, especially that bit about Birnam Wood, when the security guard piped up.

"He's already on his way."

"What?" Mac and I said together.

"Sheriff Birnam Wood. He'll be here any second."

That's when Mac officially lost it. He punched the security guy in the nose and bolted. For a second, everyone stood stunned—his father, Mona, the guy with the blood splurting from his beak, even me. Mona and Nosebleed sure weren't going to take off after him, I wasn't in much condition to run, and Mac's father couldn't decide *what* the hell was happening.

"Spot!" I called. "Way to me! Way to me, Spot!"

Spot leaped away from me and tore off after Mac like he'd been waiting to do it all his life. Right before Mac could make the other entrance into the woods Spot darted in front of him and tripped him up.

"Get out of my way, damn it!" Mac cried. He flailed at Spot but the dog always managed to jump back out of range. Maybe he'd learned his lesson with Beth.

Mac was so focused on getting past Spot that he didn't hear me come up behind him. I tapped him on the shoulder, he turned, and I kneed him hard in the 'nads.

"That's for Megan, chum."

Mac crumpled to the ground and coughed up a lung. I enjoyed every second of it.

"None of this . . . was my fault," Mac said. "We knew how this was going to end. We've known since that first day at Madame Hecate's."

"No, Mac. You're not some character in a play with everything you say and do scripted out. You had a choice every step of the way and you blew it. We all did. We're all of us responsible for our own actions. You, Beth . . . even me."

Especially me.

I wanted to kick Mac, hit him, make him really hurt for everything he'd done, but then Sheriff Wood—Sheriff *Birnam* Wood—was there putting handcuffs on him and Mona was propping me up.

"All right, Horatio," Mona said. "It's over now. You got him."

"Good. Yeah," I said, the forest swimming in front of me. "I'm just going to lie down here for a minute and pass out," I told her, and that's just what I did.

CHAPTER THIRTY-TWO

— 🗡 —

I woke up to the wet kisses of a dog.

"That'll do, Spot. That'll do," I said.

I looked around. There were considerably more people there than when I had blacked out. Mona, Sheriff Wood, Banks, his dad, Sternwood, even Mal. I felt like Dorothy at the end of *The Wizard of Oz,* waking up from a dream. "And you were there, and you, and you, and you—" I even had my little dog too. But the one person I wanted to see when I opened my eyes wasn't there, and she never would be.

"He's awake," Mona said.

"That's my sister," I said, sitting up. "A keen journalistic nose for the obvious."

She slapped me on the big clear floatie surrounding my arm and I howled.

"Oh, I'm sorry! Sorry!"

I poked gingerly at the thing, not entirely enjoying the view of the messed-up arm underneath.

"Air cast," the sheriff said. "You'll have to get the real deal at a hospital once we get you down off the mountain."

So, first things first: "Your name is Birnam?" I said. "Seriously?"

Sheriff Wood groaned. "Mount Birnam is covered by Birnam Wood, our last name was Wood, so my folks thought it would be right funny. Course you'd have known if you read that card I gave you. You know, the one with my cell phone number on it? The one I told you to call *before* you got into trouble?"

Because of course my story about the sheriff and the search for the sheath had all been made up.

"I've still got you beat," I said, deliberately avoiding the issue. "My middle name is Stanislaw."

"Horatio Stanislaw Wilkes?" said Mr. Banks.

"Mom got first naming rights, dad got second. It's a St. Louis Cardinals thing."

Sheriff Wood grunted.

"Oh, here," I said. I pulled Mona's digital recorder out of my pocket. "I got everything he said on here, and Mona's got pictures from before that will help. And from today. You did get pictures today, didn't you, Mona?"

"Of course! Wait, unless I forgot to take the lens cap off."

"Mona!"

"I got him!" she said, beaming. "I actually got Horatio for once. Somebody write that down."

"Mac and Beth killed Duncan MacRae together," I told the sheriff. "But Mac did everything else on his own. Including killing Megan Sternwood."

I meant that to bring down the happy mood and it did.

"We'll need to collect a statement, but it can wait for the hospital," said the sheriff. He left to speak to one of his deputies.

"So where's Mac?" I asked.

"They already took him away," Banks said. "I think he was happy to go to jail just to get away from his father. Man, you should have heard Mr. Mackenzie. I'm surprised he didn't wake you up."

"You know about the tax foreclosure," Mal said. "Dad couldn't pay, so he had apparently already agreed to sell Mr. Mackenzie the mountain."

General Sternwood harrumphed. "If your friend had done nothing, he'd have really inherited the mountain one day from his father. Now he's blown it for both of them. The contract's all torn up, and nobody ever saw Duncan's signature on that piece of paper except me and you. And seeing as I'm a crazy old man, my memory is kind of hazy on the subject."

"And mine's never been the same since Mac hit me on the head," I said.

Sternwood grinned.

"And I sure won't sell it to him now," Mal said. "Sell to Mr. Mackenzie so Mac can inherit the mountain one day? Never."

"He's not going to inherit much in jail," said Mona.

"What *will* you do with it? The mountain I mean," Banks asked.

Mal frowned. "I don't know. Let the bank have it, I guess."

"But then Mr. Mackenzie can just buy it from the bank!" said Mona.

"Mr. Banks," I asked, "did you write that song? 'Angus MacIron'? You didn't borrow it from some older folk song?"

The question seemed to derail the conversation. Everyone stared at me like I'd been hit on the head. And I had been, which I think is why they were worried.

"I, well—yes. Just like I told you."

I nodded. "General, I think Mr. Banks is going to need your services as a lawyer. The company that makes IRN-BRU has been using his song in a multimillion-dollar ad campaign without paying him royalties. They think it's a traditional Scottish tune."

"They've been—they've done what?" Mr. Banks stammered.

Again with the stunned looks. Only Sternwood seemed to have gotten it.

"If that's true we can sue them for a pile of cash," he said.

Mr. Banks was clearly flabbergasted. "I—I—I don't even know what I'd do with that kind of money. The Highland Games circuit is my life. I couldn't want for anything more."

"Then I've got a mountain to sell you," I told him. "Or Mal does at least."

It would have been entertaining watching recognition dawn on their faces if only my arm didn't feel like a tossed caber. Whatever the medics had given me to ease the pain was wearing off.

"I can go to college!" Banks said.

"You can *buy* the college!" Mona said with a laugh.

"Hey, the psychic was right," Banks said. "Madame Hecate. You remember? She said that Mac would be king of the mountain, but that one day I would own it. She was right all along!"

That I had been the unwitting agent of Madame Hecate's all-knowing, all-seeing flimflam did not make me as happy as it seemed to make everyone else. I closed my eyes and leaned back and tried to ignore the pain.

"Let's give the boy a rest," General Sternwood said. "I'd say he's done quite enough today. And when you're done with school, Horatio, look me up. My firm could use a man like you."

"All due respect, General, but I don't think I'm going to be a lawyer."

"Who said anything about being a lawyer? I mean when you open up shop as a private investigator."

Sternwood and the Banks boys left together, no doubt headed for the IRN-BRU booth before it was packed up. Mal told Mona to send him a text message—for real this time—and left us alone.

"By the way," Mona told me, "nice skirt."

"It's a *kilt*," I told her.

She looked at me.

"Okay. Yeah. It's a skirt."

I scratched Spot behind the ears, and Mona let me have a little space.

"It's stupid," I said, "but there's a part of me that still can't believe he did it."

"That's because you're a good friend, Horatio."

"I don't know. Being a good friend of mine can get you hurt."

I watched as two of the sheriff's deputies used a trash bag to collect the claymore as evidence. High above us the peak of Mount Birnam cut through the clouds and made me feel small and powerless again. Maybe because I really *was* small and powerless.

"He must have followed her to the hospital. Paid off those Hell's Pipers to keep me busy."

"Horatio—"

I spun the green bracelet slowly on my wrist in what I already knew was going to become my own personal rosary prayer. My fingers rubbed the smooth Celtic love knot on top and the rough, undyed leather on the back where her name was written, and I wondered how I could say good-bye to Megan Sternwood, or if I ever would.

"Horatio, it wasn't your fault."

It had suddenly gotten cold again, very cold. I shuddered and pulled a blanket over me.

"You know what they say, Mona. The mountain makes its own weather."